Jim Huck

By Michael Otieno Molina

Text copyright © 2022 by Michael Otieno Molina
Cover art copyright © 2020 by Temilade Koleosho.

Learn more about Michael Otieno Molina at www.mikemolina.org.

Educators, teacher trainers, and librarians can find a variety of *Jim Huck* teaching tools at **www.mikemolina.org.**

ISBN - 9798631650015

For those who survived and strived
in the hope that we would be.
For those who fought and died
to leave us hope in their stories.

Chapter 1
How Jim Became a Slave

There is no such thing as a slave.
There are only we souls enslaved
and the perpetual war enslavers wage
to keep us in such a state.

****

A man named Jim sat outside in a heavy sleep leaning deep against his favorite Weeping Cherry tree. Though he was a powerful man of great reach, Jim's body bore baggy rags that made him look raggedy. Drool dripped through his beard and turned to mud as it mingled with the dust of day and the crusted muck of a meal of mush.

Jim chortled with a snort as he dreamt a snarky dream. It was a fantasy of a slapstick calamity he was causing to befall someone who'd done him nasty in reality. In his dream, he widened the hole of the poo-pew in the outhouse so the Miss's narrow hips wouldn't hit the toilet lip. In his dream, Jim sipped draft as the Miss missed and fell in her own ass-trash in a splash of shit.

Aw, shut up that yelling. You ain't dead. But that's how you 'bout to be smelling, Ms. Luellen, he mumbled and laughed in his head.

Jim had collapsed against his cherished Cherry Willow tree—as if he fell against his only friend—when his busted bare feet could no longer bear the lash of the path. With one glance, one could see that circumstance keeps a certain cruelty for a man like Jim, cursed to a life of being worked like a beast of burden and only offered mean dreams as brief rest. Jim rustled for comfort and arched his back off a knot of bark that he could barely feel hurting him, and heaved in a deep breath.

The dream that had been humoring Jim bubbled up as a frown as it took a turn for the *uh oh.* Jim's head sunk down into his coat before he woke with a rough yawn gargling in his throat. He blinked open his heavy eyes—eyes dulled over with a fatigue that was doused with a grief as wide as it was deep. Jim stretched his chest like a sea swells—from somewhere beneath. His brief relief was done. *Here come the goddamn sun,* Jim spoke with the grump of a malediction.

You might think a man who would speak such must be in pain or trouble, his soul crushed under the weight of his days; his spirit must be broken in ways that only death can let a body escape. But there were no dead dogs in Jim's eyes. This was not a man ready to surrender his life. Quite the opposite, Jim looked like a focused falcon perched for flight. Jim walked the wood that night after a hard turn in his life had come to light, and in order to truly understand the trouble that had just bubbled up, let's step back to grasp a gasp of what life was like for Jim coming up.

Jim was born a phantasm of his father, Bill, and though Jim was a mirror image of his father's visage, Bill was much different. Bill had been reckless, particularly feckless when it came to women. He had dropped seeds—like a farmer, scattering ancestry far and farther, like a pirate burying treasures on isles across broad waters.

Bill had been given a measure of freedom from the man who enslaved him (his enslaver was also his father). Bill's mother, Jim's old Gran, always said Bill wanted every one of his distant buds and different offspring. She said he would point up and say *they all see this same sun,* and she'd say a day would come when he'd reap all his children, one by one. She was wrong.

Bill's father was his enslaver and a loud Christian, the Big Man in his community, who preached every Sunday about the sanctity of slavery. That man was so afraid that a shadow— Bill's dark resemblance—might be spotted near his family, that he set Bill free to roam evenings after set day hours wrangling animals and crops. Sometimes he hired Bill out to do weeks of blacksmithing in town shops. That man did anything he could to keep Bill from being around at night, when it would be even more clear that his skin was a light, dark shade of White, that Bill's chin had the family cleft, that the enslaver's bounty of slaves was built on rape—body theft.

Bill's enslaver father wanted him, as much as possible, gone. So Bill spent his nights on the roam, and a roaming man will sometimes run into a woman willing to home him, even for an hour or so. Thus Bill developed a powerful pull on a steady constant of women, each of whom would have followed him to the kingdom if he came to get them. All except for one, Jim's mother, Liza May, who wouldn't follow Bill any more than she might follow the night to find the day.

Even though he never knew her, Jim always kept a healthy fear of his mother, Liza May, based upon what the old people would say—that she knew voodoo from Barbados[1], that she used her voodoo to turn her master to her slave, that she made him spend his days staring her way till he sent his wife away because he couldn't stand the sight of anyone else in his home, that he sold all his other house-enslaved so that he and Liza May could be alone, that she had whipped her enslaver with infatuation and drove the man wild—so wild that one night he grabbed at her intending to snatch her body to make a child. That's when Liza May, gashed her enslavers grabbing hand good with a shiv of wood to remind him that he had never touched her and never would.

They said the enslaver swung a fist at Liza May, but she ghosted the blow to slip the strike as the man flew askew, landed in the fire, and burnt up his face. He rolled and rolled, scrambled and crawled into the kitchen cursing and spiting and feeling around for something with which to get to head-splitting. He'd gone from obsession with Liza May to violence against her, like many men do, but he soon knew that he picked the wrong one for sure and for true.

---

[1] *Moi, Tituba, Sorciere Noire de Salem (I, Tituba, Black Witch of Salem)*, a French novel by Maryse Conde, tells the personal history of the real life Tituba—the Carribean woman accused of bringing witchcraft to Salem. Tituba is also a character from Arthur Miller's play, *The Crucible*. Conde's book brought Tituba alive from the margins of American history and literature. Conde's story was assigned to me by Dr. Michelle Levy, who in 1993 was the chairwoman of the English Department of Xavier University of Louisiana. Conde's example was the seed that, twenty-five years later, flowered into the idea for *Jim Huckleberry*.

That man was on his knees as he grabbed a pot off the counter and turned to face Liza May. He pointed the pot at her, *bitch-witch be gone!* he was heard to have said. But Liza May narrowed her eyes and approached him in a sort of silly slink. He was dumbstruck still. She reached down slowly and took the pot from him with ease, tossing it into the sink. He sat there looking, slack-jawed, up. He couldn't force a blink. He couldn't move a wee bone. They said Liza May said *you'll move again in the morn, when you know better never to touch me. Oui, bon?*

That man didn't sleep. He sat slumped on the floor of his kitchen, drooling and thinking till day. The next morning, still frozen, he'd come up with how he would punish Liza May. Liza May had a child—one year old Jim—who that man let her keep lest she think to run away. The man thought to sell that child to another state, and teach this woman who was master and who was slave. Yet, Liza May wasn't stupid, on this or any day. She had a sense of what he would do and had already prepared herself a way.

The next morning, the sun came up on that man sitting with spit crusted around his lips. He sat in a smash of shit and a puddle of piss. She smelled the stench of his body release and let out a hiss. *This'll set your body free,* Liza May likely said as she served that man something she'd just finished warming.

He sat, still slumped against that counter, with eyes softened almost to tears as he paid her full mind – he studied her woody fingers, her lode-ish hand, her lithely arm, her orbed shoulder, her sheer neck, her fleshy mouth, only to get lost in her eyes' onyx shine. She spooned more warm into that man's mouth as a faint smile bunched his grey wrinkle lines. She caught the dribble that fell from his lip to make sure he got every drop of her White Toade soup seasoned with crushed up snake heads and leaves plucked from rash-ivy vines[2].

---

2 "Poison and Protest: Sarah Basset and Enslaved Women Poisoners in the Early Modern Caribbean", Cathleen Crowther, *Nursing Clio*, March 1st, 2018. This article speaks for itself. The information on the persistent resistance of the enslaved, particularly women, is out there if you look for it and you should look for it.

In two days of time, that man convulsed, vomited bile and swallowed his tongue. He was dead in the kitchen against that same counter slumped. After they found him, a mob gathered in bloodlust for Liza May, certain of some evil done, but she'd long vanished in the dusk of the sinking sun, and she had taken Jim, she and Bill's son. The word had travelled from the enslaved to the enslavers, word of what Liza May had done. No search party was formed. The enslavers considered themselves lucky she was gone. What was done was done, word to Amun[3].

Liza May dropped Jim with his grandmother, Old Gran, knowing Bill wouldn't be any good at raising a man while he was out acting like a stallion breeding himself in the callow shallows, haste-post-haste, on his way to the gallows. Liza May left Jim with Gran, and Gran hid the boy for years. Every time the overseers of her work camp would count bodies, Gran would give him a shot of whiskey to put him to sleep and hide him behind a bush or in the creek's cattail spears. By the time Jim was ten, the enslavers didn't care why their count always had one more in bounty, seeing as they wanted an extra body since the Big Man kept sending Bill out of the county.

Bill came and went, until one day he crossed a certain stream to meet an enslaver's sister—a thick little bit of ginger who'd been sweet on Bill since she'd seen him swinging his scythe to cut corn. They were found one evening in the midst of a blistering heat in the back of old man Johnson's barn. Bill escaped while her family was beating her near to death in the name of names. So she promptly named Bill rapist and turned her chosen lover into human game.

---

3 Amun, "The Obscure One", was an ancient Egyptian God who left itself mysterious, so as to let people define it according to their own understanding of what they needed it to be. The idea of gods that were humble, wise, patient, and strong enough to leave themselves mysterious contradicts the notion of the jealous he-god of "Western Civilization." More humble Godly spirits define Santeria and Vodun and all the hybrid religions that the enslaved made in the American South, the Caribbean, and Central and South America.

Bill was hunted and caught and strung up for all to see him torn to fleshy rinds before they cooked him like a hog as a message for every slave in the county to divine. Jim still saw his father's charred face in the shadows of his mind. Whenever Jim happened across a mirror he became invisible and, instead of seeing himself, he would see Bill's burned and bludgeoned phantom, frozen in the grotesque blank of death. The trauma of that lived with Jim, in Jim, and through Jim, and he'd made the kind of decision a child who has seen gross violence might make. He fused the edges of what he knew to seal off a safe space. Jim built walls around the place in his mind where he would stay.

One wall was against the White man's world where White folk were killers whom demanded to be obeyed lest they call a gang to bludgeon, hang, and burn you. Jim believed that from White folk there was no escape, no protection to turn to, and no place to get help. So Jim decided he would keep a whole world of his own inside himself.

The second wall was against time. Since there would never be enough of it to cover up the sight of his butchered father, he pushed time into a black hole. He didn't know the year or his age, and he didn't care to know. All he knew was that the seasons change and the river never stopped its flow.

The third wall Jim made was against freedom and any concept of it. Freedom had cost his father his life and with his father is where Jim left it. Jim would rather be told what to do every day than be free to make a tortuous mistake. Yet, this was the wall with cracks in its grout. The freedom within Jim—common to every human—was beginning to seep through his walls and scream *get out!*

11

The fourth wall young Jim made was against the world of intimate experience, and how when adults got to wanting on each other too hard, chaos is the consequence. Jim believed that any coupling up was bound to burn ash to dust. So Jim decided to never look at any woman with any hint of a gush, despite any gushing she might have for him. Until he found his wife, Sadie, there hadn't been one woman with the stuff to steer Jim's attention near, though many had tried their hands with flashing eyes and rocking rears.

Jim was what women called fetching. His face was lined with time marked in deep etchings about his mouth. Just like his father, Jim's look was arresting. Many couldn't help but gawk. Jim's features were an alluring, soft-sharp. He wore a full, arched thick in his lips and a broad-boned flat in his nose. He kept angular granite in his jaw with cheekbones that lifted in cliffs as they rose. Jim's skin was a tawny mix of regal hickory Ethiopian and fierce crimson indigenous with a dash of swarthy olive from some hearty southern European immigrant.

By the time of this story, Jim had earned some stately grey, clustered in bundles around his face and in silver traces ringed tight to light his hair. And those chrome flashes, curled into glints like starlight, caught quite a few hints in feathery stares—the same type of stares that pushed his father Bill to the hanging tree, where White men left his body in ruins, a smoldering heap of the man that could swing ten year old Jim up in the air with one hand. Since seeing Bill killed, Jim steered clear of mirrors and the reminder they would bring of the look on his father at the end—in life Bill was so ravishing and in death he was such a ravished thing.

It was likely Jim's look that made enslavers want him as an in-home servant. They found him handsome, yet Jim's resistance to intimate experiencing often came across his face as a fear or a loathing of women. So for enslaver men, Jim, unlike his father Bill, seemed safe for their wives. By the time he was full grown, Jim ended up kept as house-enslaved, as a man handy for the woman enslaver, day to night.

12

Now slaving in the house might seem easier than slaving in the field. Maybe it might seem painless. But for Jim, shackles were shackles whether iron or steel, rusty or stainless. The enslaved who cut crops were under the gun from the crack of day till dead of night come. The enslaved who kept house were under fire from a mistress's first whim to a master's last desire. Whether back-breaking or heart-breaking, whether broken in spirit or broken in mind, having a master makes all labors harder and takes its toll on souls in time.

For Jim, that time was fast approaching. Ms. Watson, his widowed enslaver, was getting more vicious by the day. And the only thing Jim could reason as to why she was that way was that she had begun to hate life since Mr. Watson passed away. But, feeling any empathy for her grief seemed unnecessary to Jim since she seemed to derive such glee from giving her grief to him.

Jim often thought he wouldn't own people even if he could have, being that it gives people more power than people should have. That kind of power allowed Ms. Watson to turn her troubles on Jim and find relief in causing *him* pain. And gaining pleasure from causing pain fouls a heart and rots a brain—both maladies being what one must pay for indulging any impulse or proclivity with another persons fate. Ms. Watson possessed Jim's body and imprisoned his mind, and to keep him confined in such a state required she conjure a bile-brined hate.

Though Ms. Watson was a thin woman, she held a deep belly of rage, and when she tapped that well she was mean as a polecat in a cage. She could be plenty rough when mustering up every pound of strength that she had to bring down on Jim's back, especially when that whiskey got to stabbing her liver. She'd begun to drink a brown river since loosing her child, then her man. Ms. Watson was no happy drunk. The liquor gave her the will to be evil, heaven be damned.

Randomly, Ms. Watson would sting slaps across Jim's cheek. Without warning, she'd hurled bricks down on his feet. She might go off and pinch his ears or pull his hair like he was some kind of disobedient beast, or scowl and knock food out of his hands while he was trying to eat. Most recently, she'd tossed hot water on him to wake him from sleep, which is a vile way to disrupt an enslaved man's only piece of peace.

Having another person take every day of your life makes life rough enough. Having that same person take your night is enough to make anybody go buck. House slaving had been no cakewalk, and Jim was just about ready to take off on Ms. Watson—to smash her like a cigar butt into the dust. But then what? Jim was her slave and Ms. Watson knew he could not raise a hand in his own defense since to do so would invite upon him a mob with mouths frothing white to lynch. So, for Jim, house or field, enslavement was enslavement, and if an enslaved man tried to take a stand he could expect the same reprimand whether house help or field hand: a torturous death.

Jim had seen it happen. He remembered the rash of lash cracking and lynching that swept Missouri in his boyhood days.[4] It had triggered some enslavers to jettison their enslaved to get paid rather than face mobs coming to take them away in enraged fits of bloodlust. It was then, during this whitelash of resentment, that Jim had been taught: for the enslaved, an accusation was a conviction, and a conviction was a death sentence. And he had been taught that vengeance for any resistance, would be swift and wide in its dispensing. That even his Gran, whom her enslavers swore they loved like a maid-mother, in a second, could be shoved away, cold, rough, and without a stutter.

---

[4] In 1901, Mark Twain wrote "The United States of Lyncherdom" after a murderous race riot of Whites on a Black settlement. Twain never published the essay noting that if he did, "I shouldn't have even half a friend left down there [in the South]...." In the essay, Twain suggests bringing Christian missionaries home from China to work in Missouri instead "to stop this bloody epidemic of insanities." Twain, at the throat of U.S. hypocrisy as usual, left his anti-racism unsaid to keep Southern friendship.

Jim: *(remembering)*
Old Gran had roots
shooting through her hands.
They were filled and pumping
with blood,
my blood.

She said Paw got killed for being a man,
for not running when they were coming
for blood,
my blood.

When they sold old Gran,
to finish a life of wrongs,
she took my hands and sang a song—
Steal Away[5]

When they sold my only family—
my flesh and bone.
I knew one day I'd got to be gone
to steal away.

I was ten when they took her,
a sapling, thin-trunked,
when they roughed and shook her
pointed barrels of guns.

They made sure I saw
to remember.

---

[5] *Steal Away to Jesus*, according to an August-September 1970 issue of the African American political journal founded by W.E.B. DuBois, *The Crisis*, was "a password for slaves to go out and discuss revolution… an escape from white oppression." (DuBois 261) Great African American artists, from composer Roland Hayes to renaissance man Paul Robeson to gospel icon Mahalia Jackson, have sung this beautiful song.

And I remember every one.

This all was in Jim's mind the whole time he sat, barely woke from his sleep against his favorite tree. And with this thinking, the deep grief in Jim's eyes turned cold, then heated up and shown bold, black as sky when the world turns and we all know the sun is just one star. When the blinding light of day and its blue veil goes away—that is the bold black in which Jim's eyes were laid and set. He looked around, swinging sight through the depths of his surroundings, the rhythm of disquiet gritting a riot through his teeth.

And they kept me, he thought. A male child, sure to be strong, had too long a life of labor left to sell away. *They mean to work me 'till my last day, to till my soul 'till my body breaks.*

Jim:
(under his breath, almost moaning)
They bled my mama[6]*.*
They bled my daddy.
They bled my granny.
They bleeding me.
They won't bleed my seeds.
Come hell or high water,
they won't bleed my seeds.

---

[6] A play off Melvin Van Peebles' charging chant of self-defense through rebellion in his self-made smash success of 1971, *Sweet Sweetback's Basdasssss Song,* which sparked the market for 'Blaxploitation' movies. "Blaxploitation" mythologized Black urban legend heroes who fought aspects of systemic racism with funk, style, and Black power. Here Jim takes the original chant further by refusing to have his 'seeds', his children, bled by slavery. Rebellion, for the enslaved and their descendants is a necessary act of resilience and resistance.

16

Chapter 2
How Huck Became an Orphan

*No matter what we are looking at
when regret hits,
but especially when looking at ourselves,
we feel blame,
the shame for that blame,
and the heat of the need to escape it
in any bit of trouble
we can double down on.*

****

Inside a window nearby, a boy named Huckleberry stood dressed in all white facing a wood-framed mirror that stretched twice the tape of his height. He was eying himself with a vigorous disgust curled in his top lip—his hate lit with flicks of light spit from a candle's hot tip. Huck's starch stiff outfit wasn't fit for a buck such as he, and so he twisted and squat in indignant glee hoping to rip a hole and mole himself free from the civilized man that the Widow watching over him hoped to train him to be. Huck snatched off his tie, snapped off the reins of his suspenders, and threw his clothes, growling at them as they flew, like some chained beast or a dressed dog might do.

If he could, he'd go stark, like the stork brung him from heaven, just to shame every reverend and their sexton. Huck preferred dirt on his hands, pants ripped at the knees, and no shirt—better to fish with. Plus if his Pap ever saw him so clean in these airs, he might catch a fist quick-quick.

Huck paused at that unnerving thought. The memory of his father jumped him. And his father wasn't a good thing to be remembering. Huck's Pap had been courting death and destruction by bottle, and he had the tendency to be slap-happy full throttle, and punch-happy, and kick-happy, and pick-up-a-stick-and-beat-Huck-with-it happy.

For Huck, thoughts of his Pap were kin to his own mind being hostile to him. And in such a situation, where a boy can't even trust his own imagination, a boy becomes like Huck—letting rain or pain or blood stains roll off his back like water off a duck. And this was for the best since Huck's young life had been put to the test in ways that would rip the heart from the roughest man's chest.

Try to imagine a thing so hard as to watch your mother killed. Well Huck did. And to make the story more tragic, his mother died under his Pap's fists. Huck watched his mother's face open, her body shaking in fits, and her life pouring from her in gaping slits.

And in the moments after her murder, while Huck crouched behind a chair and hid, his pappy yelled out that if Huck moved the width of a nit he'd be whipped till he was stripped of his hide. And if he cried? And if he so much as glanced with a hint of judging in his eyes, he'd be buried with his mother, food for mudbugs and flies.

Huck survived. But the kid in him had died that night.

So when the Widow, Jim's enslaver Ms. Watson's sister, took him in as if he were her own blood, she acted like Noah saving a beast from a flood of sin. She hated when Huck went out at night for thinking he might be backsliding. She wrapped him tight in proper clothes thinking it would restrict him from river raft-riding. She tried to teach him to read so that a book might shine some light. She tried to stop him from cussing and smoking so that he might have a chance at a wife.

The Widow tried and tried all that she could and Huck tried to give her some hope, but deep in his heart the weight of what he'd seen had torn a giant sinkhole in his soul. And Huck was filing it with adventure and stuffing it with risk, and he was covering it with rationalizing, quick as a lawyer, and mostly, he was lining it with loyalty to his main partner, Tom Sawyer.

And that is who he was hoping to see, once he'd gotten free this night. Maybe they'd run the town robbing, stealing, and killing like a band of bad knights. And so Huck's mind wandered over the wicked possibilities, leaving him so lost in devious glories that he hadn't even noticed another figure in a dark corner of the room sitting with elbows on his knees.

The figure, a man, was not asleep, but stuck in a gaze that looked much like a daze as he peered at Huck with a rough mug that struck of the doom of blooming enmity. His clothes, as baggy as Jim's, but much more dingy, bespoke a man to whom hope had been stingy. His glacial blue eyes, dank with desperation, flanked by perspiration, didn't blink or hesitate as they stared to berate his son. It was his Huck's Pap!

Huck, as yet unaware of Pap's presence, spoke himself a monologue that shucked him of any pretense of conscience. Stripped of the pressure of the Widow's rules while alone (he thought) in his room, he rooted for his own ruin, hoped to be a hellion bound for rebellion.

He made himself a pledge, doubly conscious of a past full of luck, splendid and horrid, and a future of few options other than wending and exploring.

Huck (*to himself*):
The widow treating me like a mother
is hard on my druthers.
It's enough to make me forget
all the ducats I discovered.
I'm 14 years old
six thousand dollars rich in gold[7],
but the Widow got me trapped
in these itchy clothes.
Blabbering on 'bout Moses,
like he kin to me.
Trying to make me quit smoking.
Now that's sin to me.
She is a dismal good one to take me in
after my Pap, that catfish,
went and left again.
But I won't be civilized
when there's skies to see,
when there's rafts on the river,
life inside of me.
So I'ma set out for the West now,
and earn my way
and ain't a dern thing the Widow can say.

---

[7] *Adventures of Huckleberry Finn* is a sequel to *Adventures of Tom Sawyer*. That book ends with Tom Sawyer and his sidekick Huckleberry Finn finding a treasure of gold worth $6000. That's roughly the equivalent $172,000.

Off in the dark, Pap cracked a sinister mumble that rumbled, then crumbled into a rough cough. Huck jumped up and almost humped his rump off. He turned and saw Pap, in full view, was cadaver pale. His face was withered, cracked as fractured shale. He had the physical funk of stale liquor. His long oily hair and ratty beard shone slicker in the candlelit night as light flickered.

Huck's head snapped to look away from Pap as the sinkhole in his heart bottomed out, and, in that deep, a scream screeched, but nary a squeak got out. Huck's soul was sunken in horror, under a begging that the nightmare of the sight of Pap wasn't real. But Pap was quick to make sure Huck knew that this hope was a boat that done capsized and keeled.

Pap spoke in a slow nasal whine dripping with the chittering of a squirrel, the hiss of a coon. It was putrid with the pungency of rotten rinds. It was electric with the sharp pops of castanet spoons.

As Pap spoke, Huck's spine creaked and shivered him from his mind down to his feet.

Pap:
Starchy clothes, ha boy?
Think you a big bug now?
Think you better than your Pap?
Full of book stuff now?
Heard you could read and write.
Who told you learn that mess?
I can't read
nor could your mama
'fore she went to rest.
Now fess up.
If you can read,
then read this.

Pap threw a Holy Bible at Huck's cheek with a near miss. It thumped the wall and landed as his feet.

21

Pap:
If you can read it,
then that Widow will come to mind
her bastard business.
You don't need her pity,
nor her preaching for a witness.
Tryin' teach a boy to be better than his paw.
A bastard such as you I ain't never saw.
Now go on boy, and read that there,
and if you can,
I'll put you in your place
for putting on airs.

Huck didn't want to look at his Pap. Pap's words hit hard enough for him. To have to look into his shot-drowned blue eyes would have jellied him to his stuffing. He squatted to pick the Good Book up and dusted it off as he lifted it. His breaths were heavy and fast. His guts ripped and twisted. His neck crooked up. His shoulders shrugged. Huck struggled to speak, but eventually spoke up.

At first the words were jumbled from tumbling through his stumbling speech, but then they proceeded to cascade over his barely parted teeth.

Huck:
The eye never has enough of seeing,
nor the ear its fill of hearing.
What has been will be again,
what has been done will be done again;
there is nothing new under the sun[8]

And Pap was as disgusted as he could be. He started rubbing his forehead and his greasy hair vigorously.

---

[8] Ecclesiastes, 1:7-9, in case you want to read the rest.

Pap:
Well, well, well I'll be damned.
Before you know it you'll be praying
like a lying church man.

Pap struggled to get up from sitting, falling onto his knees. Then he slumped forward, almost face to floor, onto his forearms with a wheeze. He got himself back to all fours, then slowly up to his feet, but not before wobbling in and out of sways like a sapling tree bending and mending itself straight in a heavy breeze. He stumbled over to Huck and snatched his arm rough as if he needed it as a crutch to keep from crumbling back to his knees in a rush.

Pap:
Look here,
empty your pockets.
Gimmie what you got.
Quick!
I need to head down to town
to get me a sip.

Huck reached deep into his pocket to give Pap one dollar, half of what he had, and held his other dollar back. Pap snatched it with a nastiness as classless as the dastardly rascal cad could. He waddled towards leaving the room, and stopped to scowl, turning to face Huck with an expression hollowed by wormwood.

Pap:
And there's more where that came from.
I'm sure,
and I'll have it.
Have your things packed up
by the time I'm back here.
You belong to me

23

and I'll learn you to learn.
You will work till your back burn,
and struggle till your ash urn.

Pap left. Huck was quieted as he paced the floor. His thoughts were congested with what he was sure to endure:

Huck (*thinking*):
I got to steal away if Pap's back again.
He's gonna beat me bloody
for the slightest sin unto him,
or for no reason.
He thinks anything mine is his,
and anything else is treason.
He can't know about my six thousand
or he'll take my only chance at freedom.
He may as well kill me then.
What's the way?
Gotta be a way.
Think of a way.
I can't let Pap snatch it
and drink it away.
I got to put it away.
Got to keep it away.
That's it!
Tomorrow, I'll give it to the Judge to keep safe.

And there it was—a plan. Give the money to Judge Thatcher and keep it out of his Pap's hands. And though Huck felt a slight better about that, there still remained the bitter fact that Pap was back. Huck sat and stewed in that, the guts in his belly jellied as chewed fat.

A rap at the window snapped Huck from his quiet panic. It was his partner in crime, Tom Sawyer, and, as usual, he was a might manic.

Tom:

Come on, let's go Huck.
I got the band back together.
We gonna strike the town down
rough as stormy weather.
We gonna steal and kill
like Bobby Baba's forty thieves
and ransom girls like Juan
the Don of Coyotes!

It was a welcome break—an invitation to some trouble.
This was just the steam Huck needed to release to shake the
white out his knuckles. Tom Sawyer was about that do or die.
He wouldn't mope about Pap or ask 'why me?' He would go
out and slash a path past that, and dash fast whether he flew or
crashed into a tree.

Huck:
You know it!
I'm always down for adventure.
Let's get a skiff and drift
Till we get down river.

And with no more pause for thought, Huck joined
Tom and started to walk with the broad, charged steps. This
was the hard-swinging stalk that is the mark of a boy with a
hardened heart. Huck was heavy with Pap's final straw.
Wasn't any way he would stay and be bled red by his paw. He
was stomping hard and breathing even harder, he would be free
of Pap whether he had to barter, steal, or slaughter.

Chapter 3
Jim, An Invisible Man

When friends come together,
from when they first meet,
there is a sea that parts before them.
It is the hand of God
that waves the world aside
and fingers the two forward
to walk a path that no two before have known.
Those who have lost a friend
know the vast hole,
full to its lip with emptiness,
that follows.
But when friends meet,
or whenever they come together,
the universe has bent itself to itself,
and the connection forms a charge
and that charge is a lightening.
It is a lightening of the earth itself
when two carry one thing
such as friendship.

******

That night Tom and Huck marched the trail looking for trouble. Maybe they'd set fire to a bale or leave a porch with a yellow puddle. For Huck, almost any trouble would do. With the heat of his Pap's return in his boots, Huck felt rough enough to rip a tree up by its roots.

Tom saw Huck's face lit with a fearful courage, and Tom was quick to instigate their first flourish of wickedness. He looked ahead and saw Jim, who was awake but feigning sleep against the tree as he ear-peeped the boys in hidden witness from a distance. Tom saw Jim and, for the show of it, felt he had to go and victim Jim something vicious.

Tom (*with white a hot thirst, licking his chops*):
Oooh look at that big black figure, Huck.
Is that Ms. Watson's buck, Jim,
lazy and sleep out in the woods?
Let's creep up and trick him.
We got to thug him up something good.
Rope him to that tree.
Wait in the bushes and see
if we can catch us a snicker.
Light a flame under the critter
and get his instincts to trigger.
Maybe he'll quiver,
like a frying chicken liver.
When the watermelon-licker
wakes up stuck,
he'll figure himself
with the luck of a chigger on a duck.
Let's make a picnic[9] of this jigger, Huck!

---

[9] Black urban legend has it that the word 'picnic' derived from lynching(s) where mobs of White men, women, and children would 'pick a n*gger' and lynch them. Who knows if this is true? However, considering the picnic-like atmosphere like that at the lynching of Jesse Washington in Waco, Texas in 1916, this legend is understandable as a constructed mythology to explain the unexplainable comfort and glee some White folks posed with while torturing, burning, and dismembering Black bodies.

Now Huck knew Jim, and he saw no season for hunting an innocent man just to treat him like a demon. He'd rather rob some thieves and hide the money in a cave.[10] Why waste evil making life harder for a slave?

But Huck couldn't show no sense of shame. Then Tom might think him not fit for game. A boy's got to be a gangster to hang with a gang. So Huck thought he had to think of way to get Tom to keep it moving, while proving he could act as much a donkey[11] as any mustang.

> Huck (*gruffly, smartly*):
> *No. He'll make a ruckus*
> *and blow our hush.*
> *Make us miss our chance*
> *to do real gangster stuff.*
> *Forget him.*
> *We got river ground to rush.*

> Tom (*the thirst is now a hunger*):
> *Nah Huck.*

---

[11] Language is a magic that casts spells of meaning over what is. In New Orleans, language is a magic and a sport. We compete to make up ways to shade experience as if we were German. That might be the French in us. Growing up, one of my favorite New Orleans phrases was 'act a donkey' (pronounced kind of like 'dawnkie', fyi). I loved the word play of it. An 'ass' is a pejorative label for a donkey. That folks have made pejoratives for animals is silly as is, but this particular label seems to play with the fact that humans call a donkey an ass, but that's just what we have to stare at if we work behind a donkey. It's a self-rib imbedded in a rib about another animal. The way New Orleans Black folk of the 1990s used 'act a donkey' inverts that by turning 'acting an ass' (acting foolish) into 'acting a donkey' (acting fearless) by giving the creature back its name and its dignity. *Acting a donkey* means being hard-headed in some of the best ways. That word-play might be the Bambara in us. Black language is magic; Jockomo fina nay.

I gotta.
I gotta get him.
Trick this cotton-picker into a superstition.
I got to do it Huck,
I got to do it.
I'm itchin'.

Huck (*annoyed*):
Nah, scratch that Tom.
Leave him alone.
Man, let him sleep
'fore we get stuck up at home
and can't sneak out to town
to really get it on.

Tom (*incredulous*):
Huck, don't you know
that if you let a trick get past,
you make more work for witches
and them witches'll get you back?

Huck (*bordering on disgusted*):
What fun is tricking Jim?
A sleeping slave?
That's like taking milk from a babe.
Ain't we above that kind of trifling?
Let's go and get to this night, kin.

Tom was quiet for a moment, which was hard for him unless he was scheming on bartering a tit for tat. He couldn't cope with being told no. Anything he wanted, right or wrong, Tom supposed the liberty to go and get that. His face was flushing pink as rare meat. He narrowed his eyes and, with bared teeth, began to speak.

Tom:
I'm liable to think you sideways, Huck,

29

like you a slave-lover, hag-cucked.
The way you talk don't add up.
Better know your side
and keep your flag up.
We need to treat a coon this way to teach them,
keep them clean from that dropoffmania[12]
keep them from the demons
that set them to dreaming about freedom.
Freedom don't belong to them.
It's impossible under nature's law.
Everybody knows that--
from Dr. Cartwright to your own paw.
No, I'm gonna do to Jim
that which witches demand
and trick this devil's kin
like a responsible White man.

Jim heard that last crack and peeked an eye through his lashes. He'd been awake the whole time listening to Tom and Huck going forth and backwards. In his mind, he mused on these two fools, as he sat and thought through what to do.

Jim (*thinking*):
Well it sure is a might White of Tom
to blame his evil-doing on witches,
same way a man born with slaves
say White skin made him destined for riches,
same way a man who calls vanity a blaspheming
will say he's made in God image,
then invent sin and blame it on witches.

---

[12] New Orleans doctor, Dr. Samuel Cartright (in a very different fit of New Orleans language-making), invented the disease of 'drapetomania'—a mental illness of slaves that 'caused them to desire to flee from slavery.' One can't make such ridiculousness up. But if one were looking to make ridiculousness up to explain why a "slave" might resist his station, mental illness is as good as any other lie. It (and witch) has been used against women who resisted oppression as well. As in most things, labels say more about the labeler than they say about the labelee.

Witches?
What these boys know 'bout witches?
They don't know a switch 'bout which is which
between a grave and a ditch
both of which is a hole in the ground
for poor or rich,
and how a blown wind
once set my hat on a stick
and gave me mind
to spin a trick up like this:

Jim cleared his throat hard to startle Huck and Tom,
and the deep bellow of his body rolled like the echo of a bomb.

Jim:
U Ummm!
Why great clouds of trash, it's Tom!
And dripped pigeon chips, it's Huck!
Shucks, what luck I done got
to size up the two of you mallard bucks!
I just been hibernating,
a bear waiting to spring.
What can I do you for, young men?
Must be something,
I avenge I kin.

Huck looked suspicious at Jim's offer, and the
histrionics of subservience with which it was dripping. He'd
never known Jim to speak with such hook and hedge, and he'd
never heard of a few of the words Jim had said. Huck had seen
Jim in many a situation, seen Ms. Watson berate him with a
look that like to splay him, but Jim always seemed steel. There
was always something of a dignity on him, a skin that the old
lady couldn't peel. Something was off and that was something
Huck could feel.

Tom, on the other hand, was drunk on gloat and very
satisfied by Jim's suspicious bootlicking in its pretentious coat.

31

Huck (*trying to hustle away*):
Didn't mean to wake you, Jim.
We'll be on our way.
You can go on back to sleep.
It is late.

Jim (*with a glint of a smile*):
Naw, my sleep is done.
I done had a frightful dream
'bout a witch that took me all the way down
to old Orleans.
It wuz the same witch once took me
to Timbuktu
and give me a marble
that could tell the future to you.

Huck (*ears piqued*):
Say what now Jim?
Tell the future? For true?
You think you could tell me something
'bout what my Pap's up to?

Jim (*poking a bottom lip of a frown*):
Your Pap? That old salty cracker
done squared himself back?
Well dog, Huck,
Jim ain't so happy to hear dat.

Tom (*consternation in his brow*):
Huck, don't let him speak such truck
about your paw.
Now ain't this boy
like a boy I never saw.

32

Now you might think a man born in Missouri when it was still a French territory might get used to a boy calling him a boy. But a man, at the red heart[13] of his heart, only adjusts his pride to deploy the ploys that could come from a fool's underestimation. And Jim was a man and knew how to snatch a fool up in his own presumption.

> Jim (*with calm eyes, his voice deepened*):
> *Jim ain't like the others, mars Tom.*
> *I got powers you ain't yet seen*
> *straight from a witch's lap.*
> *See this here marble*
> *it came right out an oxen's belly,*
> *and it can tell Huck all he want know*
> *about his Pap.*
> *And it can tell mars Tom*
> *about that devil in de shadows behind his back.*

Tom jumped around and stared into the dark. He backed up a lark, and as he did, Jim pushed a stick behind him to trip him a whip. Tom let out a yelp and Jim began to storify one of them warbling mixes of truth and lies only the enslaved can preach to glorify.

---

[13] FYI, Toni Morrison is as much the responsible for this book as Mark Twain. It is the foil needed should you ever teach *Huck Finn*. If you are desperate enough to turn to the internet for literary interpretations, you will read that "red heart" is a symbol in Toni Morrison's *Beloved*. You'll read that it is a symbol for, alternately, feeling emotion, hope, violence, rage, pain, death, or oppression. I believe that all of these surface readings are as wrong as the surface of a lake is the sky. They are as wrong as a drop of water is the ocean. None of these things can capture the notion of "red heart" individually. They only make sense when taken together and in full, "red heart" symbolizes life itself as the foil to the undead nature of the title character Beloved. Undead means not dead, but not alive. The enslaved are the undead, their "red heart" alive amidst the death of enslavement, until they are resurrected into their God-given freedom. *Jim Huck* is a story of Jim's resurrection.

Jim:
Let me tell you all about the invisible man.[14]
You never know if he behind you,
(whispering, through closed teeth)
never know if I am

Jim smiled and Tom couldn't tell if the disembodied
voice was coming from him or from the pits from hell.

Jim:
He slides around without a sound
like a snake on the ground.
He a flood where you spit,
a pit where you look down.
He right there!
There he go!
He a flare.
Then he smoke.
He a swear.
Then a croak.
He a snare,
a trap door,
a black crack in mirrored moors.
He the fire next time[15]*--*
the lost cause of war--

---

[14] See Ralph Ellison's *Invisible Man*, a cornerstone of the African American literary cannon. The invisibility that Ellison laments in beautiful sentiments derived from painful experience of early 20th century Black experience is Jim's main weapon as a future escaped enslaved man. In Jim's 19th century day, invisibility was often the only way to stave off being slayed. Here Jim also uses it as a way to haunt Whiteness from its own blind-spots.

[15] See James Baldwin's *The Fire Next Time*, a work of African American socio-political, intellectual discourse. The title of Baldwin's brilliant collection of essays refers to lyrics from the "negro spiritual" *Mary Don't You Weep*, as in *God gave Noah the rainbow sign; No more water but fire next time*. And this time, Jim threatens the fires of guilt, shame, and vengeance for the legacy of lynching.

34

He rumbling in burnt bone,
stumbling through brimstone,
long after floods of sins done been gone.
He the shadow in your marrow,
locust screaming at the Pharoah.
He's the white winter sun—
a crack of lightening quick stung.
Oaks moan when he comes,
guilty branches low hung
like
Creeeeeeeeeak,
shooka, shooka
sheek, sheek.
That's the whisper as his feet sweep.
Your throat choke, knees weak.
Creeeeeeeeeeak
Shooka, shooka
Sheek, sheek.
That's the branch bent from his weight.
Hear him coming?
Too late!

Tom, usually full of brag and boss, shrunk by the
breath. His shoulders rounded off. His confidence drained
from his chest. Jim moved forward, a sickly rhythmic shiver
bubbling through his flesh. A cold red moonlight reflected off
of a ruddy puddle on to Jim, his shadow swelled a might right
behind him.

Jim's reflection grew larger and larger in Tom's eyes
with every step. Tom stepped backward and stumbled over a
rock, on to his backside with a plop. Jim laughed a deep bark,
then cropped it short to snatch the rest of what was left of
Tom's throbbing heart.

Jim (*speaking slowly, solemnly*):
Now I done seen him once,
hanging high right there.

He came nigh out of nowhere.
It was a frightful scare.
It was a night like this.
Torches flared in a bright white mist.
I seen his body take form
as it turn and twist.
He look kinda like my daddy,
'cept his neck was crook.
His eye bulged like a crappy.
His back bent and shook.
He kinda slid on his toes.
I like to froze at the sight.
He almost spoke,
but I broke,
and ran deep in the night.

And you could still see him.
Just turn you back on the light.
Turn your eyes to black mirrors.
See yourself in spite.
Even if he just a memory…
He a bad dream that screams
remember me!

He be like
Creeeeeeeeeak,
shooka, shooka
sheek, sheek.
That's the whisper as his feet sweep.
Your throat choke, knees weak.
Creeeeeeeeeeak.
Shooka, shooka
Sheek, sheek.
That's the branch bent from his weight.
Hear him coming?

Do you?

Do you hear him coming?

Tom and Huck were looking around and out into the woody night. Jim froze in silence. He craned his neck up a heron's height. His ear reached forward like a spider web in the wind, stretched out to take in any hint of grim. Tom and Huck cut their movements short, lifted their heels off the ground. Jim waited, then waited, then wailed a sound.

Jim:
Too late!

Huck and Tom jumped clean out of their shouts. Their mouths dropped agape, then closed into pouts. Jim laughed long and hard at the growing cracks in the grout of their guts. Huck started to laugh with Jim. A safe fright from time to time was a joy to him. But Tom's face bore no semblance of a grin. He didn't speak, but resolve crept from his mind down to his cheek as it bunched up in a snarled smile. Knowing Tom, he planned to avenge this embarrassment with steam and style afterwhile.

The ripples of laughter pooled into a few human hoots. Huck turned to Jim with a few serious questions to get into.

Huck:
Jim, can you read the truth in the roots?
In the leaves and shoots?
In the dirt on a boot
or the ache in a tooth?
Tell me the time from the shine on a dime.
Can you read minds
and find signs
in the guts of a swine?
I need to know my Pap's road map.
Can you show that to me, Jim?
I'll pay you for your wisdom.

Jim (*thinking*):

Oh, pay will he?
Pay with what?
What truck could this young buck hutch?
I can't imagine a poor boy
such as Huck got much.

Huck *(thinking)*:
I won't tell him 'bout the buck I got tucked.
I know better than to let him know
whether my pocket is full
or full of holes.

Huck:
All I got is this fake quarter
but it's showing its brass.

Jim *(thinking)*:
Now this little sucker is really showing his ass.

Jim *(speaking)*:
That's alright, honey.
I'll take that play money
and put it tween a potato
'till the brass get scummy.
Then the whole thing'll look like a old ducat,
And that'll get old Jim a lil' bit of a come up.

Jim held out his hand. Huck flipped the coin to him.
Jim caught it and moaned with disappointment.

Jim:
Mm, mm. No indeed, no.
Say Huck, don't you know
it's bad luck to toss money at a man.
It'll gather bad spirits before it land in his hand.

Huck:

Well I'll be damned.
Jim, I didn't know that fact.
Well then, Jim, go on and give it back.

Huck looked at Jim with a facetious smile.

Jim *(thinking)*:
He can forget that.

Jim:
Aw, I'll let it pass, Huck.
I know you didn't mean nothing.
Let me go on and read my magic,
and let you know lil' something-something.

Jim was having fun now and ready to play this thing all
the way out. He pulled the marble out his pocket and held it to
his ear. He held it close to his eye and licked it like a steer. He
rolled it between his palms and let it drop to the ground. He
got down on all fours to give the marble a closer listen. Then
he spit on it until it glistened.

Jim *(certain)*:
Well, your Pap got two angels,
one grey and one blue.
And they both tryna to tell him what to do.
The grey one mad,
tugging at the worst of his soul.
And the blue one sad
at the bottom of a hole that old Pap can't fill.
Your Pap can't act
'cuz of the angry, the sad
and some kinda guilt
that done kilt his will.
There's a part of him wants to stay,
something he believes he can get
if he sets and sticks around.

39

In time, he'll find it he bets,
whether under water
or under ground.

Huck looked out into the night. He was shook by this
evidence that Pap knew about the $6,000, that Jim was right.
Huck turned away and stopped listening for fidgeting trying to
stuff his pipe. Jim looked at him with a curious inspection and
continued with his insight.

Jim:
There's a part of him wants a go,
and try and find what he been looking for
in some other place far away
from the Mississippi shores.
I say he might go.
I say he might stay.
I say old Huck gon' have trouble either way.
I say stay off the river.
Ain't nothing for you there
'cept trouble on the double if you dare.
Now listen at me good, Huck,
you gon' have a bunch a bad luck.
And something hard to love
to add to all that rough.
But by and by and by
you'll find your way,
and find your self happy one day.
Even if for just one day.

Huck was in his own head. He wasn't listening to a
word Jim said. He'd heard enough to know that Pap was after
the treasure he'd made, and to know he was smart to give it to
the judge to keep it safe.

Jim:

Huck, you listening?

Jim (*thinking*):
Not much I can say to this young fool
to free him from having his Pap for a paw.
Sometimes life is cruel
and slips you hands when you need claws,
fits you for a hat when you need drawers,
hits you with a clasp when you need a saw.

Chapter 4
Jim Decides it is Time

There comes a time when one must move.
Yet as time is not a thing
—only a figment of the infinite
set to the machinery of a gravity wrung around a sun
spun around an interstellar whirlpool
that blooms from a pull
more massive still—
one always moves.
Even when movement is still potential,
that potential is heavy
as a bearing woman
with a basket full of crop
balanced atop her head.
The heft of that potential,
for those of us who have never sensed it,
is greater than anything known.
The universe sinks around it
and we all lean
one way or another
to stand upright.

******

For good reason, Jim walked through the wood, looking dumbstruck. He stumbled forward and peeked nervously behind. He saw Pap's cabin in the distance and made his way towards it with absent mind.

When he got close, he could see Huck huddling in a corner. He knew what was happening. Huck's Pap was at it again with the drunken madness. The whole town knew how wicked he would get when lit with bottom barrel whiskey. The sight of Huck clutching his knees in fear was too much for Jim to let be. He stopped and crouched in the wood, and every now and then he stretched his neck out a bit to peek.

The inside of Pap's one room cabin was a filthful mess. Trash and tools were strewn about the room, clothes piled in a corner like a squirrel's nest. The walls, swollen with gaps, were mildewed and damp. The floor was dirt. There was one cloudy lamp of oil. There was one chair. Pap had coiled himself in it. A nearly empty bottle of rotgut laid by his side, tipped. Pap picked it up and shook it hungrily, and poured the last swig down his throat numbly. Huck watched him from a corner of the room, his face shadowed with fearful gloom. Jim saw this and thought of his own doom.

Jim was coming from Ms. Watson and the fall of the last straw of a million cuts of roughness she had stuck in his craw. It all started when she called him inside. She whistled and spit a *here boy*, and belched a *hump to me* which she said sometimes just for the pleasure of showing her nasty power in full measure in front of company.

Jim always had the urge to walk off when she whistled for him like a dog, but it was a might hard to listen to his own heart with fear gnawing at it like a hog. And so he lumbered and took his time. She whistled again and barked, *BOY,* loud enough to creak his spine. He hurried a bit. He knew that if he took too long she'd get the whip, and for a small woman she had quite a strong wrist, and when she was liquored up like this it stiffened her delivering of licks.

Jim walked in the door to a face full of spit that she had curled around her tongue and dug up from that dungeon she called a grin. She flung phlegm dead in Jim's face in front of some stranger and the stranger laughed as the mucus slid down Jim's chin. Jim had never been spit on before, though there was always a chance, so instinctively he clenched fists out of his hands.

The stranger said, *Boy,* with the menace of a slave society, and Jim limped his wrists. The stranger then laughed again and began to speak on what he just witnessed— something about the natural order of civilization and the slave's place in it. But Jim didn't hear a thing. His ears were all asting with rage at what Ms. Watson had done for no other reason than to let ugliness ring. And she had been pretty rough[16] with Jim in every way you might imagine, almost like she wanted Jim to lash out at her in some fashion, like she wanted an excuse to have him strung up for the world to see. Ms. Watson, as enslavers go, was a an insidious beast.

Yet, she hadn't always been viciously mean. She used to be temperantly so. When Mr. Watson was alive, in her younger days, she was a sheepish fiend behind the pretense of a doe. She'd only grit her teeth from time to time like she had a mind to beat Jim to smithereens, but then softened herself in order to stay the lady of Mr. Watson's dreaming. A White woman had to keep herself a woman, even if slavery required her to be a demon.

---

16 In the text of *Adventures of Huckleberry Finn,* at one point Jim tells Huck that Miss Watson had been "pooty rough" with him (translation from Twain's strange bastardization of Black dialect – "pretty rough"). This is mentioned in passing, but think what an enslaver would have to do to be labeled as "pretty rough" in a book that featured the horrible brutalizing of a child (Huck), multiple murders, a savage feud that ends in the slaughter of children, the most despicable criminal acts (of the Duke and Dauphin), all under the umbrella of a slave society built on violence and the threat of violence. Make no mistake, even in Twain's imagination, Ms. Watson, was a junkyard dog.

It would have been unseemly for Ms. Watson to rage and spit and curse and whip a man, even if enslaved. And so she bit her tongue at times, as if she were saving her venom for future days. After Mr. Watson died, she was the enslaver of the house, and those days had come. And she relished the freedom to snarl and grunt and holler. But spitting was another level of nasty in which she now wallowed.

Ms. Watson pursed her slits for lips and grit out a *NOW GIT*. As he turned to go, she slapped Jim in the back of the head so hard that it sounded like a pistol shot.[17] Ms. Watson had hands as hard as an old rope knot sealed with a scorch. Jim paused to breathe, then turned the corner of the porch. He had to take a seat to put a stick between his teeth. This is how he swallowed the anger, like gulping bitters without the whiskey's warm burning, to keep from finishing Ms. Watson's enslavement of him by pounding her down like a rigorous butter churning.

But while seated he heard what he hadn't heard before. That stranger was a slave-trader and he'd come for more than just a bite to eat, or to enjoy a slave berated and beat along the way. He'd come that day to take a look at Jim to see if he was fit[18] to take away to Old Orleans, to the selling block and all that that would mean—Jim being sold to anywhere but Timbuktu, with no way to get back to his family.

---

[17] On your own time, find Mr. Richard Pryor's storytelling in the voice of his recurring character, *Mudbone (Little Feets)*, who moved up to Illinois from Mississippi after cutting the bottom out of the outhouse so that the new "mistress" of the house could fall "in her own ass-trash with a nasty splash" [my words, in honor of Mr. Pryor, on page 9 of this book. He did so after she had slapped him on the back of the head for no reason at all. Resistance to racism came in all forms and fashions.

[18] What would a "fit" slave look like, be like? Probably physically strong and capable, but submissive and controllable. Miss Watson wasn't just being a dog, she was being a dog and pony show—greedy with the nasty to show that Jim would take it, easily. Little did she know, that the enslaved, when they could get their hands on them, most certainly kept receipts.

Jim got up and walked away, his mind flashing and panicky. After all that he'd done and done took from Ms. Watson, how could she? He couldn't understand it.

As he walked he traced his steps back to when Mr. Watson was dying and he carried the man's limp body, Mrs. Watson whimpering and crying. He carried him to the cart and rode him to the doctor as if there were some hope. And all the while he kept a soft heart to make sure Mrs. Watson was consoled.

As he walked he sweat, like when he built Mr. Watson's casket, even though he'd treated Jim like some worthless bastard, like Jim was some shame or disgrace that had befallen his family. And Mr. Watson would remind Jim all the time that his father was lynched for being a "walking calamity". And Jim still built the man's casket, carved with a rose, and stitched the inside with velvet to soften and warm his way whether he rose or fell. And Jim thought likely he'd fall and spend his velvet eternity burning in hell. But he still built the man's casket.

As Jim walked through the thicket on his way from Ms. Watson's house into the wood he remembered this: when Mrs. Watson lost her baby, it was Jim who took the child's poor lifeless body and buried it in the field, and built a wooden cross from a thick branch of cherry tree. It was Jim who prayed over the grave when Mrs. Watson couldn't lift her face from her pillow, while Mr. Watson was drunk as a skunk out under the willow. And Jim knew that this child would have one day owned him and learned the ways of his parents, learned to treat him with miscarriages of justice as if it were the natural balance. And he still built the child's casket and fit it with a cherry cross.

And as Jim made it to the edge of the Watson property, he recalled all he'd done to keep Ms. Watson from poverty. Like when the bank came for her farm the first time, it was Jim who hired himself out, to make extra money to pay the balance and keep Ms. Watson in her house. And Jim knew she would still call him *boy* though he worked like her man. And Jim knew that she couldn't remember his wife's name to save her right hand. And that she had used that right hand to whip him with all the force she could muster as if breaking Jim's back would crack open the past to bring back her husband and child... And after he built their caskets and saved her land, she would inflict this last treachery on this man?

And after all this she would send him from the only home he's known in Missouri, down the Mississippi to the big city at the bottom of the south? Sell him away from his family into the heart of darkness and doubt? To where he could be sold to anywhere but Timbuktu, she would ship him off with no regard for all that he'd done to help her through?

As Jim crossed the threshold of the wood, Jim paused as he finally understood. All this time, he knew he was enslaved. But somewhere inside he was choosing to endure slave days to make it to what was next, like all this suffering was a test he would pass once he made it to rest. He could have chosen, like his father, to live life fast and die trying by doing whatever he wanted whenever he pleased. In some ways, he was bearing his condition by planning on a better life for his seeds. And that's why he stayed even when he shouldn't—he hoped that life with the Watson's might offer a chance to build for his family something that being on the run wouldn't—a plot built atop his lot in life. Now he would be scattered to the wind, one of millions of black dandelion wisps, a chained and yet untethered kite. And as Jim stepped into the wood as he had a million times, this time he stepped anew, since he was certain of what he was about to do.

He thought a last time of Ms. Watson. All this time, she never understood Jim as a man enslaved choosing to live for another day.[19] She just thought him a slave born to do whatever it was that she might say. And any service he gave, building caskets for her husband and child per se, was just a part of his station. To her, the privilege *of breath* was his payment. That she let him live and work for her was something she felt he should feel grateful for in this nation. For she could have easily thought up a reason to have him beaten, burned, and hung for some social treason like his father, the libertine. All this, the perpetual threat of death, is the power Ms. Watson held above him like a guillotine.

Things hadn't ever been as clear to Jim as in this very moment—enslaved life was hell. After all he'd done and done went through, Jim's eyes could see clearly now. His heart had swelled to full, and the gravity of freedom became an irresistible pull.

To save her farm, Ms. Watson had planned to sell him tomorrow, and that would be the beginning of new and shifting sands of sorrow. He started to moan a tune as he marched swiftly through the wood.

---

[19] The question that haunts the teaching of American enslavement is why would antebellum Black folk accept that condition for so long. How could they? The answer is simpler than you might think. Wherever you are sitting right now, you are hoping for a better future. Whether you are in jail or on a private plane, you are hoping things will be better for your children. The enslaved were no different. The choice they had (which was no choice at all, Kanye) was to survive to raise a child who they hoped could be free or escape and take the chance to never again see their families because they were now dead or up north. What would you do? On top of that, if they were captured while escaping and sold down to trading posts like New Orleans, they would still be enslaved and likely never see their family again. What would you do? Before you say you would run away, think about all the little indignities you eat every day at your job to provide for your family. Multiply that by violence and torture enforced by law. Now what would you do?

This familiar melody was one old White folks would sing about when times were good as gold, but Jim made it new; he made it blues to reflect the truth: he could take almost anything but being sold.

Jim (*half singing, half mumbling, half thinking*):

Way down yonder in Old Orleans
this old lady-dog is selling me
far from my family
far from my seeds.

Way down yonder in Old Orleans
to the land of broken dreams
where the lashing rains
flood the fields with pain

There is hell right here on earth
where the labor is worse than work
in the land of broken dreams
way down in Old Orleans

Big old city with a trail of tracks
beat deep in the soil's back
oh the land of broken dreams
way down yonder in Old Orleans[20]

---

[20] I love New Orleans more than any of you do. But true love tells the truth. My hometown was the bottom of the American South and the top of the European Caribbean. That's a hell of a geographic location since it made for the perfect redistribution of bodies throughout the Western Hemisphere of slave society. Many of your favorite places to tour the French Quarter, to sit, listen to music, and eat, to get served with Southern Hospitality, to walk in the warm nostalgia of living history, are warm because they are still heated with the embers of the hell of slavery. Now, I know everybody loves New Orleans, but I love my city more than any of you do, and true love tells the truth.

Now back from his flashback to how Ms. Watson had broke the back of his camel-hump of submission to a slave's station, Jim hummed nervously in the wood outside Huck and Pap's shack. His face was tepid with trepidation and sullen with contemplation. He heard another voice singing, and he stopped suddenly as if his body were stunned by its reverberation. It was coming from a raggedy cabin shack. He crept in towards an open window and peeked in on Pap, who was singing an old pub song in the throes of luck lack. Pap slung the words against his wall with the exhausted crestfall of snake eyes in craps.

Pap (*singing, slurred*):

I walked down to the city
I wandered for a while
Looked high in the sky
Looked upon a child
Between the two I found myself
I measured what I am
A man is measured by his work—
The effort of his hands

I pondered on my purpose
What am I here for?
I walked upon the bank
and thought upon the shore
Epiphany she come to me
And measured what I am
A man is measured by his work
My work is what I am
A man is measured by his work—
the effort of his hands

Pap's voice cracked as his song devolved into a mumbling scoff, briefly broke down into a maniacal laugh, then choked into a cough. It spilled into ranting. He was panting as he found someone to blame from deep inside. Pap snarled about a free Black man he'd seen get off a train he himself couldn't afford to ride.

Pap (*mumbling to himself*):
It is evil. It's evil this ... This...
This gubment is the root of all evil. State's rights!
They want slaves to vote and women to think they's equal.
They hate life.
Pretty soon there'll be a mulatter president. That ain't right.
They'll let all them Mexican devils in to rape my dead wife.
Chinamen, Mooslims, the goddamned Jews!
What's a poor White man to do?
Look at my hat. Look at my coat. Look at my shoes.
Am I a white man or a back-broke mule?
Where's my rights to the riches of the country I built?
Where's my slaves gave as pay for the Injuns I kilt?
Where's all the land
they 'posed to grant [21]
to keep this country White filt?
Am I just some frothy filth
in the land of honey and milk?

---

[21] The Southern Homestead Act of 1866 granted free land to any person, regardless of race, who was willing to build a home in the west. As with any law, it is only as powerful as its enforcement and enactment. At best, long-held White stereotypes about formerly enslaved Black people's intelligence, moral worthiness, and work ethic probably led to denials of land grants in practice. On average, cold ambition probably kept White folks jumping the line on vulnerable Black folks in the minority. At worst, pure envious and fearful hate led to Black people being outright denied the opportunity to build wealth after slavery. Here, Pap's rant expresses all three of these sentiments during the decade before the Civil War.

That free slave[22] in Ohio
had the whitest shirt in the north.
I never seed such a cool cocky slave walking for sport.
He got off that train
like some kind of disciple of the lord.
He wouldn't give me the road
till I shoved him off my course.
I yelled about for a slave patrolman to come down off his horse.
And you know what he told me?
That this slave was free!
And they can't sell a free slave
till six months down South he be.
What kind of gubment
allow this kind of trav'sty?
They let a prowling, infernal,
white-shirted free slave
go free!
They said he was a professor,
could write and read!
I saw his gold watch on a chain,
his silver headed cane,
disinguishin' hisself
like the thieving slave he be.
Well let me out!
I got a mind to leave!
What kind of gubment
let's free slaves go a-walking free!

---

[22] This whole passage is derived from a passage Twain's *Huck Finn*, except Twain has Pap use the n-word everywhere you see "slave" here. As non-ironic as Pap's use of the n-word is in Twain's book is, the use of the word 'slave' is as ironic as can be. Here a free Black man is only a free slave, as if the state of being enslaved is as natural to the Black man as the privileges Pap expects are natural to the White man. As old and ridiculous as these sentiments seem, they aren't too far a stretch from garden variety White Nationalism of today. See Derek Black.

Pap stood up, enraged and stumbling forward, he was consumed with grumbling and mumbling. Jim, outside the window, heard the heavy racket of his tracks and ducked off behind a tree of the wood. But something told him to stay right there as long as he could.

He thought of the boy Huck and the fortune Jim had told him, about his Pap and how the world would scold the both of them. Thinking this drunk madman might do just about anything today, he thought he might wait to make sure that little unlucky mutt, Huck, was okay.

Meantime, Pap kept up his rage.

Pap:
With the nerve to open his mouth up to talk to me!
Why, we can't have a country with slaves free
so they may earn money that belongs to me!

Pap turned to Huck, his eyes maniacal with need. Spit foaming at the corners of his mouth, he grit his teeth.

Pap:
I want that $6000 boy.
I'm your damn pappy!
And that goddamn judge is a thug
for snatching that cash from me!
I'll cuss his Custer
with a bluster buster
and stuff that butt-sucker
in the gutter!

Screaming uncontrollably, he fell forward into a large trash pile. He went wild with fury, throwing and kicking refuse around the room in a flurry. Huck cowered in the corner knowing what was coming next. Pap scrambled to his feet and charged him, determined to catch him a wreck.

Huck covered his head as punches and kicks rained down. The muffled thuds pounded in awful, solid blocks of sound. Huck didn't cry out. He didn't whimper. He knew better. Pap wanted dead silence so he could hear the thumps of his blows in their deepest register.

Jim heard the whole thing, a few steps into the woods. But what good could he do? He stood behind a tree and broke a little inside for what slavery would have him be witness to: a child being mauled by his own father. It reminded Jim of a moment with his own daughter, and he almost took a step towards Pap's cabin. But then he thought about his daughter again.

Jim (*thinking*):
If I stop this,
I'll die.
I'll die for the act.
If I save this child,
what will become of my own?
I'll be sacrificing myself
and my family's chance at freedom.
No.
If I have to sacrifice this child
to be sure I can get mine free
then so it be.
God forgive me.
Forgive me, Huckleberry.

Jim sunk down to the roots of the tree. And as much of torture as it was, he listened to Huckleberry get beat. He said that if Huck got too quiet, he would knock on the door. And if Huck had died he would sure be the witness, and he would go to the judge to bear the truth on the chance that someone would listen.

Down on the roots of that tree, Jim felt the devil of guilt gnawing at his hilts, his fists, elbows, and knees. Jim could have kilt Pap easy with his bare hands. He could have beat the savage out of that man. But he let him maul his own child.

Jim stared into the dark, into the horror of the fact that Huck didn't even scream. As bad as he was getting beat, he was taking it all in steam. *Huck strong as a buck*, Jim thought as he drifted, thankfully, off to his dreams.

Dreams meant a lot to Jim. They seemed to tell him what he couldn't see, and he did his best to remember them and figure out what they might mean.

The sense in the dream he had that night wasn't easily found. The main thing he could remember was the thickest of fogs, but the fog only came up to his hands hanging down. And every time he would pull his hands up out of the fog, they no longer looked brown. His hands had turned grey and wrinkled and loose-skinned, as if they belonged to a corpse. There were spots where the skin was wearing down to reveal bone between sores.

A little sickened, Jim looked all around to find he was alone. But he could hear a sound, what sounded like a song, but wasn't. It was more like a moan. Jim realized he was moaning.

Then he felt pain in his hands as if hidden spiders and rats and snakes were on him. But he'd pull his hands out only to find he was tearing his nails into his own skin. And the dream went on in that fashion, with Jim unsure who was doing what, only to find out it was him doing everything, and with the fog all the while half swallowing him whole and, while the pain in his hands would come and go, every time he looked at his dead hands, they were pocked with holes.

An hour into Jim's dream, Huck sat in the corner with a trail of dried blood crusted down his face. He clutched his legs to his body. Purple bruises bloomed on his arms in the shape of Pap's boot. Huck's calf was swollen and knotty. Huck was leveling a shotgun at Pap, holding it up between his knees. He was shell-shocked, but determined. Through his stuttering, Huck got to muttering a survival sermon.

Huck (*to himself*):
He said it was snakes.
I don't see no snakes.
He's got the shakes again,
D... D... Delirium tremens.
He's asleep now,
but that won't last.
If he comes for me now,
I'll have to blast.
Where he put that knife?
He wants to put it in me.
He says I'm the Angel of Death...

He rustled up the gun and made sure it was aimed right at Pap.

Huck:
Well we'll see.

He sucked air and covered his mouth to keep a tearful yelp inside.

Huck (*to himself*):
Too many blows on my back.
Too many punches and kicks.
Too many times he snatched me up
to slap me down,
to whip me with sticks
till my back turns brown.

Am I a boy or a slave to be beat this way?
I'm not staying in this place another day.
I already thunk up the plan.
He's got to think I'm dead
or I'll never be a free man.
I'll cut that pig like a ham
and pour the blood from his head.
I'll take everything
and make it look like some tragedy,
like some villain broke in
and I stood my ground
and so the villain axed me.
On Jackson Island, I'll lay low
'till Pap and the widow let me go,
and then I'll set westward ho.
I'll follow the sun
through the sky.
I don't need spit but my wits
and Pap's gun
for my life to be mine,
for to be free.
Mr. Huckleberry Finn,
A free man I'll be.

When Jim woke from his slumber, the first thing he did was wonder if Huck was alive. He took a moment to wipe his eyes and breathe. He was recovering from the frightful dream by shaking his hands and tugging down his sleeves. His jacket tore at the shoulder and he didn't notice, he couldn't possibly care. He was staring at Pap's cabin, still wondering what he would do if Huck was dead in there.

He mustered something that was somewhere between courage and responsibility, and he made his way over to Pap's cabin, quietly. He'd made it to a corner that had a crack between logs and peeked an eyeball in. He saw Huck awake holding his shotgun ready to pop Pap, who was snoring in a heap of a drunken mess, flat on his back.

Jim backed away from the crack and worked his way back to the wood, thinking *if that boy shoots his own Pap it'd be his Pap's own fault for making the boy so hard that he could. Life fights to live whether bear, buck, or kid.*

Jim(*to himself*):
I got to get away from this.
This a madness.
Power done got these people so savage.
This boy rather make himself a bastard,
put his Pap in a casket,
than take another beating.
That's tragic,
but that's what you get
when you used to treating men
less than a dog.
It makes it too easy
to get lost in the fog
of the freedom to find something pleasing
in being a tyrant over men.
White men take that bloodlust home
and put it on they woman and children.
I got to get away from this.

I'm going to Jackson Island
to take some time
'till I can find the plan
somewhere deep in my mind.
By river or through rough
I won't live in a place
that let's a man be Pap
and beat his son like that,
but won't let me
protect my own kids
from another man's lash.
That dream I had,
me tearing at my dead hands,

58

that's me rotting from inside
every day I accept being a slave
and not a man.
I got to get away from this place.
I got to trust my legs,
even if I can't see where they leading,
push through the fog
half-swallowed
but still believing.
I got to trust my legs,
even if I can't see them.
I got to ride my own body
to freedom.

But what of Sadie, his wife? What of their children, his life? Would he take the time to tell them so as to spare them some strife? This was one of the most difficult decisions he'd thought through a thousand times or more. Through all Jim's calculations, he'd come to one conclusion—no, and no for sure. He figured the less they know, the more safe their souls and the more secure their bodies. If they were as shocked as anyone when they find out, maybe they wouldn't be pressed to confess. If they'd cried or if they wailed loudly, they'd seem true. It tore a wound in his heart to think of their worry, but he hoped that's what they'd do—scream out in fear that their dear father and husband had run off. Jim said a little prayer for the protection of their hearts.

Jim (*in a whisper*):
I ain't ever ask you much, dear God.
I know You busy
with the whole world in Your hands.
But I'm begging You for Sadie and my boy,
for Sadie and my baby girl
to remember what they know of me
and to know I must have a plan.

59

Chapter 5

Jim Escapes

*Negotiating escape
is an act of erected dignity.
It is the resurrected eternal
yearn to be free.
Freedom has no end,
no place, no nation, nor creed.
Freedom is simply the urge followed—
the choice to be free.*

****

How Jim escaped was sweet wine he made out of water. It was whole loaves of possibility he'd made from the crumbs life had offered. It was as if Jim were his own personal lord and savior. It was hard and got harder till it got done for him to savor. It went like this from sun to sun, as Jim never waivered once he'd begun. He'd gone over the plan in his mind more times than he had years under the gun.

When Jim heard Ms. Watson's treason, he lit out with perfect time. He knew what time to go and he knew the proper signs. Jim knew how to follow the smoke to find the wind, and how much traffic any particular hour of river would bring. He knew that when the owl howled it told him which black of the night sky made for the best cover. He knew when each creeping White man would be on the prowl for his lover. He knew when the dogs were fed and done for the evening. He'd run them extra hard all day and fed them double so they would be heavy sleeping. He knew what to do.

The only thing he hadn't anticipated was hearing that demon Pap beat his son Huck red, black, and blue.

After having heard the torture of poor Huck, which left him feeling miserably, Jim went down to the bank of the river expecting to swift off in a skiff. But the canoe that was usually there wasn't there to lift. So he ducked out in the barrel-maker's shop to wait for the coast to clear, till all hosts to toast their moonshine. He waited all night till about evening-time nine.

At that point, he wasn't worried about Ms. Watson missing him since he'd had plantation patterns down to the minute; he knew Ms. Watson kept a church camp meeting that would keep her preoccupied with praying about sinning; she was used to Jim heading out with the cattle about when the sun starts to grinning; the rented overseer wouldn't miss him since he'd holiday as soon as Ms. Watson was in the wind.

As soon as the river traffic allowed, he slipped in and went to pounding strokes out, humping across the river with the rhythm of a beaver. That rhythm made him sound like a swimming retriever. He knew water was the only way to make himself some luck. If he went by land the dogs would catch his sent and no matter how far he got, he'd be sitting duck. So water was the only way.

The river was rising and the current was strong and you might think that was good favor when a body is trying to get gone, on to the free bank of Cairo then on as far away as Decatur. But getting down the river wasn't the hard part; the difficulty was getting across. The river's push isn't easy to crack, no. This is the Mississippi, boss!

He felt every bit of billions of drops of water tugging him forward, each a tiny horse, each with its own little bit of force. When added all up and moving together on one course, the entirety of the thing could make the most power-rich steamboat miserly, and could rip and throw a thousand trees with the ease of a breeze, and do it all quietly. That was just the power Jim needed to get away, if he could push himself to cut across the flow. So he kicked and pulled and pushed and frog stroked.

Jim made it to a gaggle of logs loose in the river and grabbed to one and kept his head low so all that would show of him was a sliver. Jim never felt so good to be brown—to match tree bark. He thought, *my hat will look like a stump lump; my arms will go unseen. White man say my skin a sin—please. That's because it help me steal away with from him ease.*

Jim rode that log for miles and miles till four in the morning, awake the whole time with eyes wide for any canoe coming. This was a lot of time to think, and think Jim did. His mind was a marathon with all the thoughts running.

Jim ran through the terrors he'd heard and horrors he could name of what would happen to slaves who'd grown weary enough to break their chains. The names would come and go, he couldn't remember if it had been Emmit, Tray, or Floyd, Garner, Sandra, or Philando, but the faces though, their faces froze hard and cold into Jim's memory, iceberg casts of ghastly faces gnashed by the white teeth of mobs with their children in tow. Now, on the river, he saw those faces in the nobs of bark of the logs, in the eddies shimmering dark, in the spaces between the leaves of branches hung and rocking in the breeze. He saw them in every blink. Every time he felt a bit of hope in the distance, one of those faces would float by and his heart would sink. Maybe the next name would be Jim. Maybe the next face would be him.

But then, Jim remembered Ms. Watson wouldn't have him murdered. He was worth too much to her for that. Jim had done the math and found himself Ms. Watson's most valuable possession, and that was a fact. But because he was worth more to himself, he had made his mind up that he would die before he went back, and that meant the man who tried to catch him would catch Jim's hands and his hands had been strengthened by holding writhing pigs and his hands were big and his hands were thick and his hands were hard as red brick and his hands were fast as blood is slick. So the man who tried to catch Jim would catch them hands, and the heap Jim would leave him in would be his last stand—his next step would be to death.

So it wasn't so much the catchers who had Jim's heart and mind racing, but his own will, which had made its mind up that it had the heart to kill anyone standing between him and getting free. Hard as Jim tried to consider another way, no other way could be. So Jim was shook by the thing in him that had made this decision. He was shook because he knew he had it in him, and the moment to let it out might be soon coming. He had to calm himself ready.

To stay calm he started to watching everything. He watched the bugs zip and zoom sending tiny waves sweeping like a broom. He watched the bird's bellies shine with the reflected the light of the moon. He watched the frogs sit in clumps, little lumps of gloom. He watched the snakes whittle away at the water with hard-earned ease. He watched the fish wriggle their tails to leave the water cleaved. He watched everything, and everything was free, and he felt a lift in his spirit because soon, so would he be.

And yet Jim knew soon ain't never now, and soon ain't done till now comes, and soon becomes never as regular as the moon becomes the sun. And so till then—when soon becomes now, there's work to be done.

There were a couple of close calls with rafters riding by, but their rocking lamps threw light with a rhythm that gave them away long before they could get close to Jim's side. But one particular canoe was keeping pace with him, and Jim felt the need to get some distance.

Now, a log is just a log, and kicking off was not an option because the sound would bend off the surface of the river and slip right into the sense of any man with an ear, and he'd know there was somebody swimming near; and he'd likely think they were coming for him. In a state as rowdy as Missouri that could mean anything from a runaway slave willing to do anything to get away to a robber coming to swing his blade. And Jim didn't want any vigilance tweaking the nerves of a White man when he was trying to find his way to free land. So as he approached Jackson Island, a mount in the middle of the river, he started looking for a bank shallow and near enough for him to glide to a crouching stand. But no such luck. Most of the banks were too bluff. With no grip, one slip and he'd come crashing back into the water loud enough to wake a drunkard up.

The log he clung to was almost to the end of the island before he found a suitable bank, and once he did he left the river to regroup. Water weighted his clothes as it streamed in streaks off his flesh. He'd long lost his shoes, so his toes sunk in self-made mud with every step. But, he'd kept his pipe and matches dry in his hat, and so he looked for a stump to rump on, to serve as a stoop to sit and smoke and calm his nerves for a spell. As he did, he dipped down deep into the well of courage that running had dug for him. He said, *well*, and sipped the bittersweet wine of time again.

Soon, Jim popped the cork on a grin, slapped both knees with both hands, and said in a weirdish whisper, *Call me Free Jim!*[23]

---

[23] One of the deeply disrespectful developments of the story of Twain's Jim over the years was the constant literary references to him as "N*gger Jim." Twain never wrote those words in the book itself, and apparently never said them when he publicly read from *Adventures of Huckleberry Finn*, at least in front of Black audiences (see *Huck Finn's America*, by Andrew Levy). Some reviewer or critic or reader or teacher came up with that little bit of viciousness. But is calling him "N*gger Jim" any worse than calling him a "runaway", as if he were some obstinate child running from the inevitability of his situation, as if people ran on a whim, in a fit of being fed-up with their station? Escaping slavery a lot of times must have been meticulously planned and thought through. It had to be worried over and agreed on after first being refused. The enslaved knew the consequences would fall on those left behind, those they might never see again. Escape was the most difficult decision the enslaved could make. Should you stay to raise your children in the hope that they might be free one day? Should you run in the hope that you could somehow make it to make a way? Few of us know that difficult a choice. But we should know that the escaped enslaved weren't just throwing themselves to fate when making up their minds get free. They were making a holy choice, a grave decision, a powerful use of their inherent and indominable human agency against all odds. So Jim, calling himself, "Free Jim" is a nod to that and to himself. "Free Jim" is title deserved—a new name—made out of deep respect for a man who broke his chains, and another way to free Jim from the hold of Twain.

Chapter 6
Jim and Huck Meet Again
and Strike a Bargain

A deal lays the cards out
till each hand is set.
Yet, how each plays their hand,
and how one bets,
is the crest atop which fate is pressed,
and the eternal mountain of chance lays underneath,
at rest.

******

Let's back back a few days to how Huck got saved because the boy deserves some word play for the way he managed to steal away. We only know this part of the story because Huck told Jim, over some of those dark nights to come, about why the boy would sometimes wake up screaming and crying like from the devil himself he was on the run. This story, for Jim, was one of those moments that he couldn't help but feel for Huck. It made Jim think of his own youth and why a poor boy would have to go through so much.

Huck's get away plan—to butcher a pig and flood it's blood about Pap's cabin as if he himself had been stabbed and dragged away—Huck's plan proceeded swimmingly up until it was time to kill the swine and swill the scene with blood. It wasn't that Huck had any problem with gore. He had seen more than his share of gizzards and guts. It was just harder than he imagined it.

As he axed the pig, he saw flashes of what his Pap had did to his Maw. The noise the pig made sounded like a scream. And the slits in its skin looked most like the long seams that came open when his mother was beat for that last time. And it took Huck an awful long grind to finish the kill for the tears that kept rushing from him against his will. He hadn't cried so hard for his mother up until then, out of fear that Pap would snap out of a dark corner to kill him.

And he cried and cried so much he had to stop, and bent over in a crumple like a human rock. And the screams of the pig and his own chokes and wails made a sound that might make a gator tuck its tail. Huck couldn't stop, wouldn't stop crying.

That was up until he happened to hear a nightingale gurgling, trilling, and whistling from wherever it was perched up above, resting from flying. And before long it begun to sound like a song, more like a song than any bird words Huck had heard whining. In fact it sounded like his mother, and how she'd shush him to sleep.

Huck could have sworn he heard the bird peep, in his mother's favorite melody. It was a song she always sung to shush him to sleep. The song sucked Huck into a memory.

It was his mother bent over him, water wetting her eyes, her mouth moving slowly above him spreading and folding like a pinkish sunset cloud. And she sung with the force of a storm of feeling. And she sung with the gush of a waterspout. And she sung with the warmth of summer soil. And she sung quiet, not loud.

Ma (*in Huck's memory*):
Oh baby, babe
It's time for you to sleep babe
Oh baby, babe
It's time for you to sleep
And when you sleep
The world will calm around you
And in that calm
You'll dream the night away
And when you wake
The sun will come to greet you
And when you wake
The moon will wave goodbye
And I'll be here
To hold you so close to me
Oh baby babe
I love you so

Huck settled into that, that the bird sung his mother's song. That even though she'd been gone so long, she was somehow still watching over him. And that was a revelation of light in an outlook pure dim. And despite the throngs of what could go wrong, the song was just what he needed to be strong. And so he kept on.

Huck took what he needed. He laid his trap for Pap to think that he'd been hacked. He felt good when he looked back at what he'd done, like God on the seventh day of creation or on the third day, after resurrecting a son. After taking a canoe, Huck was set to ride the river dew away from Pap, away from the Widow, and on and on to whatever was new.

He slipped the canoe into a seam sunk between a braided bulge of river run. Under the weight of one foot, then another, the vessel sunk ever so slightly due to the light weight a boy bears. The canoe waddled as water humped by its sides brown as a bear with flecks of dried mustard orange and tufts of gumbo green and plumes of white burped up from some river creature's spleen.

If he had been a diving bell spider the current would seem a mountain range and the colors, the aurora borealis. If he had been a guppy, his canoe would be a cloud and the trail of his path the aftermath of a streaking comet. If he had been a demon shrimp his paddle might be the hand of God come to sweep the river sod and wipe him and all his kin to hell to rot. But Huckleberry was a man to be, an adventurer ready to cut his teeth on a river he knew about as well as a river rat ought to. And so he rode on not knowing that the town would soon catch word of his death, and a search party would soon start blasting the river to force Huck's body up from the depths.

His river trek took him to Jackson Island, a mile-long wooded stretch, a mound rounding out of the middle of the Mississippi. It split the Father of Rivers[24] in two till the two currents reintroduced themselves to their common destiny. Once there and satisfied with having gotten away, Huck found himself in a thicket of lonesomeness sitting restlessly.

For three days and three nights, Huck was stuck in a mess of regrets. Was this really better than being trained by the Widow? It was certainly better than being beat. But think of the heartbreak she would have dreaming of his body reduced to bloody meat. Those three days were the worst of freedom, the freedom to dwell on all the things that might condemn him to hell, and on all those things Pap had done him that he could never tell, and on why he was ever born at all, and on how at any moment he might be mauled, on so many things of which he was ashamed, and on Tom Sawyer and never seeing him again.

---

[24] "Father of Waters" is a poetic English interpretation of a merging of phrases in two different indigenous languages. Most American's don't generally think of Mississippi as a state of self-awareness. Having grown up a neighbor of Mississippi (the river, the state, and the people), I can tell you most Americans are wrong. According to the Mississippi.gov website, the word Mississippi "comes from the Chippewa words 'mici zibi' meaning 'great river' or 'gathering in of all the waters' and the Algonquin word 'messipi.'" The preceding quote, for those unfamiliar with Mississippi ways and means, means "we don't know what the word means, but it meant something important to somebody and it means everything to us." The Mississippi River's impact on America can't be overstated—The Midwest nursed from it. The South was its slave. The North was draped in the bounty of its delta soil. The lifeblood of the West (oil) came from the land the Mississippi made. Mississippi, Father of Waters, is what Jim leaned on to escape.

So on the fourth day of his escape, Huck rose to escape his mind and explore his new life on this land bubble carving the center of the river like a whale's black might crack the ocean open with its flat shoulder. Before long he wandered upon a campsite and a body warming its head by a smolder. Huck took cover and waited to see who this lone companion might be. Before long, the body stirred and revealed its owner to him. Huck felt a flash of upful relief. It was Jim!

Huck:
Hey Jim! It's Huck!
What luck to end up
finding a familiar friend in all this rough!

Jim (*thinking quickly*):
Damn luck and buck friends,
a man don't need this boy's trouble
following him.
I knew his death was faked soon as I heard it.
Don't nobody drag a bloody body half a mile
once they've murdered it.
Can't say I blame him for running
from that hell of a Pap,
but I can't have him on my back
slowing my path
I'll make him think I think he's a ghost
and be gone
as fast as fright might make
a poor, ignorant fool
get on

Huck saw how Jim was looking at him, with a mix of fear and concern. Thinking Jim might think him a ghost, Huck was about to explain. But, before he could speak, Jim yelped like he was being maimed.

Jim (*acting more scared than he was*):

Oh no,
I 'on't wont no trouble wit no ghost!
You could have the island!
I'm gone!
But Lord bless you though!

Jim grabbed the little sack he had and turned away to
make his way away with haste, but Huck yelled at him to wait,
please wait! His voice was full of ache. It was a voice like a
prisoner begging for water, like a lamb's last shout at the
moment of slaughter, like Jim's own daughter when a
nightmare done caught her and shook her awake. The voice
stopped Jim in his tracks. He looked back into Huck's face.

Huck:
No Jim, don't go.
I ain't no ghost.
I'm alive can't you tell?
I faked the whole thing
to get away safe.
Pap done went mad
and I can't take no more.
So I'm here on Jackson's shore
to see what might be in store.
Tell me, Jim.
Jim, what you here for?

At that question, Jim's gut dropped. He was not about
to tell this boy that he done run. Jim had to make some quick
sense to put Huck on the defense about what *he* done, so he
would stop wondering about what Jim done done. With that
bit of a turned table, Jim would have to figure out an angle that
might keep Huck from sending him back to get beat, burned,
or dangled.

Jim:
Oh Huck, honey,

I'm so glad you not dead!
I felt a fist full of sadness when I heard it said
that you'd been cut up like a stuck pig.
But good gracious,
young Huck lives!
And the Widow will be so happy to hear it!

Jim (*thinking*):
And there it is.
This boy don't want to go back.
I'll hold him ransom for his silence
in exchange for mine,
and matter fact
I'll help him get away
and he'll help me the same.
A white boy with a name
can save a slave from getting hanged.

Huck:
Oh no, Jim.
I don't know why you would speak of me.
I'm looking for a new life,
a new place to be.
But, say, what you doing
so far from your place, tell me?

Now, you should know by now that Jim wasn't dumb. There is no such thing as a dumb slave. Dumb implies numb to sense and the enslaved without sense don't survive their days. Sense in the enslaved is precise as a pyramid; sense is to the enslaved what war is to the Illiad. The enslaved have to construct a perfect harmony with sense, lest they slip into dissonance and be broken into a thousand fragments.

Jim had some sense. He could smell Huck's fish from the hook. So he decided to drop all pretense and read Huck's book.

Jim:
Well, I won't speak of your run
if you don't speak of mine.

Huck:
Jim, you done run and stole yourself?
Why would you do something so ...?
How could you commit such a crime?

Jim:
I heard I was gone to be sold to Old Orleans,
and that told me it was time.
Now you promise me,
and I'll promise you
and we'll set our minds to do together
what we left to do.

Huck:
Jim,
folk will call me a rotten abolitionist.
I've never seen slave-loving forgiven
as long as I been living.

Huck paused and turned his back to Jim to contemplate. He walked away a ways so as not to face Jim's face and any influence it might have on a question as flush with contention as this.

Now, it seems an easy choice to make—help this man get free. Yet, Huck knew he couldn't get away with doing the right thing so easily. See doing the right thing when the whole world is wrong means being willing to say *if it's the whole world against me, then so it be*, and ain't many a man been made that can say that and mean it confidently. In fact there's probably only been three: Moses, Jesus, and Mohammed, rest in peace.

Huck wasn't even a man; how could he understand the nature of such a choice better than a boy of fourteen could? For a child as low rung as him, helping Jim would cost any chance at being let in a world that would rather cast him out to the streets. What would Moses, Jesus, or Mohammed do at fourteen in America circa 1853?

If Huck chose to turn Jim in, he would choose his society[25] over his freedom, and they'd both he and Jim would be bound for some type of prison. Jim might even be hung. Pap might break Huck's back for being such a son as would steal a gun and waste a pig. Should a boy of fourteen, as short as he'd lived, even carry the fate of himself and a full grown man like this? Huck thought, *why am I the god of wrong and right?*

Behind Huck's back and out of sight, Jim's hand was in his pocket. His mind was on flight as he inched out a handle, then a peek of the blade of a rusted knife. Jim gripped it tight as a child grips a candle at night, and thought to himself about how to handle this plight.

---

[25] Thomas Paine, the British traitor and American patriot once wrote about the nature of society in his famous pamphlet *Common Sense.* "Society in every state is a blessing... the strength of one man is so unequal to his wants, and his mind so unfitted for perpetual solitude, that he is soon obliged to seek assistance and relief of another, who in his turn requires the same." In short, folk come together to help each other do what they can't do alone. The hundred million deaths question that humanity has to answer every so often is this—why do societies keep committing atrocities against each other? The paradox is that society, as Paine describes it, is the problem and the solution. Huck's society, slave society, requires he return the assistance his Whiteness has and will give him. That assistance takes the form of aligning with White supremacy. Yet, that same society, slave society, produces the horrors that Huck has been a victim of by way of his Pap. White supremacy requires violent injustice. The question here is whether or not Huck will choose his society, one that empowers his collective White race at the expense of his individual freedom to choose society with Jim, a Black man. Spoiler alert, he doesn't choose here.

Jim (*to himself*):
A twice dead boy won't tell no lies.
I'd hate to do it,
but I'd trade my freedom for his life.
Yep, freedom keeps a shotgun,
and this boy's got one,
and that might just get me past a patter roller.
If I took him now
and turned his body over
to the river
to deliver him south,
then not a sliver
of a word of me
would ever exit his mouth.

Meanwhile, Huck stubbed his mind on his own
dilemma.

Huck (*to himself*):
Yeah, they'll hate me alright.
They'll make me an enemy of
all things good and White.
They'll keep me from working.
They'll stop me from taking a wife,
and all just for spite.
They might hang me
and the Pappy what sprang me.

Well that might be alright.
I druther be dead
then to be with him
or in a world what feeds him gin
and keeps him grim
day and night.
I might just take my chances with Jim
since at least with a slave such as him

I got some power.
I got some right.

Huck (*to Jim*):
Blast it, Jim.
I'll take their spit.
Honest Injun.
Your secret is our secret.
I'll keep it.

Jim pushed the knife quickly back into his pocket and smiled, but he kept his hand there. He'd be damned if he'd let the whims of a boy determine the wind and whether he lands square.

Jim wore the mask and bore the task of every slave who would survive. He looked up in a disguise of smiles and played the slave a while.

Jim:
Well Huck, I guess you my lil' partner
'tillin I's free.
And good a man as Huck seem to be
dat's jus alright wit me.
Say Huck,
you wants to hunt up something
something other than strawberries to eat.

Huck:
That's all you been eating
all these three days?

Jim:
That's all there was to find
along the way.

Huck:
Well I got a canoe full of goods

I took from my Pap.
I'll be right back
with enough to make you fat.

Jim:
Well yes suh, yes suh.

Jim (*to himself*):
This might work out alright
for a couple days,
a couple nights
till he get found by his people
and I go my way.

And that day, Huck and Jim ate bacon and catfish, coffee
with sugar –a feast! Jim called it a land of luck that Huck could
provide so much to eat. They sat back in a glaze of laze that
stretched the rest of the day and talked of signs and what signs
say.

Jim said the crickets were screaming to warn the fairies that
rain was coming sure as his chest was hairy. Then he told
Huck that the thicket on his chest was his ticket, that it was the
fur of a man sure to be rich. Huck took issue with this. For
how could a slave be rich when his whole body belonged to
another and was either working for free or thrown in a ditch?

Jim thought it a good question and worth it's weight in an
answer. So he told his motivation for the risk he was taking,
and it lit, in Huck's mind, a lantern.

Jim:
I used to think my wife, boy, and lil girl
were all I had in this world,
but they are slaves.
They don't even belong to God above
much less to me.
Once I heard I was sold to Orleans
I knew I didn't even own my own feet.

78

But once I'm free,
I figure I'll have the price of my body.
I heard Ms. Watson was to sell me
for 800 dollars.
I reckon that's mine now.
And on the value of my body
I'll speculate my labors.
I'll collect my pay
from my friends and neighbors
till I can buy my wife and children out.
And then I'll have them,
and they'll have me,
and between us three
we'll be rich no doubt.

And there was a long silence then, as Huck considered Jim and while Jim considered himself. They sat and listened to the currents washing along, and watched some other suns[26] whisper prayers or songs from the purple-black felt upon which throngs of white stars knelt. And for the first time, Huck tried to feel what a slave's life might be like if he were free. Yet, Huck couldn't get past the belief, in his mind, that a slave was all a slave was ever meant to be.

---

[26] Shout out to Isabel Wilkerson for her Pulitzer Prize winning historical masterpiece, *The Warmth of Other Suns: The Epic Story of America's Great Migration*. Read it and weep for pride, pain, and predictions about the future of the United States.

Then, just as Jim had said, the rain came to thrash the trees and rip the wind, and everything began to bow and bend to nature's whims. And Huck and Jim took off to find a cave so they could hole up for the night as the thunder throes grunted and rolled under lightning strikes. The storm crackled around the cave and burst the air into whipping whiffs of warm, wet river breath. Jim and Huck sat to chat as the water rose to crest. Jim told Huck another way to be keyed to oncoming weather; be worried if the birds hurry in one direction. It was the second of many such lessons on how to stay present to presages in nature's messages.

Jim stopped Huck from catching a bird. He said it brings death to catch something meant to be free. Jim said his father had died after catching a squirrel and getting it in his mind he had powers no White man could see. That he was quicker than a gun, faster than a dog, and too heavy for a tree.

Jim's granny had warned his daddy, to no avail. She had warned Jim too. But sometimes a sign just lets a man know just how rough it will be to do what he's got to do. Jim knew all the signs, the many signs of bad and worse luck. And Huck ate it all up like a pup lapping from his master's cup. And Jim liked his attention.

Jim talked of seeing a dead body at a medical college[27], but didn't tell Huck why he was there, and then he told of his many speculations on fortune and dare. He'd bought and lost a cow, invested in a bank, and tried dumb luck; but all these things had tanked and he'd ended up with nothing but his hairy chest and arms – a sure sign of future come ups. Jim said that this sign had already come true because here he was with Huck and almost a free man, too.

Huck thought *this was nice* and *I wouldn't druther be anywhere but where I am tonight.* They stayed in that cave for over ten days, the river rising the whole time. They ventured out to check on things from time to time, open to whatever they'd find.

---

[27] In *Huck Finn*, Twain made a reference to Jim's visit to a medical college in passing. Was it random? Read this and weep for shame, suffering , and crimes of a slave society's rot: "The Use of Blacks for Medical Experimentation and Demonstration in the Old South" by Todd Savitt in the Journal of Southern History Volume 48, Number 3, pages 331-348. (1982) Here's a quotation for you: "Black bodies often found their way to dissecting tables, operating amphitheaters, classrooms or bedside demonstrations, and experimental facilities." This article acknowledges two other important aspects of experimentation on Black people. First, that poor European immigrants in cities like New Orleans, Louisville, Memphis, Charleston and Mobile were also scooped up for experimentation as "clinical material". Learned lesson: if you allow it to be done to one, you allow it to be done to all. Second, Black people were experimented on more frequently because they "were rendered physically visible by their skin color but were legally invisible because of their slave status." These were crimes of opportunity made opportune by America's slave society.

The river was a ravenous mess on the North side of a curve; it had spilled its banks to become a mile wide as it dispersed. It bit through tree trunks and gobbled up their root guts; it chewed fences, swallowed their rubble, and took wagons on wild rides. And even before the flood, the river was a treacherous beast ever since the government had flooded free states with bounties for human hides[28]. Jim, a fugitive slave in the act, was in season and there were plenty poor White and Black with reason to treason against freedom to hunt and trap his flesh.

---

[28] The *Fugitive Slave act of 1850* requires that any enslaved person who escapes to a "free state" must be returned to enslavement, that those attempting to return an enslaved person to enslavement may use force to retrain this escaped formerly-enslaved person, and that any enslaved person who resists being re-enslaved or any free person who aids an escaped enslaved personal will be committing a crime. Well actually it says this in Section 6 - when a person held to service or labor in any State or Territory of the United States, has heretofore or shall hereafter escape into another State or Territory of the United States, the person or persons to whom such service or labor may be due, or his, her, or their agent or attorney, duly authorized, by power of attorney, in writing, acknowledged and certified under the seal of some legal officer or court of the State or Territory in which the same may be executed, may pursue and reclaim such fugitive person, either by procuring a warrant from some one of the courts, judges, or commissioners aforesaid, of the proper circuit, district, or county, for the apprehension of such fugitive from service or labor, or by seizing and arresting such fugitive, where the same can be done without process, and by taking, or causing such person to be taken, forthwith before such court, judge... *blah, blah, blah, legalese malarkey*... with authority to such claimant, or his or her agent or attorney, to use such reasonable force and restraint as may be necessary, under the circumstances of the case, to take and remove such fugitive person back to the State or Territory whence he or she may have escaped as aforesaid.

And this in Section 7 - *And be it further enacted,* That any person who shall knowingly and willingly obstruct, hinder, or prevent such claimant, his agent or attorney, or any person or persons lawfully assisting him, her, or them, from arresting such a fugitive from service or labor, either with or without process as aforesaid, or shall rescue, or attempt to rescue, such fugitive from service or labor, from the custody of such claimant, his or her agent or attorney, or other person or persons lawfully assisting as aforesaid, when so arrested, pursuant to the authority herein given and declared; or shall aid, abet, or assist such person so owing service or labor as aforesaid, directly or indirectly, to escape from such claimant, his agent or attorney, or other person or persons legally authorized as aforesaid; or shall harbor or conceal such fugitive, so as to prevent the discovery and arrest of such person, after notice or knowledge of the fact that such person was a fugitive from service or labor as aforesaid, shall, for either of said offences, be subject to a fine not exceeding one thousand dollars, and imprisonment not exceeding six months... https://avalon.law.yale.edu/19th_century/fugitive.asp.

The river on the South side was as it always was, high white bluffs like a prison fortress. But they had no time for thinking back; they had to go forward to progress.

Up ahead, they saw a house cracked in half; a two-story, half-sunk, was floating down—a casualty of the war between land and water. Jim and Huck loaded themselves in the canoe to see this domicile slaughtered. As they approached the smashed out windows they could tell someone had been living there due to all the human life story puddled into piles of rubble everywhere.

They called out and there was no response. Jim looked closer and cocked his head for a better look. There was a body there, white and naked as meat hanging from a butchers hook. Seemed like the dead man had been shot in the back and stripped to his craw and buffers. He told Huck that a flood is a trouble that brings out the best in some and the worst in others.

Jim climbed in the house first and moved over to the man to take a long look at his face, then covered it with a piece of cloth and told Huck to stay away.

Jim:
Stay back Huck.
You shouldn't see this.
No boy should witness
such a mess as a body
shot by men and whipped by the Mississipp.
Go on and look for things to keep.
It'll be your death gift from this body.
Then we'll leave it to Old Man River
to take it where it was bound to be.

Basically, this law deputizes every single part of society, from the courts to police to private businesses to private citizens, to help recapture any enslaved person who escaped… and creates a poor folk (White or Black) feeding frenzy.

Jim and Huck looked around the room and saw the most ignorant words and pictures scrawled with charcoal, some old greasy men's clothes and clean women's clothes hanging from the ceiling in a web of chartreuse. They took it all thinking some bit of this grimy refuse may be brought into some timely use.

They found a sharp knife, a hatchet, and a fishing line. They found a wooden leg, a roll of buckskin, a horseshoe and a kit for shoeshine. They found medicine with no label, a tin cup, a fiddle bow, and a shitty shawl. Jim, for the life of him, couldn't understand the depravity in which some White men crawl.

As Huck left to go look for useful items, Jim looked at the body once more and thought. He looked perturbed and unsure, and spoke to himself about what he just saw.

Jim (*to himself*):
Yep, it's Pap,
Huck's daddy,
which means the boy is free.
That's good for him.
Better a bastard be
than the son of bastard such as he.
Yeah, this is good for him,
and not so good for me.
If I tell him
he might go back and stay.
I won't have him as cover
for my mission away.

Well when old Moses split the sea,
he told his people follow me,
and didn't tell them about the dusty days of trouble ahead
once they got free.
Moses could see
that this was the way it had to be.

84

No, Huck should never know,
not till Cairo[29],
about the death of his pappy.

Not till old Jim is free,
will young Huck be.

And that was that. Jim had made up his mind to leave the truth flat on the floor of the house that necessity built. He decided—in the face of opportunity, he will not wilt. Huck was a luck struck and Jim was certainly willing to tap that to the tune of two or three fateful riffs. You can try to judge him for keeping it from the boy for his own benefit, but if you think you can judge an escaped slave for anything, I got news for you, fool: You can't. Freedom is as freedom does, and it is liberty or death for all those whom freedom loves, and freedom loves everybody. Take that as you will.

They rummaged the room and took almost all. It was a decent, if random haul—the remainder of a random life led by a random fool who couldn't read nary a clue nor context to suspect his own downfall. They took all that made some bit of sense and pushed on, leaving the house and Pap's body to chance as the current rushed on.

---

[29] Read up on Cairo, Illinois if you want to understand the living history of enslavement. Start here – "Cairo, Illinois was once a Booming City—Until Racist Violence Destroyed the Entire Town", by Daniel Rennie published January 24th, 2019. The short story is that a once booming town at the crux of the Mississippi and Ohio rivers never had a chance due to long simmering White resentment for the enslaved who escaped to settled there and who refused to accept violence, segregation, and disenfranchisement any longer. The town is, apparently, still dead and dying, despite a most fortuitous geographic location. As of the year 2020, you can buy a five bedroom, three bedroom, 4,214 square foot house in Cairo for $46,200. Cairo shows the limits of economic explanations for all things racist in American capitalism.

Chapter 7

Jim and Huck Head for the Border

There are borders between people
as there are between nations.
Whether the border is skin or religion,
blood or portion of rations,
all borders are porous.

******

With the big haul, Huck and Jim were feeling all bucked up. Escaped man and runaway boy be damned, now they had some stuff. They both got to feeling comfortable, boocoo[1] comfortable with things and with each other. And some comfort, as warm a tone as its bell can ring, can be a bellwether for conflict between two brothers. Comfortable as they might be on their rocking raft, at some point they'll have to agree to take some position in order to balance or they'll both fall, and sometimes none of those positions is comfortable at all. Huck and Jim were gliding toward their first squabble, easing toward a squall.

Huck wanted to imagine the story of how the dead man came to be shot in the back. Jim was still keeping him protected from the fact that that dead man was Huck's own Pap. Jim said let it go else they be haunted by his restless soul. Huck saw that as good sense and gave Jim what he thought was a compliment.

Huck told Jim he had an uncommon level head for a slave, and that he'd certainly shown himself *worth $800 to a White man today*. Then Huck added that he'd rather own Jim than own magic beans, and that he'd never sell him off his *team of cotton-pickers*, should he ever get rich enough to *own one who could spit a litter*.[30]

---

[30] Here are some definitions for the word 'litter' in case you are confused about how dehumanizing it is for Huck to describe Black children this way. *Litter* (noun) – a number of young brought forth by an animal. *Litter* – Litter (noun) – objects strewn or scattered about; scattered rubbish. *Litter* (noun) – a layer of slightly decomposed organic material on the surface of the floor of a forest. *Litter* (noun) – straw, hay, or the like used as bedding for animals. *Litter* (noun) – pulverized absorbent clay used for lining a box in which a cat can eliminate waste. *Litter* (verb) – to scatter in disorder. I think this qualifies as a *microaggression*, how about you?

And that word *litter*—when associated with the children Jim loved enough to pull a trigger for quick—that word, *litter*, triggered in Jim a rictus of a grin that was cover for an internal feeling of rigor mortis. It left Jim cold as death inside, and it took him a breath not to let that rusty knife he kept slide across the red flesh of Huck's skinny neck. The thought of taking such a drastic step led Jim to another breath to calm himself down and to melt his frozen smile into a warmer thing—a frown.

And after a moment plastered in the puss of preening privilege spilling out of this child, Jim took a chance and tried to school Huck for a while.

Jim:
Let me tell you something, Huck.
You can't judge what's level from a hill
or what's in a room from a hall
any better than a fish
can tell a cloud from a pall.

You heard the story of Solomon, Huck?
The wisest king 'cording to the Bible?
He had a harem of 'bout a million wives,
which ain't wise at all.

Anyhow, there's a story
where Solomon gets the credit
for fixing a trouble between two women,
which must have come easy
considering all the humbug must have come with a thousand-deep
harem.

Anyway, they was fighting over a baby,
so he said he would split the baby in two
to test who really wanted the child
and this is told as a smart thing,
but there ain't a more ignorant thing a king could do.

Think now,
what is a child to a king
with a million wives
who'd just as soon lose one,
so as to loose one ball of chains from his life?

He ain't value a child like a man like me does
and never understood
the madness of a mother's love.
See, a mother might done beloved[31] a child enough
to take a dead half
rather than give the child to trouble,
and a mighty king
who owns a million women
and ten million children
might laugh at that a might,
but I know what it means
to be hungry enough
to trade a cow for beans
if them beans might be just enough
to feed some hope through a night.

---

[31] If there were one book that is responsible for this book more than Twain's *Huck Finn*, it is Toni Morrison's *Beloved*. It was a struggle to teach them both the same semester, the first semester teaching at a Baltimore prep school, the year after the uprising following Freddie Gray's funeral. It was a tense time. And reading *Huck Finn* early in the year, raised the stakes. *Beloved* was probably too challenging for most of the 11th grade students, but the book broke others hearts open with its founding act of loving violence. A woman killed her child to keep her from being a slave to "school teacher", a horridly curious enslaver. Jim's wisdom here, is the wisdom of the enslaved. One might accept a dead child over an enslaved child. Is there any more merciless a condemnation of slavery? Likewise, the people of a (West Baltimore) neighborhood might attempt to burn that neighborhood down rather than continue living next to nests of lead-poisoned rats in the crumbling caverns of addiction (read: vacant houses) left to them by earlier generations of targeted neglect.

Huck looked at Jim with the cocked-head confusion of
a dog and thought, *that is 'bout as dumb as a moss strung log.*

Huck:
Jim, you done missed the point,
done missed the point clean and whole.

Jim:
No, Huck, the point is deep underneath
what the preacher tell,
and it's all just a make believe
to help the children sleep
hoping they lie above hell.

Huck (*half-joking*):
Jim, you done mixed kings and bibles
and children tales.
Why you the most tangle-headed coon what ever tipped a scale.

Jim (*half-serious, but intent on learning Huck*):
I'm a coon?
Well ain't that the donkey
calling the ass, Jack.
That's the ass calling the glass cracked.
That's the salt
calling the sugar white.
If I'm a coon,
you a coon
as sure as the sun comes after the moon.

Huck (*a little dig-bit, but intent on learning Jim*):
That's a good one, Jim.
But, look, kings ain't fairytales.
They are real.
Take Louie the Sixteenth of France.

He was so real
they chopped off his head.
I would tell you what he said
to end up dead,
but he talked French.
Like 'polly voo fransay.

Jim (*half-joking*):
Boy you lucky you a boy, Huck.
I'd bust a knuck on a man if he talk to me such.

Huck (*serious*):
No Jim, it's just Frenchmen.
They speak different.
Like cats meow and cows moo.

Jim took quick stock of the dumb nature of a boy—so
sure in his ignorance that his ignorance seems a ploy. Huck
couldn't be serious. Did he really think Jim didn't know people
speak in different ways? What Black man didn't know how to
speak one language with White folks and a whole other with
the brother enslaved? *It's still people speaking, if they using strange*
words even, Jim thought. Now Jim was going to give Huck, for
free, a bit of the wisdom his many years had bought.

Jim:
Huck, is a cow a cat?

Huck:
No.

Jim:
Is a cat a cow?

Huck:
No.

Jim:

Is a cat or a cow a man?

Huck:
No, fool.

Jim:
Fool yourself.
Ain't a man a man?

Huck:
Yes, and?

Jim:
Then why wouldn't a French man
say some of the same things a man like me do?
Huck:
Jim, you really couldn't catch a point if it stuck you.
Couldn't make a crack of sense
if it up and whipped you.

Jim was right tired of being talked to like a child by a child. He'd had to eat such truck for most of his whiles. Now he was beginning to see that there is no point in being free if he had to swallow indignities—from a dumb little White boy at that, one who would make a laugh out of catching the lash? Jim snapped.

Jim (*bitingly*):
Well you can catch a bird splash
with your lil' raggedy head ass
lil' dirty, bad bred river rat.

Huck (*bitten*):
What's this Jim?
Why talk to me this rough?
What's gotten in to you
to speak such?

Jim recognized the look on Huck's face as the heat he'd seen in masters past. It was the mix of fear and power that cracks and blasts in the whip's lash. To see it in Huck was a reminder, not a shock, but a realization of the ticking clock on Huck's interest in helping him. But Jim was deep into feeling free now and taking salt from a boy isn't how freedom tastes, and so he let out a sting of ugly to remind Huck of his place.

You should clutch your pearls for this next bit of unexpected raw. Jim had heard many a whisper that Pap wasn't Huck's real paw. And not only that, Jim suspected, and had heard more than a few suspect that, a chink along Huck's real father's chain was Black, black as the back of Jim's hand[32]. There are a miniscule few things that would shake and rattle a White man as flat as that can.

Jim (*with a mean hint of a smile*):
You remember your maw, Huck?
I remember her.

---

[32] Shelly Fisher Fishkin. Was Huck Black? Mark Twain and African American Voices. New York: Oxford University Press. 1993. Pp. xiv, 270… since some of y'all need that. Fishkin refers to a Mark Twain short story called "Sociable Jimmy" in which he wrote about a real Black boy he met working at an inn where Twain once stayed. Twain wrote about the boy because he was, in his own words, "a wide-eyed, observant little chap" who was "the most artless, sociable, and exhaustless talker" he ever came across. Fishkin found that Twain's characterization of 'Sociable Jimmy' had these similarities with his characterization of Huck. Fishkin writes: "The cadences and rhythms of Jimmy's speech, his syntax and diction, his topics of conversation, attitudes, limitations, and his ability to hold our interest and our trust bear a striking resemblance to those qualities of speech and character that we have come to identify indelibly with Huck." Fishkin argues that Twain may have built Huck from this Black boy "Sociable Jimmy" in every meaningful way except for Huck being poor and White like Tom Blankenship, the boy from Twain's childhood that many assume was the model for Huck. Here we take some time to run with this theory. What if Huck were really the son of a half-Black father, someone other than the whole "fishbelly white" (as Twain described him) Pap? What if that is why Pap was so hateful to Huck? What if that's why Huck had some seemingly innate resistance to slave society?

She was a good woman…
seemed too good for your Pap's timber.

Huck's lip twitched a bit at that, but he knew it was true.

Jim:
Boy, your Pap was meaner
then a tread on rattler.
You ever wonder why?

Huck (*looking away*):
Nope. Never had the time.
Too busy duckin' his eyes
'lest I catch a knuckle in mine.

Jim (*with a sigh and a lowering his voice*):
Well your Pap was mad,
very mad at the world,
and especially at your maw.
See,
he had it in his mind
that she wanted something
other than him
something not so sharp…
something she might have saw
in another.

Huck (*seething as a reflex*):
Jim,
I don't know where you going,
but my mama was a Christian.
And there ain't a thing
she would have done
outside Christian living.

Jim (*looking a way with a smirk*):

95

You probably right, Huck.

Huck:
And you probably best shut up.
You taking your inch[33] too far.
That's enough.

And Jim did shut up mostly because he didn't want to play in a graveyard by digging dead things up, and partly because he did feel that talking about the boy's dead Maw was a push too rough. That's what Jim told himself, but he also shut himself up in that basement of a Black man's mind—that cave where he translates the world through the double-bind of seeing himself from both within and without, both privy to and prison to the worst in White men—the venomous, envious fear mixed in their grout. It was there, in the cloud of his story's dust, that a Black man's courage crusts over with rust. It was there where he trained his voice to be loud about its rush to hush.

And the voice that tells that tale needs-must be both flush and frail in the shush of heat gone stale. Jim changed his voice by choice, and became the minstrel of slavery's groove—a song of playing dumb as the only intelligent move. And in the throng of all that, Jim shifted his tongue real quick as if he were changing his coat. Jim reasoned for a diversion, to focus Huck back on himself, to make him choke up the mucus stuck his throat. Jim swallowed and spoke.

Jim (*obsequiously*):
Oh, honey, old Jim done done it again.

---

[33] In his 1845 autobiography, *The Narrative of the Life of Frederick Douglass: An American Slave, Written By Himself,* Frederick Douglass quotes a former enslaver man who chastises his enslaver wife for teaching a young Douglass to read: "If you give a n*gger an inch, he will take an ell. A n*gger should know nothing but to obey his master—to do as he is told to do. Learning will *spoil* the best n*gger in the world." Clearly, Huck has been told this as well.

Huck (*confused*):
Done what again?
What have you done Jim?

Jim:
My daughter, Huck, I'm thinking of her,
more exactly, of a time I roughed her.
Maybe I'll tell you that story one day.
But all you need to know
is that a man sometimes be hard on his child
to make them ready
for the world that's awaits.
A man sometimes swing his hands
before he can hold back his rage.
A man sometimes
lets his beast a tearing out his cage.
And I ain't nothing but a man.
And much as I love my daughter,
and her most precious laugh of all,
it's one of the saddest lessons I ever taught her.
A quiet man can be a squall
a'ripping with gall
and a'dripping with cruel.
Best you learn that lesson too.

But that's a lesson Huck knew all too well. With Pap for a paw he'd seen the tidal wave of a man's rage swell. But one thing he'd never seen is a man own up to himself. Huck had never experienced a man bow his adulthood to a child in the manner that Jim was now. And Huck questioned himself, *maybe Jim only did it because he's a slave.* But either way the move was made, and Huck was moved.

Huck:
Jim, I never seed a slave such as you.
You seem to love your child
as much as some people do.

It's a surprise, really Jim,
I didn't know it could be
that you could feel family.

And there was silence again. This time it pressed with a
heft in Huck's brow. His head dipped a bit, his eyes hit the
ground.

Huck:
I wonder if the widow or Pap
might be still looking for me.
Jim, I got to find out.
It would be good to know.
I need to see.

Jim nodded his head, with a genuine smile this time. It
was quite wise of the boy to know what he needed to know for
his own peace of mind.

Jim:
Well you gon' need some cover,
something that will keep you
from looking like Huck.
Why don't you take that dress from that truck we hutched
and pretense to be a girl
to seek some information and such.
Why boy you'd be the ugliest girl in the whole world,
yeah you might.
They'd give you all the word you want
just to get you out of their sight.

Huck (*laughing*):
Well you ugly enough a boy
to be the big bad wolf,
but that might just work today.
You can dress as my dog,
and hang back
like a good boy,

and lurk in the shade.

And the word 'boy', the way you call a dog, reminded Jim of that lady-dog Ms. Watson, who he wouldn't have minded butchering like Huck's hog for all the times she used words to try to bury him in a self-hating bog. And those words, heard coming from this child, felt even worse and silenced Jim for a brief while.

He let out his heat in a smile, as his reflex had taught him to do. They had been joking each other, that's all, but a joke on Jim that reminded him of his place beneath seemed laced with some kind of White man's voodoo. They weren't just words, they were a curse, a spell that sunk his soul a bit. Jim caught himself before his mood went too low and finished their ribbing tiff.

Jim:
I'll hang alright.
I'll hang if I go with you.
Naw, I'll stay here and hear all about it.
You go and find out what you need to.

While Huck costumed in his dress, Jim walked around to the other side of a big rock and reflected on himself: A grown slave teamed up with a white boy for whom he might be no more than a toy[34]. Huck is playing runaway, he thought, like he might play through a day in his boredom with freedom.

---

[34] Shout out Richard Pryor for one of his most shamefully poignant movies. In *The Toy,* released on December 10th 1982, Richard Pryor's willingness to even pretend to be a White boy's toy, was a glance into evidence of the undying zombie that is White supremacy. It was all around sad—a great Black actor and comedic genius reduced to playing a broke writer willing to sell himself to a confederate flag wielding rich, southern White man as a human toy for his spoiled brat son. There were remnants of Twain in the comedy. The residue of slavery was comedic fodder in 1982.

Jim twisted a tight curl of his hair even tighter and pressed a fist against the boulder. He leaned in to speak to the rock hard space between himself and Huck. And though Jim had seen the kindness around Huck's mouth, he heard him speak with the poison of the South, all he's ever known. Jim wondered, *if this giant rock was chipped off a mountain, then maybe slavery is just a thinning creek sprung from the river of freedom, a leak bound to run as dry.*

He remembered how the creek near his Old Gran's shack used to come and go. It would rage after a rain and then sometimes barely flow. In the middle of the heat of the summer it might turn to a vein of mud, with a little trickle of water like how a cut might spit a little blood. Then the rains would come and turn the creek's fickle into a flood.

Somehow the animals always knew before hand. They'd get to changing up their way of living to fit the creek whether rush, muck, or sand. *That's freedom*, Jim thought, *to be natural and do things that make sense in life and not have to squeeze yourself into the chicken wire of some other man's likes.*

The image of a chicken popped into his mind. Not just any chicken, but a chicken he knew. And he recalled how the animals on a farm act just like the farmers do. They learn society the same as a child. And if you pay attention, they will teach you about the world around you and about life. This particular chicken taught Jim a deep lesson about his own position, and the thinking that kept him there. Unlike Jim, who had to bend and constantly freeze himself cold, "Mister"[35] the chicken was a cocky cock that was allowed to strut everywhere true to his own bold.

Jim (remembering):
I remember Mister the chicken,

---

[35] "Mister" the chicken embodies the psychic violence against free will that is American enslavement. "Mister" is a creature of directly from the mind Toni Morrison in *Beloved*.

nothing but a chicken,
but he was freer than me.
His name was his
and he was king of all he could see.
He seemed to chuckle at me working
while he strut for his scratch.
He knew he had something I didn't
and was proud of that fact.
He was allowed to be what he was,
a tamed beast.
But me, I ain't allowed to be a man
and then called less-than
due to what I'm not allowed to be.

The slave is made of the fear of the Whites;
their fear that they are weak,
their guilt that they are Caining their brothers.
So he blinds himself to my flesh,
clear as night,
and binds me to his dreams
of shadows and shudders.
He thinks me a slave
and calls me so
as though slave
came before the name,
before he made
this cursed creature
so long ago
with guns, bibles, brands, and chains.

So I hear myself called slave
for song and show.
Slave is a balm
that keeps White fear calm and froze.
Being slave keeps my body alive
just as it kills my soul
and walks me in shadow

101

where every dawn is cold.

Huck uses "slave" as a simple word,
not knowing what it means
and that's probably the same way
I use the word "free."
But what each man does,
tells the story of each.
So what I do now will explain me
and unbind the twine
of the twain we be,
both chained to the same strange story—
slave and free.

Chapter 8

Huck Meets a Woman and Jim Listens in

Eve kept a bone to pick
from between her teeth,
from under her tongue.
The bone was sprung
from the rack of ribs
she's accused of coming from.
Since the lie Adam told,
since Adam's betrayal was done,
woman been enslaved,
woman been enraged,
woman been in wait
for her day to come.

******

Jim decided he'd follow Huck without the boy knowing so to see what was going on. He watched Huck stumble in his dress as he begun to make his way on to a nearby cabin sitting behind a dirt lawn. Jim pressed in, settling in a nest of a bush just past the left side of the dirt.

Huck peeked in the window and saw a woman sitting alone sewing. The cabin looked clean to the dust specks. All the women Huck had known seemed too busy, too biblical, or too shy to suspect, so one sitting and sewing was just about what he might expect.

He walked up to the door and knocked softly, probably trying to remember any girl he ever knew, so he could get into character and know what to do. The only one Jim had heard Huck talk through was Becky Thatcher, the Judge's daughter. Huck had mentioned to Jim that if he had Tom's class, maybe he could have caught her. And so as the lady approached the door he likely had Becky in mind as he figured out how he ought to talk. The Lady opened the door and stood a moment to gawk. By this time, Jim had inched in close enough to listen in through a slip of a window in the muddy mush behind a gang of cattail stalks.

Lady:
Well looka here, who are you?

Huck (*pretending to be some girl named "Sarah M."*):
Sarah maa'm, Sarah McAdoo.

The Lady opened the door to let him in watching him the whole time. She seemed to almost immediately see through his disguise but didn't seem to mind. She probably thought it was funny. She told Huck (pretending himself "Sarah M.") to take a seat, 'right here across from me.'

Lady:
Sarah, huh?
Well what a girl doing out late at night?
You know there's a runaway

killer slave on the loose?
Took a boy named Huck Finn's life
then likely set off on a river route.
My husband's looking for him now,
out for that $300 reward.
That's a might of money for a family like ourn.

Jim hunched quick at word of this and started looking
left and right. He ground his fist into the muck and looked up
into the night, thinking *here we go, I should have seen this coming.*
Damn these folk for always aiming to blame a slave for something.

Huck (as "Sarah M."):
Oh, well that's a shame.
You think he did it?
Did he kill the boy?
Buck, was that his name?
And if he did, then why?
What sense is it for a slave
to act so untame?

Lady:
Well I don't think he did it.
I think it was the boy's pap.
The boy had come into a load of money,
and the boy's pap wanted that.

Damn right, Jim thought. *Good thing women got good sense to*
see right to the heart.

Lady:
And the boy's Pap warn't too good to do it neither.
Went to the judge to get a loan for a search party
then showed up drunk the next morning
like he'd gone out to party.
Then he left off with some hard-scrabble fellas
and never came back.

He'll likely stay gone for some years
till it blows over,
till it's too late for anybody to prove the facts.

Jim nodded with relief. He thought, *leave it to a woman to see through to truth when men be dumb as beasts. Maybe she can talk some sense into them.*

Huck (as "Sarah M."):
But your husband's still out for the slave?
Why come?

Jim nodded and spoke under his breath *good Huck, damn good question.* For a second, he felt for the boy a bit of affection.

Lady:
Well didn't you hear me?
$300 dollar reward?
If the slave didn't do it,
we'll scare out of him that he did.
We gonna get that slave
and get that money
and do something productive with it.

Jim was outside grinding his fist again in the wet dirt, angrily. *Well ain't that about a witch. How quick she'll trade her good sense to get rich.*

Visibly nervous, Huck wrung his hands unconsciously. The Lady looked at Huck (as "Sarah M.") and cocked her head to the side to study him, closely.

Lady:
Say, what you say your name was?

Huck (as "Sarah M."):
Mary, maam, Mary

106

Huck couldn't remember the rest and he could feel his heart thumping in his chest. Jim, outside listening, slumped down sunk. *The damn boy done forgot his damn name, now the jig is done. Time to get gone, son.* He was about to make his way back to the raft, to prepare to push off without Huck. Jim wasn't daft. But what the lady said next stopped in his tracks.

Lady:
Mary huh? Here, Mary. Sew this for me.

The Lady tossed a needle and fabric towards Huck. Huck closed his legs together to catch it. He picked up the needle and looked at it curiously before beginning to stab the needle into the cloth furiously.

Lady:
Mary huh?

And just then Huck remembered that the name of his character was actually Sarah, Sarah McAdoo. And now he knew that she knew he was a fool, and he was unsure of what to do.

The Lady recognized the fear in his eyes and set him at ease. She left him with a small piece of wisdom when it come to the life of a girl who must one day take on the role of woman-to-be.

Lady:
No need to be nervous, boy.
Now what's your real name?

Huck (*as himself, now pretending to be "George"*):
George.

Lady:
George, huh?
Well look here, George.

107

I think you out here hunting for that slave
and I don't blame you neither.
But you better be careful
because a hungry, runaway slave
might just snatch you up and eat you.
That cannibalism run in they blood.
That's the curse of Ham
that was Noah's son that saw him naked
and liked to carve his father up like ham.
And a boy?
A little boy like you?
A runaway slave liable to put you in a gumbo stew.
Go home and count yourself lucky.

Huck (as "George"):
Yes'm.

Lady:
And one more thing.

And she began to speak, almost as if she would sing, to lay out some things about girls that might seem confusing if one hasn't been taught the nature of a woman's living.

Lady:
You make a poor girl.
Might fool a man, not me,
from how you stab that stitch
to how you open at your knees.
If you must perform a girl
you must work at it endlessly.
Refine yourself.
Design yourself a fool.

You mustn't ever hit
what you can miss.
You musn't ever let on you can.

You mustn't throw with verve,
mustn't have much nerve.
You must never out do a man.
No that will not do.
Refine yourself.
Design yourself a fool.

If you will get what you aim for
you must never ask
till they get their wish.
You've got to smile your eyes.
You've got to pout your lips.
You must cross your thighs
to spread your hips.
Refine yourself.
Design yourself a fool.

And a fool you'll be,
until you can get away.
Women rue the day
they don't do what a fool man say.
Then he'll gnash his teeth
and thrash his hands our way,
and try to take what we won't give
as if it was his anyway.
I done had to fight them off at night,
beg them away all day.
I done refined myself,
designed myself a fool.

But the fool he'll be
for as long as he breathes,
then even moreso after his last breath
when we are finally free
and all the jigs are up,
all the pretense released
once we see him to his death.

Then we will waltz on up the street
to some other beat
and resign ourselves
from designing ourselves
his fool.

Now, by George,
don't you forget
this little bit of school.
If you ever find a woman
willing to put up with you,
bow your head.
Resign yourself
before you find yourself a fool.

And Jim leaned to listen in as she finished with her eyes up at some place high on her wall. And Jim didn't know what to think about her at all. He had always thought of White women as characters in the White man's story. They were possessions in his coffers whether daughter or wife, something to ransom for glory or to hang on his arm to decorate his life. Even Ms. Watson's natural meanness depended on her husband—whether she flew off like a demon out of hell or whether she kept her evil reluctant.

But listening at this woman Jim figured since Adam supposedly sold his soul to Eve for a tasty bite, the world call a White woman born trouble, double if she hoped to be anything more than a bit of rib that God took to give man something to play with. Because of that, underneath it all, after all the love White women had shown him, Jim believed White women to be a lesser, dumber, weaker half of White men.

Now he knew he was wrong, and he never forgot it the rest of his days. He said in a whisper, under his breath, *White woman is another one of the White man's slaves.*

110

But like what Jim had known of the enslaved, this White woman showed him that they weren't what most thought. They were a whole lot more than the lesser half of Lot. *All this time White women been pretending to be less strong, so to keep a White man thinking he's stronger?* Jim wondered. What would a White woman do if let loose, what would they hustle to without the bustle[36] of a White man's wishes slowing them down like a overstuffed caboose? *Probably run around trying Black men till she got one killed,* Jim thought, *like the one that killed my paw, Bill.*

Jim had listened from a distance at the woman's instructive lament and still imagined she and him might be a might the same. Jim had known how to bend his back to keep a White man tame. To keep a White man sure of himself, of his superiority, Jim had betrayed his better sense and his better abilities. He thought of all the lost ideas, all the lost wisdom, all lost to the lies told to White men to keep their fear pinned in them.

As he made his way through the wood back to the raft, he thought of what a slave is to a woman White: cousin of the same fate, compelled to the same summons in life. She must see, he believed, what they both bear, and that they both dare the same wish, a same hope shared—to choose what they love, to love what they choose whether a man, or stars, whether a leather-wrapped bible or some snake-bit blues bars.

Regardless of all this, Jim now knew he had to vamoose, since she—White woman slave or not—she was on the hunt for him too. Jim needed to get gone poof with the quickness of a poot.

---

36 That big fake donkey butt-looking hump Victorian women used to wear under their dresses… that's a bustle, and a strange premonition of post-modern things to come in the 21st century.

By the time Jim got back to the raft, he began to contemplate whether to trust Huck or just go. He sung himself a lullaby of soft philosophies and such, high ideologies that dreamers reach to touch when the glow of a rainbow isn't enough, when a pot of gold is like a trunk of trinketty truck next to a spot of bold light that might debunk the shuck and the jive that is a life designed to confine some for the freedom of others. He throttled his mind in a quick swaddle of time, and went to rest under this cover: there is no profit in the slavery of another.

> Jim (*whispering to himself*):
> *Refine yourself. Design yourself.*
> *Go find your wealth and be.*
> *Go make a way and choose the day.*
> *Go forth and be free.*
>
> *And what I want*
> *White men can't give me,*
> *for he doesn't have it himself.*
> *I want to be my true and my best,*
> *to love my work*
> *and choose my rest,*
> *to not need another to crouch down*
> *for me to feel tall.*[37]
> *I don't want the White man's rank at all,*
> *or his brands of liberty.*
> *I just want to own myself,*
> *to own my body's wealth*
> *to work for myself, free.*

Jim made up his mind to go, Huck or no, and the decision was easy as feet hitting a floor.

---

[37] Shout out Toni Morrison on Charlie Rose… look it up, and look up every Toni Morrison interview you can find while you are at it.

112

Meanwhile, Huck had left the Lady with a brief thanks and also made his way away quick. With this new news that Jim was being hunted, there wasn't much to do but git. So he worked his way back to the raft in a quick fit, to warn Jim of the woman's witness.

Jim was at the raft set on his next move, still unsure of what Huck might do now that he knew he could score $300 for cashing Jim in. A slender creek of hope in him believed the boy true, that he'd hold fast to allegiance like boys spit-swear to do. But the better part—a river of common sense—was the sentiment that blood is thicker than spit all frothed in its emptiness, pushed from hollow throats by expectorant or swallowed by expectation. For White boys are the seeds of White men, part of a tribe before aware of the nation. And as a man's friends are all that he ever has and a boy's tribe is with whom he has been, since Huck has been with masters, and masters know the absolute sin of absolute power over another living thing, Jim thought it foolish thinking to think anything other than that Huck would perform his duty to turn him in.

Over the time of Jim's contemplation, Huck rushed to return ripe with the news that though his own plan had worked and that his own tide seemed turned, Jim had been blamed and was set to be burned. Somehow Huck hadn't considered this consequence of his plotting, that a slave would be the natural blame for the savage butchery of his body. Now Jim, Huck's only help on the run away, was doubly unsafe for being a runaway and being wanted for Huck's fake foul play. Huck's mind and feet raced to the place where Jim was already prepping escape.

> Huck (*all caps FRANTIC*):
> *Jim hump yourself up!*
> *They coming for us!*

Us? Jim thought. *That's a weird way to say it, when he is scot free and I'm the one in danger.* He laughed a bit at the thought of it. *The boy thinks we are a team.* Jim *hmphed* and finished the prep to back-back into the river's seams.

Chapter 9
The Fog of White[38] Falls

Witness is borne
like weightlessness
in water—
so massive that we float inside.

****

---

[38] By now, you may have noticed the capitalization of "Black" and "White". You'll notice that at times neither are capitalized. Capital "B" Black, in the universe of this book, refers to the ethnic and cultural consistencies that exist across the African Diaspora—the fact that black-eyed peas, okra, and gumbo are on both sides of the Atlantic; that dancing a casket through a street happens after some funerals in 7th ward New Orleans second line just as in some South African townships; that the "habitual be" adds an efficient and logical tense to English in Black communities from Seattle to St. Augustine, Florida; that layered gradations of skin color, hair texture, facial features, and all types of phenotype reflect the mixture of Black in every corner of humanity from Martinique to Madagascar—that these ethnic and cultural consistencies exist across an entire planet offer proof that Black is a diasporic culture of hybridity which has unity in inclusivity as its core. Shout out to the one year of graduate school in American Studies at NYU for the thousands of pages of readings that led to this perspective.

However, White reflects a power built on exclusivity—power rooted in who can be left out of any legal designation of rights and privileges, the welcome, the access, the opportunities, reverence, grace, presumption of ability, claim of historical primacy as a creator of modern civilization, claim of dominance, claim of intellectual superiority, or claim to cultural hegemony incorrectly associated Whiteness. "White" and "Black" are very much opposite cultures that define each other.

Once the raft was packed, Jim and Huck shoved off and that was that, off to where the river offered all. All the zigzags never found on a map, all the towheads and eddies hidden in the waters' belly, all the rips and tides of a current that whips quick enough to smash a ship to jelly, all this and more is what the river had in store.

The river—the writhing snake—to Jim, was like riding a quake. No telling where it might take his fates or what breaks he might see. An ocean may be wide as witness and deep as eternal peace, but a river is as total as time, as impossible as infinity. Never in your life will you ever touch it in the same place twice. Like now, it is here and at once gone. What happens on the river stays on the river as the river rolls on.

Down river, Jim and Huck witnessed a drunken brawl on a barge—a squall of big talk that led to men getting mauled. The things said that night were burned into Jim's memory, for the sheer mendacity with which poor men will craft raving hyperbole to bully for some sense of dignity. Jim replayed the scene and laughed at the lies these men cast on the wind, the big-talking that served as a sort of caulking between lives cracked, to challenge the pitiful facts of lives loaded down by plentiful lack.

Big-Talker One was a mean poet and his rhymes settled in easy folds. His words, harsh as they were, had music in them, hard music, hard as a rock rolls.

> Big Talker One (*groan-talking*):
> *All you scrubs better bow and pale*
> *before I whip the wind into a gale*
> *that'll pluck the feathers out the quail*
> *of your frail pride,*
> *that'll swallow the tide of your tall-tailed lies.*
>
> *You'd best shut your damn clams*
> *before I sheer your hides*
> *like some summer lambs,*
> *bake you to the pink*

like a honey ham.
Think I won't?
As hungry as I am
to break a foot off
inside a lesser man?
Go on and try your hand
and I'll cut your deck
till I leave your head hanging
from a slit neck!

Big-Talker Two was cold and quick, words hopped from his hip like a ready blade tip. The words seemed to split the air as he spit them quick as a sickle leaves a cornstalk nipped.

Big Talker Two:
Oh your talk is big
as a cow patty is wide.
You bark a whistle
but got as much bite
as a mite on mice.
You couldn't carry my sack,
you two-bit bitch bit with lice.
You couldn't marry my dog,
you puss-bucket of hog tripe.
You shouldn't walk in my path
if you want your life.
Cuz boy lightening can't flash
fast as the blade of my knife,
and thunder don't roll
deep as I'll put it in your life.
The undertaker loves me
for all the business I've been giving him.
The worms gonna love you
when I leave you filthy as the hole
you was born in

Big Talker One:

118

Enough!
Put your goddamned hands up!
I'm coming for chin and your guts!
I'll crack your nuts!

Big Talker Two:
Let's go!
I'll throw blows at your nose
till your brains rain down
like the Mississippi flows!

Big Talker One:
Die dog!

Big Talker Two:
Fry hog!

Big Talker One:
I'll lay you down
hollow your ass like a log!

Big Talker Two:
I'll leave you black, blue, wet and stinking,
moldy as a bog!

And those were the last words Jim heard before the rumble of bodies tumbling, so he and Huck got to strumming at the river, paddles humming, just in case the trouble was coming their way. Wasn't a use to sticking around to see who won the day, when either one would have Jim's hide for that $300 slave-ransom pay.

Time passed and more adventures passed with it. They survived a close encounter with some murderous bandits on half-sunk wreckage. There was much narrow trouble that was hard to get through, but none of it as thick and heavy as the fog that came to break Huck and Jim togetherness loose.

Clean clouds look so soft in the sky—in the distance, majestic. But when they fall on your body as fog and crowd your eyes, your mind is congested. In the thick, cotton dream where all you see is white, you can forget you're riding a dark river, the giver and taker of life.

Fog on a river is a snare of highest rank when you have to dare blind between rocks and sands, shot docks and gnarly trees hunched over banks. The safe way is to shoot the middle, but there the fog is thickest set and wisdom says that this is where you find your quickest death from a white whale of a boat barreling dead for your deck.

None of this was lost on Jim, who kept his body still and his head swiveled as a riveted owl, scanning the white darkness with intent and scowl for any hint of a sound. The front of Jim's mind was full of the awful probabilities. The middle of his mind was sunk in the inevitability of this whole adventure splintering, probably. In the back of Jim's mind, he was spun down in spirals, spinning in the feeling he'd missed the turn up the Ohio[39], floated right by Cairo and the land of the free. The bottom of Jim's heart was sunk in a thought that they were heading to the southern deep, being brought straight to where he'd been bought to, old Orleans. Jim didn't know the states nor the rate of flow.

---

[39] The Ohio River was a way to the North and a line of demarcation between states of Slave Society and Free States. Ohio was central to the Underground Railroad, White allyship in self-emancipation, and White attack on that allyship. From Ohio History Central: "Although slavery was illegal in Ohio, some people still opposed the ending of slavery. These people feared that former slaves would move to the state, take jobs away from the white population, and demand equal rights with whites. Many of these people vehemently opposed the Underground Railroad. Some people attacked conductors. Other people tried to return freedom seekers to their owners in hopes of collecting rewards."

Jim didn't know about taxes or Black Codes[40]. Besides Huck, Jim didn't know a soul, yet here he was, sure that he'd stole deeper into slavery's hold.

Together, in the midst of the thick mist, Huck and Jim decided that, once the fog had passed, they'd sell the raft for a pass on a steamboat to find their way up to the free territory of Ohio. But the fog would make that plan homicidally hard. They'd have to make their way through the thick mucus of air without the raft being smashed to shards. The dangers and obstacles are invisible. White is all you can see till you right up on some trouble. You could easily be befuddled, since what looks like heaven is really hazards hidden, calamity cuddled and doubled.

Huck had the idea to tie the raft still till the fog passed. Jim thought such a task was sure to fail and that such a failure was bound to last. Tied down, there would be no way to avoid getting smashed. Jim thought they should stay on the move so they could dash one way or another out of a steamboat's path. But Huck wouldn't hear that and, in the midst of the anxiety of the moment with the pressure of decisions that must be made fast, the boy had gotten brash and begun to act like a man with his own mast set on enough cash ($6000) to be a master.

Jim (*attempting to calm Huck to sense*):
Look Huck,
we got to think straight.
If we are stuck in one place
and get hit
we'd be quick to sinking
in less than a blinking of fate.
Let's keep loose
so we can move.

---

[40] Just look up "Black Codes"... then look up late 1990s and early 2000s state criminal laws created during the echoes of the 1994 Violent Crime Control and Law Enforcement Act. Coincidence or conspiracy? You be the judge.

Huck:
No, Jim!
Tie her up like I told you now.
Do it,
and rush!

Jim:
Now look, boy,
I just told you that's a bad thought.
Don't be afraid,
we can just stay ready
if trouble pops off.

Huck:
Now I done told you what to do,
and I ain't gone say it again!
Do what you are told
or get off my raft
and get back to slavin'!

Huck gnashed his teeth like he was sure to set sail his own
way, even if that way was disaster. Jim went silent, rather than
argue with the little brat bastard. And that was that for a solid
rack of silence. But then Huck felt bad for the way he'd spoke
and said something he thought was soft, but was just another
poke.

Huck:
Look, Jim
Most people would turn you away.
I don't listen to a word they say.
They don't see you like I do.
I wish they would try to.
I'm sure they'd think again,
If they had a friend like Jim.

122

Jim cocked his head at the song the boy just spoke. *Boy, we ain't friends*, he thought.

Jim (to himself):
I might as well be this boy's pet rat
needing on him for food.
If he think that's friendship,
he in for something rude
once I dump him for my route.
But I'll just keep that fact
tacked in my mouth.

Huck shimmied ahead and could only find saplings, which wouldn't offer enough grappling to keep a raft and canoe from rushing and rafting. Jim watched him, but didn't say a thing, still unsure of how to handle a child master helping him get free. You can tell a White man when he's wrong, but only if you're willing to be blamed no matter what comes to be. If it works he'll say he did it despite your lack of belief. If it fails he'll say it was because you didn't do your part to make it succeed. And blame for a slave is to be beat at best, and, at worst, it was certain death. And despite the fact that Huck was a child taking baby White man steps and couldn't beat Jim if he would, in the midst of a fog so thickset, Jim settled into the sense that had always saved him; it's best to let a White man alone to learn he's dumb on his own than to try to save him.

Huck went to tie the raft to a skinny tree. Even though Huck was young and dumb, Jim followed the boy's lead, and sure enough the raft snapped the young tree. The force of the break threw him and Jim careening on different sides of a towhead mound that neither, due to fog, could see around nor through. The raft went with Jim and Huck found his way to the canoe.

Jim realized quick that this towhead wasn't no mere bump in the river, but a full-blown island, with a full-grown forest to separate Huck from hither. And with the fog what it was, Jim knew Huck was lost and so was he, and that they were no longer lost together. Huck called out; Jim could hear him, but he dare not lip back for the whip-crackers that could be near them.

This is the second time he heard this yearn in Huck's voice—that pleading for him—the second time Jim had a choice to walk away from the boy and never see him again, to get on with freedom without the burden of the boy's presence. But then Jim thought back to when Pap was beating Huck, when the thuds of Pap's blows were thumping on him, cornered and curled up. And Jim sat in silence while Huck's tendency to panic unfurled flush. That's why he stopped the first time Huck begged Jim to accompany him down the line.

But this time, Jim knew better. H e had to put himself before this boy. Any noise and he'd be jumped by body-hunters poised in the bushes with poison in their clutches in the form of a page stating Jim was in season, as if they needed a reason to beat him and keep him enslaved. No Jim would be leaving Huck today, and send the boy to the wind and take off on his own. It seemed there wasn't any other way for Jim's freedom to be born but alone. And still the thought troubled Jim.

Jim factored Huck's chances to survive and his own chances to get free. And the math added up to the same conclusion he'd just reached. Huck must adventure and Jim must be free.

But, as Huck's calling out for him began to fade in the distance, the thought still troubled Jim. He began to think of the reasons he should stay with the boy and the reasons he should leave him.

> Jim (*to himself*):
> *Huck's white*
> *might blend in with this fog.*

But my black will show me to be
a rack of lamb on a bundle of logs
to a White man that's hungry.
Yet I'm a man
and if I can,
I will fight being traded for money.
But Huck is just a boy
a young body to steal
and to the starving scoundrels
running this river
Huck is veal.
No telling what they might slave him to:
a prop in any number of schemes
a ploy for undeserved sympathy
a child servant trying not to get beat
a wholesome cover for a murdering thief
dear God please
not a plaything for something sick,
and all that
if he isn't smashed to bits
by a steamboat steaming hard
with no regard for a little nit.
The south is savage
in ways the boy can't imagine.
The deeper we go down,
the more chance for the savage to happen.
But if I try to save this boy
and I am caught
I already know the consequence
I will have bought.
They might tie me to a wagon
and get to dragging me for kicks,
might clamp a slave bell
round my neck,
mask me in spear tips,
strap a scolds bridle to my tongue,
chains round my wrists and hips,

they might just let the dogs rip me,
bit by bit,
and lap up my blood
like an after-dinner sip.[41]

Jim noticed his thoughts as they flicked and scattered, like flames across the white dark of fog. As he sat and listened to Huck bang pots now that his voice could be drowned out by the peep of a lark, he sunk flat on the raft so as not to be a bright black mark. And his mind kept on tearing at his hope like a great white shark.

It wasn't in Jim to weep in a time of trouble. And panic on a raft is as daft as a cat jumping on a coyote's back. So what to do? What to do? What to do? The refrain was like a lullaby singing Jim to sleep, and Jim hadn't slept well in so long it seemed that his mind was reamed of good keep. Since a toddling boy, Jim was self-aware of such moments, when worry had hold, because his Gran, who watched him close, would notice him gripping his nails into the folds of her apron. She would notice the boy Jim grinding his teeth. The boy Jim's disease would be visible in the twisting and curling of his feet; he couldn't keep still. The boy Jim would get to tapping the tips of his fingers against things, seemingly against his will.

---

[41] If you are skeptical of the violence (perpetual warfare) that kept slavery in place, look up "Slave Punishment" on google. No potential consequence noted here is hyperbole. Enslavers and their society used terrorism and torture as the threat against self-liberation.

126

Old Gran would see Jim sucking his bottom lip, his eyes darting around. She figured it was the memory of seeing his father as a burning mound of death on the ground surrounded by flesh—smoke shrouded, proud White men with their approving White women holding their smiling White children—who were no older than Jim when his daddy was lynched—all standing in some cannibal's orgy toasting his father's flesh to their own health, holy before eating him wholly. That memory was a horror burned onto Jim's soul like a brand gone swole in keloid coal black cold.

So here, surrounded by the fog, trying to catch his breath, all that came to Jim was his Gran's voice and the song she would sing to help him rest.

Gran (*Jim remembering*):
Oh baby, babe
It's time for you to sleep babe
Oh baby, babe
It's time for you to sleep
And when you sleep
The world will calm around you
And in the calm
You'll dream the night away
And when you wake
The sun will come to greet you
And when you wake
The moon will wave goodbye
And I'll be here
To hold you close to me
Oh baby babe
I love you so

And so Jim turned himself one way and then the other. He stretched himself straight as heaven's gate and softened his breath from its nervous stutter. And with slow drags and pulls, he began to drift free. While hearing his Old Gran's song in the wind of his memory, he nestled the wool of his head into the cool of his hands and closed his eyes and went swift into a brief sleep.

Jim dreamt a quick, odd dream. It was nothing like what life seems. It was he and Huck in some sort of schoolhouse room. Huck was one of a gaggle of children hassling over something on a table. Jim walked over to see what it was they were fussing about since, from where he stood at the front of the class like a teacher, he wasn't able.

Mister Jim! One of the children shouted. *It just moved!*

And Jim noticed that the children, most all of them, was a different color. Some were peach like Huck and others red as a pale radish. Some were toast covered in cinnamon dashes. Some were ruddy brown as the bark of pine and others deep purple as blackberry wine. One or two were banana pudding, a few were the skin of honeydew, still others were pink as swine, and a few were midnight blue.

As he approached them they turned to look at him excitedly. *Mister Jim!* They shouted again and again, and it was taking him a minute to get used to the 'mister' but he settled in to whatever dimension this dream was in. Jim laughed loud.

Yes children? He said and smiled, somehow and for some reason, proud.

Mister Jim it moved! It moved while I was watching! Said the girl that was honeydew.

Ooooh! I saw it too, the purple boy said with a coo.

They were so excited. All except for Huck, whose eyes were as full black as that of a buck. Jim stopped when he saw his eyes and realized that among these children, Huck was very different. Jim walked closer and saw that Huck was as grey and worn as a crinkled newspaper page and that his skin was wrinkled as an old date.

Jim looked down over the shoulders of the children. They were looking at an egg. It was shaking a bit as if whatever was inside it was just about to kick out a leg. The children made way for Jim as he leaned in, just as a dot of the egg's shell gave way and let loose a spot, a mere corpuscle of blood. Then it cracked and let out a red, black flood.

The blood poured over the table and the children scattered. Jim reached for the egg just as it shattered. Inside the egg, there was a boy, contorted and stiff. Jim leaned in and saw the tiny creature for what it was. It was the greyed, wrinkled miniature of Huck.

Jim reached down to the Huck-looking thing, to pick it up. Its flesh seeped wet and cold between his fingers. He was quick to set it back in the eggshell. But a slick residue gleamed and lingered, dripped from his palms. What had been Huck melted into a bloody yolk, and Jim was ripped from calm. He shouted, *Huck!*

Just then Jim felt something brush up against him, the arm of one of his school children maybe. When he turned to look see which one it was, he thought he must have been crazy. It was Huck, not the shriveled little corpse, but the real boy, fleshed out and alive. It was such a shocking relief, Jim let out a cry.

Huck! You survived! You ain't dead in an egg!

Now simultaneous with the end of Jim's dream, Huck had canoed back to the raft after slipping through the seams of the river's wrath. The whole crash must have been like a bath to Huck, a short baptism in the way of the path. Somehow he found his way back to find Jim sleeping like a dead man on his back.

Huck had put it in his mind that now was the time, that he would carry out the charge that Tom gave him that one time. It was time to play a trick on Jim, and what came to him was to pretend the whole crash was all a dream. It seemed to Huck that such a thing would be a perfect end to such a troubling bit of struggling. But that's a child's thinking, a child with the privilege to play with a man's mind because that man is enslaved.

Jim for his part, still half-awake from slumber, went to mumbling all kinds of loving words on to Huck. He was actually happy to see the boy alive. After the trouble and troubling thoughts and dreams that had just struck, Jim couldn't help but smile.

Jim (smiling):
Boy, Huck, you something else.
Your little ass survived!

Huck (*playing*):
What you mean survived?
Survived what?
You fell asleep
in the middle of the rough
of the river.
I wouldn't believe it
if I hadn't seen it myself.
You just bent
and went to sleep
like Snow White did the elf.
It was a damn shame, Jim.
I needed you right then,
but you collapsed and went to dreaming.

Jim (*serious*):
What?
You telling me
all that was just a dream?

You didn't get lost
and swallowed by the fog
and tossed to the river's fiends?

Huck (*playing*):
What fiends, Jim?
The only fiend was your laziness
come to take you
to where all the slaves went
before they was slaves
and made to work for a livin'.
You went off into dreaming
when there was work to do.

Jim (*playing too*):
For true?
You trying to tell me I falled asleep
in the midst of all the fog
that had us calling out
for each other because we couldn't see.
Brother,
you must forgive me.

Huck (*serious*):
You didn't answer when I called out!
And why didn't you answer?
I was banging pots and yelling
and you were quiet as a panther.

Jim (*serious*):
So you were lost in the fog?

Huck (*caught*):
Well, I was just...

Jim (*serious*):
You just talking some truck,
and that truck there is trash.[42]
That ain't no way to act
to a friend
to pretend he was useless
when you needed him.

And there was a long quiet then, the kind of quiet that keeps people at distance. It might have been fifteen minutes till someone spoke, and it was Huck apologizing for the mean joke. He did so with a whole host of hesitation and jerking at his own yoke as to keep himself from falling into the throes of humility. For a White boy like Huck, apologizing to a slave had to trigger some memory of his low station in White society. But he knew he was wrong, and he knew Jim was right for calling out his impropriety. And still his face, while apologizing, looked like he was chewing on rotten cow tongue fried in the fat of pork belly.

And this is what made it plain to Jim just how young and dumb Huck was in his stupidity. Though to Huck, the whole thing was play, to Jim, a grown man who knows what was at stake, wasn't a damn thing funny.

---

[42] Any student reader of *Adventures of Huckleberry Finn* will recognize this passage as the one where Huck briefly mentions that it took him fifteen minutes to get up the nerve to "humble myself to a n*gger."—Twain's words. It is a complex moment where Twain is both offering the possibility of White people humbling themselves against White supremacy while using the n-word to immediately undercut that possibility. More importantly, one thing is made clear. Twain's Jim describes Huck's behavior, in trying to convince Jim that he abandoned Huck and fell asleep in their time of trouble, as "trash". It is a moment, for Twain, where Jim acts as Huck's first true father figure.

When Jim slathered Huck in honey, happy to see him again, it wasn't as a slave hoping the boy would help him to freedom. It wasn't as a lonesome traveler happy to have some company. It wasn't some overwrought token of emotional nobility. It was because he cared. He cared if Huck lived or died. And to see him again was like a light at the end of a tunnel. But all that was lost on Huck's sensibilities. He was still a child full of childish inability to understand empathy.

But something else was lost in the distance of that silence. Huck's struggle to humble himself to apologize brought square the whole of the resistance they were up against. It wasn't just the river and the steamboats it hurled. It wasn't just the whip-crackers with their fingers curled around triggers aimed at Jim's curls. It wasn't just slavery. It was the fog and all that the fog seemed to mean.

It was the confusion and the lack of surety of what to do caused by the distance between what was believed and what was true. See Huck had been taught, since as early as he could interpret what he was seeing, that White people were human beings blessed with supreme faculties and mentalities. To Huck and all his teachers, this was the destiny that god himself had guaranteed, to place White men above all things and beasts. To them, all things with any hue were either things or beasts or something in between, not White, like human beings. And Huck believed this because it meant he was made of good and might have good things, despite his trash ass Pap. And the $6000 he'd come on was some proof of that. And finding Jim on Jackson's Island was more of the same. And maybe Huck could make something out of his name. And all that was due to being born in the light of being White.

That's what Huck must have believed. Yet what he'd known to be true, was being the son of Pap was as dastardly a fate as anyone could be born into. He knew his mother was dead, beat to death by his father who could do every depth of cruel. He knew Jim was as good a man as any he had ever happened on and that Jim loved his children as strong as a peak pushes down upon the mountain it is grafted to. What Huck knew to be true was that, already, Jim had cared for him more than his father had ever even tried to.

Yet he believed, by natural law, that Jim was a slave and that a slave was the property of White men due to the power and privilege that their god gave. So the burning friction between what Huck was raised to believe and what was true, made a smoky fog as thick as his own skin, and as important to his own survival as any believed truth.

Jim for his part wasn't confused by the fog's fall. One of the basic privileges of the enslaved, if there are any at all, is to blessed to be alive and be awake, to see through it all. Jim could see what Huck believed as what it was, as it were—a mythology that men create to generate some sense of strength and self-worth, when the world is cold and seems on the attack. And the White man's world, for sure, was that.

Jim had seen White men, furious in feuds, butchering each other from toe to tooth. He'd seen them lynch each other at high noon and bring their wives and children to cheer the convulsions of the doomed. He'd seen them, drunk, sip a last gulp before beating their wives and children to pulp. Jim had seen how they'd torture each other with rumors as practice for how they would treat his kind, so he knew the White man's world was, for certain, unkempt and unkind.

What Jim didn't know was that White folk done attacked each other in more wars than one could count, more dark ages than dark caves under a mount, more diseases than a devil could devise, more starvation than the poor could survive, more oppression than a king could reign, more conspiracy than Shakespeare could name, more pain than in hell's flames, more death and destruction than there are stars. Jim had only a sense that the White man's world was hard and that's why he always seemed to look for someone to blame it all on, and its always easiest to blame a brother—a brother to punish for all the strange and merciless clangs of swords, bursts of guns, pounding explosions of bombs that they hurled at each other.

And Jim knew that he was the thing, the one thing dark enough in the fog of White to spark fear on sight, the one thing that could make a man believe it was good to be White when history knew better. So when Jim looked at Huck and saw how the indignity of apologizing to a slave had festered into a sense of confusion, he wasn't surprised.

And when Huck looked at Jim he probably saw all the difference between them—mainly skin, but also hair and nose and lips and sound-sense, since Jim didn't sound like White men, and thoughts because Jim didn't think like White men and although along this journey that had been a good thing, the deep resonance of Jim's vocal register when he spoke had been, for Huck, unsettling. Huck must have thought about wrong and right, and how he'd been taught that everything right in the world was made by somebody White, and that God was White, and Jesus was White, and Thomas Jefferson was White too. And Thomas Jefferson owned more slaves than Solomon had wives, for true. And right was what he had been taught and what he was used to, and that was the righteousness of masters owning slaves. And wrong was everything else—any kind of freedom that wasn't God-gave. So the weight of society had fallen on the raft just like the fog fell. The fog had passed, but it left a thick, humid air as heavy as a spell.

135

Now, Jim and Huck were both fidgeting, circling the raft, each daft of the math of what to do with the other. The raft teetered under Jim and tottered under Huck, but found a balance in the rhythm of its bob and buck. On Jim's mind: his proximity to freedom. On Huck's: his proximity to hell. And between them a mighty silence fell.

Huck stole a glance at Jim with fret and frown in his eyes. Jim read the look and lied a smile to hide a feeling he despised. It felt as if a hummingbird were aflutter in his veins. It was rage, as curdled and trilled as the songs of pet birds caged.

Huck (*to himself*):
Now the widow ain't ever
did me a thing
but try to school me 'bout clean living,
and here I am setting a slave free
after all the widow done done for me.
I'm bound for hell by the bible.
Unless I tell,
I'm liable to feel down right filthy,
and just as I should,
because I'd be hound-bite guilty.

Jim chucked a look at Huck. It was neck full of suspicion. Huck recognized something familiar in that. Jim might have looked something like Pap, who was ever-enraged. Huck felt the rattle of fear in his ribcage.

Jim (*to himself*):
This boy is wavering.
He is favoring
what he's been told.
That I'm born to be a slave,
a human bought and sold.
No matter what freedom we might find
in friendship

136

that fog will always clog his soul.
Well if I must be a slave,
he must be my inch.
I will take an ell and more.
I'll fight before I am lynched.
Before I'm burned, I'll war.
Huck can have his White.
I'll take my flight.
I will bury myself
on freedom's shore.

As they circled and the raft creaked, Jim flashed hot eyes. Huck sucked his teeth. And simultaneous as sound and beat, each began to speak.

Huck and Jim (*simultaneous*):
Where we headed?

Huck:
Think we passed Cairo in the fog?

Jim:
I don't want think of it, Huck.
If so, it means we unlucky
as two two-legged dogs.

Huck:
Maybe we should take the canoe
and head back.
Deeper south
can't be better than that.

Jim:
Ain't no back, Huck.
I told you that before.
Besides,
what we want to go back for?

Jim sang a reasoning in persuasive verses, like a preacher. His pulpit was the raft. And atop that shaking lattice of dead wood he stood and channeled his flow like a pipe shaft. And Huck caught the wind to chime in with questions, like a thinking child investigating biblical cataclysm in catechism.

Jim (*spitting in rhythm*):
Back back?
What's that for you?
Broke rules and the caned hide blues?

Back back?
What's that for me?
Work till I hurt and never earn a penny?

Back back?
We know what's there.
We left that for the better side of fair.

Back back.
Huck, can't you see?
Back there, we'll never be free.

Huck (*almost pleading for guidance*):
But, Jim, what about all the good they done?
The widow treated me as her favored son.
She fed me first and fed me well.
Prayed for my soul to stay from hell.
She hoped to raise me right.
Tried to raise me White.
And here I'm off with a slave
lost in the river's maze.
Jim, it's a sin.
I done stole you free.
And I'm wondering what good could come of me.

138

If I could do such thing
in selfish haste,
Jim what kind of man could I be
if I turn my back on my great race

Jim (*unmoved*) :
Back back?
What's that for you?
Did your race save you from your Pap's boot?
Back back?
What's that for me?
Die a slave
and leave my children chained like beasts?
Back back?
We know what's there.
We left that for the better side of fair.
Back Back.
Huck, can't you see?
Back there, we'll never be free.

If you go back and turn me in,
you get the reward of good regard
sure as sin.
But won't you wonder
what old Jim might have been?
What kind of father to his own children?
What kind of husband?
What kind of man once and finally free?
And what kind of man would you rather be—
The kind that turns coat on a friend
Or the kind that's trust-worthy?

Back back?
What's that for you?
Broke rules and the caned hide blues?
Back back?
What's that for me?

Work till I hurt and never earn a penny?
Back back?
We know what's there.
We left that for the better side of fair.
Back Back.
Huck, can't you see?
Back there, we'll never be free.

Huck heard Jim and he felt him too. Jim turned it black and white. Huck would either do as friends do or be a traitor—treacherous untrue. Huck plopped his elbow on his knee like thinking men do. He sat his chin in his hand to keep his mouth shut. He felt that if he kept talking to Jim he would no doubt be struck by a truth that he couldn't deny.

But the Widow had always warned that the devil is a lie, and that the devil is Black, and that the devil had slick attacks, slick enough to tempt even Jesus Christ himself an inch toward sin. No. Huck was through listening to Jim, and he just thought on what he'd been taught by the Widow and all his kin.

Huck thought and thought, and a sudden light shining from the shore bought him time. While Jim hoped it might be Cairo, Huck had made up his mind. He was going ashore. There'd be no more living this fable. He'd get Jim back to where he belonged—in Ms. Watson's stable.

Huck (*half-true*):
I'm a go see what town them lights is.

Jim (*suspicious*):
Yeah. Go see and come back quick.

Huck pushed off with the skiff as Jim eyed him from the raft in the distance and slid himself in the water to hide out of sight-line vision. Huck, one hundred yards away, had the awful worst feeling about the decision he'd made. He was going to turn Jim in. Then he heard two voices calling at him and tightened up his face.

Man-hunter:
Boy, is the man on the raft Black or White?

Huck (*thinking quick*):
Oh, that's my Pap.

Man-hunter:
Well we'll go check,
five slaves done run off tonight.

Huck (*thinking quicker*):
Well that's great
because Pap needs help a might.

Man-hunter:
What's wrong with him?

Huck:
He's got the...
uh...
he not feeling good...

Their voices fell out, but Jim listened harder, hoping hard that Huck wouldn't hand him to the slaughter, to the catchers hunting the waters, not for fish, but for people sick with just a wish to be free; for people who were like he—enslaved in a slave society. Jim had a heavy moment, as full of worry as a bag full of rocks.

The weight of worry fell from Jim's head into his pocket where he fingered his blade. He started thinking through moves that might work against the two—how to incapacitate one while he left the other splayed, what angles he could play to lull them into feeling safe just before raking them open from guts to face.

Maybe he would cry out in panic with all the pleading for mercy he could muster—just enough to invite them to make fun and bluster of him. Then, just as they were reveling in his begging, Jim would pound one a fist to the throat and chop the other an elbow to the nose on the back swing. He'd follow that by grabbing the first one by the hair and slamming his head down on his knee, then jamming his knife through the soft underbelly of the other's jaw, to spear that tongue between his teeth. With both down he could bash them with pots to the eyes and mouth, till both the dastard man-hunting crackers bled out.

But as Jim readied his plan, he overheard Huck's game. Huck told the men that Jim was his Pap, and that his Pap was lame with small pox. That was enough to make the catcher's jump out of their sox to stay away and stay detoxed.

Jim settled himself from the thoughts of stone cold self-defense and took a moment to marvel at Huck's bold, good sense. *Huck's a quick boy*, Jim thought. *And good too. When push comes to shoving off he might just be worth sticking to. Maybe then, when he's grown and some more seeds of good been sewn in his soul, he might be a new kind of White man, different from the old.* Strangely enough, Jim began to see Huck as Huck was seen by the Widow.

And when Huck came back to the raft, there was a moment when Jim looked at him, this raggedy pipe-puffing White boy born of the worst sort of truck, whose mind was as trapped-up in as much slave-talk as any whip-cracker, whose ignorance rushed fast as any river, who was as likely as his Pap to die by a shot or a shot liver; Jim looked at Huck and thought, *this boy could be my son.* And Jim thought himself just about old enough to need one—an older son to help him work some land should he find a plot. And in that one moment, it's as if he felt a twine of slavery pop. *A white boy as a son!* He laughed heart-full and quiet-shunned.

Huck (*smiling proud*):
What, Jim?

Jim (*proud too*):
*That was mighty smart
what you told them.*

Huck (*prouder*):
*Yeah and they gave me
two twenty pieces too!
Here's one for me
and one for you.*

Jim (*completely struck*):
*I ain't gon forget this Huck,
sure won't forget you for this,
for true.*

Huck (*sheepishly*):
But Jim...

Jim:
Yes, Huck.

Huck (guiltily):
*I'm pretty sure Cairo done come and gone,
and we as deep South
as we ever been.
I'm sorry Jim,
I reckon if I hadn't...*

Jim (forgivingly):
*It ain't your fault, Huck.
Don't blame it.
For a slave's luck is savage by nature.
And that's just it.*

They didn't say a word for quite a many clicks. There was nothing to say but to call the fault in it, in the way things was. And that wouldn't do a thing but draw up more bad luck.

143

Later under night, they talked about what to do and figured they had to keep floating down till they could take the canoe and push against the river. So in the black dark they drove the raft center, as daft as they were demoralized, right toward a bull of a paddle-boat that was pounding up from past where they could see.

The fog was back as a thicket in the middle, right where they were and that might have been a good thing. For when a man is blinded, his body gifts him with enhanced hearing. And Jim heard the sure sound, a split second before Huck, of the river breaking on a paddle-boat down the center of the river, dead toward them like a charging buck.

It was aiming dead for them, as they often did, to see how close they could come till the pilot stuck his head out to laugh at the damage he'd done—at a smashed raft. But this one didn't seem to see them and rang out cusses to stop the engines. But, pumping white-hot clouds, she come gunning for space like a stampede and trampled toward the middle of their way.

They both scrambled to push the raft, but which way? They had a few seconds to move and there could be no delay. And without indication of whether the big boat would go left, right, or decide the safest thing was to barrel straight, there was no way for Huck and Jim to tell the direction toward safe. Either way, it was too late.

The big boat barreled and cracked the raft with a bone-shattering sound. Jim clung to a half of the raft and saw Huck go down. The big boat kept barreling fast. Jim was tumbling with the raft. In a flash he saw Huck's arms go up and quickly go back down as he and the canoe succumbed to the paddle suck. Jim then dove under just as the big paddle came thundering down. It forced Jim to dive to keep from being beaten and thrown, concussed and drowned. Jim went down, way down deep and narrowly missed the planks as they whooshed and creaked an inch from his head meat.

When he came up he saw a good bit of shafts of raft, still tied together, enough for him to climb aboard. And afraid to call for Huck for being spotted he sat and searched starboard and port, bow and stern, straining his eyes through the dark to discern Huck. But there was no such luck and so he sat and contemplated that.

But soon he saw Huck, bobbing up ahead. His heart leapt to know that he hadn't been crushed dead. As much for the luck that Huck provided as for the ways he'd shown a heart bigger than his pride, Jim wanted to keep up with Huck. And with his hidden hopes bound to those of Huck, Jim stayed a distance behind until the time was such that he could catch up.

Jim, whose eyes were hawk and whose heart was as bullish as any big boat, kept sight on Huck quietly as he continued to float, clutching a plank. He watched Huck land on a bank and crawl up but, by the time Jim had reached the place, Huck had set on. So Jim decided to camp in the thicket to rest and get strong. Jim was sure, knowing Huck, that he'd find some luck and would use it to their advantage. And the place he'd found provided some vantage, to keep watch for Huck's return. And before long he fell into a sleep that he, for sure, had earned.

Chapter 10
Jim Meets Middle Pass

A bridge is the carriage
the axle
the wheel
the arch
the pillars
the base
the design
the sweat and skill
the time it took to build.
A bridge is the intention
and the will
to crossover.

****

When Jim came awake he took up the space around himself with a great stretch. Though still on the run, he was pretty well-hidden, and within him there was a sense of something—something different. And though his river partner Huck was gone, Jim felt a bit of good riddance since every hair of assistance the boy gave had been littered with nits of nuisance. Now Jim was alone and away from all he had known with a real, yet still really dicey possibility of being free. But even freedom takes a bow when a man is hungry. So, Jim got to his feet and surveyed the scene for what there might be to eat. He'd long ago learned, from his Old Granny, about the roots and shoots that could satisfy a barren belly.

Jim walked and with each step found himself feeling lighter. An energy bubbled up from his feet and coiled through his chest hairs to curl them tighter. See, Jim's chest hairs were sensitive to confidence which was why they hinted the promise of wealth. And wealth is what Jim felt now that he owned himself.

The fact of that dawned on him, and he let out a reckless yell, not even caring who might of heard him go *WOOOO!* He figured the river was full of kooks doing what kooks do: being wild and popping off. There is something of a rapture, even if on the run and lost, when one has freed themselves from land or from capture at any cost.

As he walked, Jim soon came to a gathering of enslaved men in one of those secret circle cyphers that offer a brief breath from enslavement—where a man can be a man. It was as secret as it had to be, since any gathering of three Black men was labeled with a gang of criminality. This would leave all three subjects subject to the law of averages that they might be hanged expeditiously. And though these three men didn't boast, brag, and fight like the men on the river barge, they did argue and they argued hard. They happened to be gaggling and haggling, with hustler's craft, about who among them would be the new owner of the remains of Jim and Huck's raft.

There were three men: one young, one less young, and one not young at all. One was short, one was less short, and one was tall. The three knew each other, seemed like for years, and the way they talked was as if every word was half a joke and every laugh, half a tear. Jim listened in with a pointed ear.

Cassius:

Whip up all you want by way of proof, Rich.
The gavel's in the footwork[43],
and you ain't carrying that raft a stitch by yourself.
Lemme help
for half the knot
that you'll get when the getting's got.

Rich:

I'll be damned!
Damned to the mud in my bone[44].
I'll just fix it right here
and ride the river gone.
I'll give you a quarter the price for a hand in fixin' it
and that's worth more than the horseshit
you spittin, Cassius.

Redd:

Now hold on, hold on.
You saw it first, right Rich?
Then you came up on Rich
trying to figure out what to do with it.

---

[43] Muhammad Ali—born Cassius Marcellus Clay— was the warrior-poet of his day, of all times great. Ali must have had an analog who was enslaved—a funny man who could break a funny bone off in your face.

[44] There had to be a prior Richard Pryor. I guess we know this because of Mudbone, the character Pryor channeled from back in Peoria, Illinois all the way back to Tupelo, Mississippi. When it comes to dropping bombs on history, Richard Pryor's was King Comedy.

Ain't that right, Cassius?
Seem like a stalemate to me.
Best thing'd be
to let me,
as the elder,
settle the disagreement quickly.
Then we split it in three
so as to compensate me
for all the trouble
of getting us out of so prickly a kerfuffle[45].

Jim thought fast of what to do. He walked up with a story to settle the truth and spoke with a sort of grandeur to match the freedom he was getting used to. He put on the act, the proper tongue, like his Old Gran used to when Christian company would come for a fellowship function. He cleared his throat with a loud, garbled *eh em* and damn near startled the three men out their skin.

Jim:
Gentlemen, that there raft
belongs to my master and me.
He a young boy of about thirteen.
We got broke by a river boat.
He sent me to find this raft
and to get it patched.
I could use some help
if any of you could use half a ten piece
to work with me
and find me something to eat

---

[45] The antebellum version of the great comic Redd Foxx must have been lick-slick with the quickest kind of slippery wit—wordplay like mixtape Wayne, spit game like Tyson with no shame, doubling the hustle through his name (double d, double x).

And there wasn't any stall in getting help from Cassius, the tall, young one. Half a ten piece was big pay for a man used to getting none. There was no haggle, no negotiation. Only the question of whether or not Jim could produce the funds. Jim, of course could, and his newly hired help was flush with ambition to get to action. Jim threw a few more ducats at Rich, to find him some food. He shared a bit more treasure with Redd, the elder, as a tribute to the right thing to do.

If there was any benefit to being enslaved, and there is exactly one ton minus a ton, it was that it doesn't take much time for life-long workers to get work done. The raft was patched before the sun went down. And since the raft was right and ready, Jim begun to ask around about Huck.

The other perk the enslaved have, but don't really possess, is a keen and quick recognition of change in the slightest. If the days of your life swung from captive to chaos on the whims of White men like the days of the enslaved do, you too would be spider-web sensitive to any trigger of change and what that change might indicate for whom. The enslaved had to be, at all times, political—at all times correct. As a result, they would collect information and share freely as a way to collectively find some sense of security.

If one of them blasted masters had a wife who couldn't stand his touch, everyone needed to know because a man frustrated such would be bound to let his frustration erupt on the backs of enslaved men and on the breasts of enslaved women. And if that master had another woman who had another man, the whole triangle was known by all the enslaved. This was so they could prepare for the day when the whole damned shame would result in a slave being blamed.

The politics of the enslaved were a maze of plays and counter-plays. This was the backdrop that Jim knew well. So he knew that if he asked about Huck, there was someone who had something to tell.

One of the men had heard about a new young boy who called himself George, which immediately let Jim know what was up—Huck was holding tight where he was.

So while Jim awaited the potential of Huck's return, he spent time on and off the raft for about half a week. It was good thinking time, time to just be. Just about the first of such time Jim had ever seen. And at the end of the first day of the week, Jim, taking it all in, began to speak.

Jim (*to himself*):
Good thing how far a body can hear
on the water,
how the voices fill up the shores.
It keeps me
to keeping my distance
from them people
and on my course.

I might say the days swim by.
The days stroke between the rains,
and when the rains come,
they thrash the trees blue and black
and make them all shadowy and strange.
When a whip of wind rips the leaves
and send the trees a bending and jumping,
like folk at a hootenanny be,
it's like they catch the spirit of the storm
and bow they heads
till she pass and leave them be—
quiet again.

The sky looks cast iron black
when you lay down on your back
in the deep of moon shine,
and I never knew it like this before.
For I never had the time.

With time, I could use my mind
to think about all that we wrapped in.
I might wonder if stars was made

151

or if they just happened.
I might suppose the moon just laid them there
like some frog eggs...
like a frog lays a million eggs in the dregs
and kicks off somewhere.
I might suppose that's me,
kicking off free,
so maybe I can lay some stars
in the mud of the river
to kick off free one day
like me.

And at that Jim paused for a long time, and there was time again, a time to think that Jim couldn't find during his enslavement. His thoughts chimed in accord with what human minds can afford when faced with space to contemplate a plan. Jim's fate filled his hands, despite the hunt on his back, despite the fact that the shield of Huck might never come back. In the slick grip of the marsh pit where he crouched, there was a hard grit that fused like grout in Jim's will to get out. It bubbled up into his mouth and came as a song he'd heard his granny moan about a time when the enslaved had their own: their own land, their own ways, their own tongue. The song come like the cool of dark after a long day done, and, quiet as a fish swum, Jim sung:

There is a land from which we come
to which we will fly away

And when we go, we will know
the hope of souls and rest in day

We will speak our tongues free;
we will walk with strides wide

And when we go, we will know
the hope of souls and rest in life

152

There is a way, a way to live—
a way we will plant our seeds

And when we go, we will know
the hope of souls finally free

And when we go, oh we will know
the hope of souls finally free

As Jim sang, he didn't know he wasn't alone. Just on the other side of a thick of brush there was another enslaved man sitting silent as stone. He listened to Jim's song with a smile on his face. And as soon as Jim was done, he spoke through the brush in a hushed way.

Middle Pass (Jack) (*in a raspy whisper*):
Seeking station to Canaan?
You baggage, brother?[46]

The voice froze Jim cold and he flattened himself into stealth as if he were stowed in the bottom of a ships hold—some pirate's stolen wealth.

Middle Pass (Jack) (*a bit louder now, clearer*):
Your humming sound good,
and song will keep you goin' on
sure is the day is long.
Song will make you strong.

---

[46] According to the Harriet-Tubman Historical Society, "conductors" of the underground railroad "used words railroad conductors employed everyday to create their own code as secret language in order to help slaves escape. Railroad language was chosen because the railroad was an emerging form of transportation and its communication language was not widespread."

But you not far from the pitter patters
of the rollers[47] of the road, you know.

As he spoke these last words, he showed himself to be a large man of mahogany, broad and healthy as a tree stout on a patch of land formed and fed by the thick veins creeks weave. There was a force that Middle Pass Jack wore like a robe. It was either courage or purpose or passion or hope; maybe it was all four. He was enslaved, it seemed, but there was something of him free and sharp and sure. His voiced buzzed with the seething rhythm of bugs moored to a moor.

---

[47] "Patterrollers" were organized groups of armed white men who policed the enslaved and enforced white supremacy through terror in the antebellum south. One of many accounts of the formerly enslaved makes this clear. See *Leaves from a Slaves Journal of Life* – Lydia Marie Francis Child, 1802-1820, The Anti-slavery Standard, 20 and 27 October 1842, p. 78-79, 83. Take Ms. Child's word for it:
"But as I was telling ye, they hire these patter-rollers, and they have to take the meanest fellows above ground; and because they are so mortal sure the slaves don't want their freedom, they have to put all power into their hands, to do with the [Black folks] just as they like. If a slave don't open his door to them, at any time of night, they break it down. They steal his money, if they can find it, and act just as they please with his wives and daughters. If a husband dares to say a word, or even look as if he wasn't quite satisfied, they tie him up and give him thirty-nine lashes. If there's any likely young girls in a slave's hut, they're mighty apt to have business there; especially if they think any colored young man takes a fancy to any of 'em. Maybe he'll get a pass from his master, and go to see the young girl for a few hours. The patter-rollers break in and find him there. They'll abuse the girl as bad as they can, a purpose to provoke him. If he looks cross, they give him a flogging, tear up his pass, turn him out of doors, and then take him up and whip him for being out without a pass. If the slave says they tore it up, they swear he lies, and nine times out of ten the master won't come out agin 'em; for they say it won't do to let the [Black folks] suppose they may complain of the patter-rollers; they must be taught that it's their business to obey 'em in everything."

Jim knew the look well, it was the swell of one enslaved to a wealthy family for sure.[48]

> Middle Pass:
> *Middle.*
> *That's my name brother.*
> *Middle Pass.*
> *That's what I call myself when asked,*
> *but the name I was given,*
> *is Jack.*
> *It's a good name, matter fact,*
> *but White folk call me that*
> *so it's something of a lifetime lash.*
> *Jack acts tame as night is black,*
> *and plays the game*
> *until such time*
> *as I must change names*
> *and tack my tack.*
> *Consider me a track*
> *on that Canaan train.*

---

[48] Let Ms. Childs tell you one more thing about what you might call the Middle Class enslaved, "some folks go down to Kentucky, and tell fine stories about how well the slaves live; that they dress as nice as anybody, and have a horse to ride a Sunday. Well, so it is with many of them slaves that are the favorites in rich families; but I tell you them favorite slaves are most to be pitied of all. They are obliged to cringe a little lower than any of the others. They must mind and please the master and mistress in everything; and please the children, and the uncles, and the aunts and the cousins, and all the relations; for the master wants him to feel it is all along of his will that he is better off than the others, and that he has the power at any moment, to cut his comb; and he is always sort of jealous, too, that the slave will think he has a *right* to any of the privileges he has been used to having. So he has to mind his P's and Q's right smart; for if he says or does anything that any of the relations don't like, he's pushed right down below all the slaves." From *Slaves Journal of Life* – Lydia Marie Francis Child, 1802-1820, The Anti-slavery Standard, 20 and 27 October 1842, p. 78-79, 83.

Jim had no latch for grabbing what this man, Middle, was casting. He was mixing bibles with trains, and chains with names, and whips with games. What he was saying, Jim could not see. Seemed like something out of a book that Jim couldn't read, but here was a man calling himself Middle Pass, as if he was a bridge to Jim's destiny.

Middle Pass:
I heard your song.
My granny taught me the same one.
You sounded good, for sure,
good as a drinking gourd
on a hot day
or a wadin' in the water
through a hot night.
I come to see if I could shepherd
one of Moses' bundles of wood
toward heaven's light.

Jim:
I don't know no Moses.
And I ain't got nobody wood.
I'm here with my massa,
and we lost our raft,
and now I done found it,
so we need to get back on our path
if we could.

Jim lied loud and clear. Escape could never let one forget that a fellow might be on something slick to get you to let slip that you running, to trade you in for some bounty right quick. No, this was not a time to be loose lipped, Jim had to keep his tongue moose bit, keep the truth holstered to the hip.

Middle Pass took a step back and angled his head, not sure if he had correctly heard what Jim had just said. He thought for a moment and smiled. Figuring Jim didn't trust him, Middle Pass played a while with Jim's wiles.

156

Middle Pass:
Your massa?
He a boy ain't he?
Two of y'all just arrived three days ago?

Jim:
Yes!
You seen him?
What he up to?

Middle Pass:
He done landed with the Grangerford family.
That's who I'm with too.
They a decent good group to stumble on to,
at least temporarily.
They got time and space
and done give him a place to stay.
They done gave the boy me[49] to tend to.
Say his name was George.
Funny he never spoke on you.

At this, Jim knew Huck was keeping Jim's cover and might have intention to get back to the river to continue to get him free. Jim let out a visible smirk of relief. Middle Pass saw that and facetiously began to speak.

Middle Pass:
He your massa, ha?
This boy, George.
How that come to be?
A boy and his slave river-rafting
the Mississippi?

---

[49] Irony. In Twain's *Huck Finn*, Huck bragged that the Grangerford's gave him a slave named Jack.

You sure you don't know Moses?
Ain't on your way?

Just then something dawned on Jim. Moses. He'd heard that name outside of the bible. Moses. White folks had spoke of this Moses who was alive and wasn't a man at all. Moses, a woman, was a freer of slaves and whether swamp, tree, or cave would gather people and give them a way out of the mouth of a place named for Jesus' mother—Mary's Land—to go forth in the north.

Jim:
The Moses you talking 'bout,
that the Moses that take slaves...?

Middle Pass:
The very one.
But there's more than one.
And listen my friend,
you musn't say anything so clear
under the sun
or even in the night.
You have to learn the code,
you have to fly the kites,
to keep distance,
make sure you know
with who you have spoke
before you go talking about something so...

Middle Pass cut himself off before it was too late. He reached into his bag and pulled out an apple to hand to Jim, which Jim proceeded to decimate.
Understood, said Jim between bites. *That's all that you was talking, right, trains and baggage? That's the code... the kites?*
Middle Pass smiled. *That be, it might.*

158

Middle Pass:
All I have in this world
is my word
and the nerve to serve freedom,
to herd sheep when I meet them.
You surely heard of the beatings,
the murders of men pleading
hung, strung, burning,
face crushed and turned in.
That's the devil's brand of learning
to leave your stomach turning
before you get to thinking of an inkling
of a yearning
to be free.
That's the savagery of White men
against we that he call beast.
Well that there don't phase me.
You might say it's crazy,
but if them whip-crackers almost catch me,
I'm taking three more with me.
Even if I die,
my name'll go down in history.
They'll be three less
of them to catch
another who seek to be free.

Naw, them ofay'll[50] never get me.
Never chop a foot from me.
I'll get slippery,
shift to mist quickly,
and be gone three days to Haiti[51]
before they miss me.

Intrigued, Jim interrupted his speech.

Jim:
Wait, what's Haiti?
I think I might of heard of that.

---

[50] "Ofay", according to *Cab Calloway's Hepster's Dictionary: A Guide to the Language of Jive* means "White person." According to many sources, it is an "extremely derogatory" term for a "White person" that has some root in some mysterious "African" (and recall that Africa is a continent) word. Really? This is more proof that language is arbitrary and powerful. It has been used to denigrate and desecrate human value as much as it has been used to deify and venerate human evils. Twain's favorite, the "n-word", is proof of the power of language to reify the mysterious and viral mental illness of anti-Black racism. Alternately, the term "ofay" shows the power of language to dismiss itself as arbitrary and meaningless, then be resurrected as proof of mythologies like "reverse racism." Language can make something out of nothing and nothing out of everything... that's true power.

[51] The Hatian Revolution (1791 – 1804) is a historical fact of mythical lore in the mind of any Black student of the past. It is a moment when a nation of enslaved fought back the lash and went on the attack. They tossed Napoleon and his French army into the sea, and fought off the Brits and the Spaniards who swore an island of former slaves would make easy booty. The Haiti you know as a scene of chaos, hunger, and poverty was made that way by waves of European and American dastardly deeds and attacks on it's sovereignty. But, throughout the African Diaspora, the Haitian revolutionary act itself (despite the facts of the years since), the act itself is enough to inspire resistance. It's enough to know that it can be done. Your homework: *Black Jacobins* by C.L.R. James.

Middle Pass:
Haiti Island?
Oh that's a nation—
a nation born black.
The slaves got together
and went on attack.
They kicked out the French,
buried any traitor in a trench,
and built they own
just like your granny's song.
You heard about that?

Jim (*in disbelief*):
That's real?
Or more secret kites of code?
Slaves fight to take a land
and the Whites let it go?

Middle Pass:
French had no choice:
die or leave.
They knew Boukman.
They knew Mackandal.
They knew Toussaint and Dessalines.

Jim:
That's French you speaking?
That's what it sound like?
The Black nation people
speak French like Whites?

Middle Pass
Black folk speak French
Spanish, Portuguese, Arabic as well.
They know the language of the Indians
and remember heaven in the motherland
before this here hell.

That's where I'm going
when I'm done in Babylon.
I'll stop on Haiti Island
to find a wife,
then I'm back home.
Gone.

Jim:
Well, I got a wife and children too.
I ain't going nowhere without them.
Haiti a place women and children can get to?

Middle Pass:
Where there is a soul there is a will,
and if you willing you can make a way,
and if the way is treacherous
the question is
what risks will you take
to see your children play days
and your wife lay safe
in a home of your own
in a land far away?

Jim began to consider that, when Middle Pass broke the last bit of the facts of Haiti Island.

Middle Pass:
Now leave it to the lord
—the great trickster up high—
that you would have to travel through
the lowest bottom to reach the highest tide.
Haiti is south of Arkansas,
south of Louisiana,
south even of old Orleans,
the opposite of Canaan's Canada.
The burning swamps under Orleans
will rot the chains away,

there the maroons
—the escaped slave children of St. Malo[52]—
lead the way
to a village of mix,
where women walk with bowls on their heads
and men war with sticks[53],
where small Manila men[54] fish
with tall Indians,
blood inked on their fists,
where they all give reverence
to the secret of the escaped slave St. Malo
and offer no signs of evidence,
where all the people turn the colors of cypress:
all black and brown and peach
and red and yellow,
to match the marshland—
Bayou Sauvage.
Yes, you must keep south
for a different kind of free.
You must face the beast
to reach the Island of Haiti.

---

[52] Juan St. Malo was an escaped slave who started a community of maroon (escaped) enslaved, Indigenous, Haitian immigrants, and Creole pirates in Bayou Sauvage just past the present day neighborhood of Michoud in New Orleans East. Your homework: *Africans in Colonial Louisiana: The Development of Afro-Creole Culture in the Eighteenth Century.* Gwendolyn Mildo Hall, Louisiana State University Press. 1992.

[53] Filipino stick fighting, called Kali, is an old and vicious martial art. Legend has it that fighting with sticks is what led to the balanced and even defensive setting of fists that became the norm in professional boxing.

[54] Manila Men were descendants of Filipinos who overthrew Spanish slave ships and sailed those ships to the bayous of Plaquemines Parish, Louisiana in the 1700s. They established a long-standing community. Personal note— my great-grand father, Moriano Molina, a Filipino boxer and fisherman in New Orleans, was likely descended from the Manila Men.

Then there was a long silence as Jim was struck dumb. All this time he'd worried he wrung the last bit of luck out of his soul. Now he done found out that instead of stuck, he was headed the way he needed to go.

Thinking of luck made him think of Huck. No need for him in Haiti. No need to nurse his White mind out of slavery, out of the tendency to stake claim to human bodies. Huck would have to understand his place in a Black nation—no better and no less. He would have to become civilized out of the wretchedness he had been taught from his first breath—that there was such thing as a slave, that this slave must be a slave, that his slave soul must be broken and controlled lest it open, become bold and throw the White man into his grave. Little could Huck know that, having tasted the slave bit, no soul could ever torture another with it. The nature of injustice is so. Once you know it, you want it gone from the face of the earth, for every body and every soul.

Middle Pass read the contemplation in the countenance beneath Jim's face and accounted for other options that might hide and provide sustenance should he succeed in escape. He told him of the railroads and how they would take a runaway west, that is if he was willing to John Henry himself to death. He told Jim of the Chinese who had come from far away to hammer, and how they were damn near slaves of another manner.

Middle Pass told Jim about the Mexican War and St. Patrick's Battalion—the Irish who had joined the other side, tired of being treated like trash no matter how hard they tried. He explained that Indians, 'the first people alive', had kept and protected runaways to grow their dying tribes. Middle Pass went on and on about all the places a runaway might be free or at least where he should try to be should he get free. All the while, Jim spied him for a sense of what was driving him.

Jim (*probing*):
*How you know so much
about so much?*

164

Middle Pass (*smiling*):
Quiet as kept,
I can read.

Jim (*shocked*):
Read! How?

Middle Pass (*proud*):
Well there was a mistress
that owned my mother,
yet seemed to believe she loved her
like a sister.
For all we know they was.
The mistress' daddy was want to do
what men who own grown women does.
Well, she taught my maw,
and my maw taught me,
and along my travels
guiding brethren free,
I pick up what I can
and read what I can read
and learn what I can learn,
and there's quite a bit of knowledge
I've earned.

Jim (*flummoxed*):
Well if you know so much,
why you put up with such
as being a slave?
Why you don't just run away?

Middle Pass paused. Not as if he hadn't thought of the question, but as if the question was the thought that crossed his mind just about every other second. It was as if he had a ready answer, an answer he gave a million times, but that something about Jim and the way he asked it made him want to change his mind.

Middle Pass:
I'm a hostage
just like you.
I got people I love
I'm trying to keep to.
What will me running away do for them?

Jim (*trying to convince himself*):
More than you can do
being kept like a beast.
Me?
I'm buying mine free.

Middle Pass smiled and nodded, as if he was glad to hear it, but there was doubt tugging at his bottom lip. So many times he'd heard a man say that plan and so few times had a man actually done it. He knew that, to push on, Jim had to have this hope, but he also felt he should give Jim some notice as to how hard it would be to make it so.

Middle Pass (*looking away*):
Do you know how we came to be slaves?

Jim (*with a brow raised*):
I don't know about you,
but I was born this way.

Middle Pass (*looking at the ground, now*):
No siree.
God made every body free.

166

But in the beginning,
who made your father a slave,
and your father's father a slave?

Jim (*looking around*):
Well, I done heard about Africa
and that being where we came from.
But I done also heard that them people was savages
who beat drums
and eat their own children.

Middle Pass (*looking dead into Jim's eyes*):
Well you heard lies.
Africa has kings, just like France
and whole nations,
older nations that'll dance
rings around France
and Spain
and will never be chained or whipped
by any white man.

Jim (*unconvinced*):
If that's true,
then how we end up in this trouble?
How we end up stranded
and branded
and muzzled?

Middle Pass (*with a pained smirk*):
It's like Judas did Jesus,
Brutus did Ceasar,
Kane did Abel,
White man wasn't even able
to get past the shores of Africa.
It was Africans that chained our people
and walked them to the ocean,
and sold them.

It was our own that did us in.

Jim *(shaking his head)*:
Damn.
Ain't that always the way.

Middle Pass *(nodding)*:
That's the only way.
You can't hold a people
the way they hold us as slaves
without some of us helping them
day after day.

Jim *(struck)*:
Helping them like I'm helping Huck?

Middle Pass *(feigning being confused,*
reaching for a stick in the ground):
Helping who?

Jim *(looking away)*:
Never mind.
What you mean helping?
All I'm trying to do is survive.

Middle Pass *(poking the stick in the dirt)*:
Well, that's what I mean.
As long as we slaves,
we can't help but help them
by surviving.
If we die, they lose.
But if we lose our life,
we lose all hope.
So what else can we do?

Jim *(grabbing his own stick)*:
We run up north.

Middle Pass (*stabs his stick in the ground*):
Up North?
The North got rich off
what the South horde.
Who loan the plantation money
to buy seed, plows, and hoes?
Who take the cotton and ship it
to distant shores?
Who bank the money your master make?
Who make the law that keep us slaves?
The North, that's who?
Go up North and see what they do you.

Jim (*bending the stick in disappointment*):
But I heard there ain't no plantations up North,
that a man can work a factory
and a factory can pay a wage
and a wage can feed a family.
I heard that children can learn.

At this Jim choked on his words a bit, or rather on some tear in his heart that hope had opened up. The chance that his children might learn, that his children might earn a way for their children was beginning to grow from an impossible hope to a real feeling. Before a drop of water could fall from his eye, Jim held his head back and looked at the sky.

Jim (*gathering himself*):
I've heard the North is where a man can be free,
that up there is where we should flee.

Middle Pass (*reassuringly, then pointedly*):
Well yes,
if you can make it there, go.
But don't be so sure that you'll know freedom.

169

Answer me this,
What do slaves provide this country?

Jim (*angrily breaking his stick*):
Free work!
A whole body!

Middle Pass (*throws his stick*):
And a mind to boot!
How you think these farmers know what crops to plant
where and when,
what diseases rot their potatoes
and when the boll weevils are hiving?
How you think they know
what types of crops can hold on
through dry seasons
and keep to thriving?
Now the master'll take credit for it—
will call himself a scientist—
he'll say his White mind
is perfectly designed
to find solutions to planting's predicaments.
But it's the slave who seen it coming.
It's the worker who knows what works.
It's the slave who tells the master
when, where, and what
to put in the dirt.

Jim (*unmoved*):
Yeah, I know.
But so?
That don't get the slave a penny
or a moment of rest.
Matter fact
all that do
is improve the chance
the slave will be worked to death.

170

Middle Pass (*haltingly, quietly*):
Well that slave's body and mind,
before he dies,
is this country's greatest crop.
To have a human
working as a beast
means they got
the labor of the muscle
and the industry of the mind
which is double, treble
many times increase on the investment
in due time.

Jim (*looking away, then at Middle Pass*):
It don't make it no better
to speak what is.
How is any of this gon' help me get a grip
on what the north is?

Middle Pass (*looking back at Jim*):
Do you think the north will let all that wealth just walk away?
Do you think they will just pay you
the pay a White man is paid?
Don't you think that poor White might have something to say?
Do you think they'll hand you the keys to the kingdom
and say 'godspeed and good day?'
Do you think they will see you
as anything more than a slave
or a slave they made "free"?
To them you will either be a crop
a charity
or a burden that they carry
and wish they could erase from history.

Jim (*resigned*):
So we got to get away from the White man

171

in order to be free?
I hear that.
But this Haiti you told me about,
is it really better for somebody like me?
I mean I can't even read the language I speak!
Now I got to learn another language
to be free?
I don't even know what them folk eat!
I don't know how they live.
I don't know what they act like.
What if I go and they put me in the field
day and night?
What if I go,
and they don't want me there?
What if I go
and they ain't got no work to spare?
I'd rather deal with the devil I know
than the one off in some strange land somewhere.

Middle Pass (*nodding*):
Well, that's logic
and that's up to you.
I just don't want you going North
thinking it is heaven under the moon.

Jim (*probing*):
But what about all that Caanan stuff
you was talking—
all that religion hoodoo,
all that promised land
you told me about
when I first came upon you?

Middle Pass (*after a pause*):
Those are codes.
I didn't know you from Adam or Cain.
That's the way I see

if you here to get free
or looking for lighter chains.
The North ain't heaven
is all I'm saying.
And in this land and country
your skin will always be the mark
that says to them
'This is a beast.
Work it or kill it,
but it cannot be free.'

Jim (*after a pause of his own, indignantly*):
Well this the land
where my old Gran slaved
where my daddy
got slayed.
I can still see his face!
And I'll be damned
if I just give my people's work
and suffering away.

Middle Pass (*slowly getting up to stand*):
This land,
this America they call it,
this land of the free
and resting place of our fallen
who lived to work
and died and left nothing,
who wore rags for shirts
and tried to make something
when they made us—
This land of the free
one day will pay for slavery.
And when that day comes to be,
you and me will be long dead,
and still we will run in the blood shed.

173

And we will flow forth
in the sweat sweat.
And we will rise again
in the arms stretched
to raise a fist against the original sin,
to breathe a new breath,
to watch revelation and its horsemen
trample with no mercy or regret,
to tear open
what's been frozen
in the circles of hell,
and tell the truth
of what made this world—
a well of sin
deep and poison-brimming.
Where will we be free?
In the bones,
in the blood,
in the breath of our progeny,
wherever they be.

Jim (*growing weary of words*):
Our who?
I don't know that word.

Middle Pass (*looking at the sky*):
If you know your children,
you know your sword.

Jim (*frustrated*):
Man, I don't know what you saying
or what you saying it for.

Middle Pass (*breathing heavily*
while speaking slowly, then forcefully):
Like I said,
they profit off our bodies

and they will always try.
They'll try to profit off our minds
till the day we die.
But they will never hold our souls
unless we give up and give in
to the story they done told.
You got to be free inside
no matter what they shackle you with.
You got to have a place in your heart
that can't be beat with a whip.
You got to keep your Old Gran
and the songs she used to sing.
You got to keep your daddy strength
as your inheritance
and crown your son with it,
a king.

Jim (*done with metaphors*):
But what, exactly,
what am I supposed to do?

Middle Pass (*calming, taking a stump for a seat*):
Live to fight.
Fight to live.
We have to help ourselves
to whatever we can.
And even if the White man
gains from our labor,
we have to always
ready ourselves
to steady our hands
to take freedom
when we get the chance
to get gone.

Jim (*nodding, then cocking his head left*):
But you watch freedom walk away

every time you help another escape?
Do you pass that up
just to help some other slave break their chains?

Middle Pass (*nodding, a pained smile*):
Some of us got to stay
to make a way.
And some of us got to go.
Seems like you done made your choice,
so I'm gon' help.
That's what I'm here for.

Jim (*shaking his head judgingly*):
All the people
you done helped free,
and none ain't come back
to see about you?

Middle Pass (*looking at the ground*):
They'd bet not dare.
If they go,
they better go
and never press a foot
nor set a thought
back here
in the devil's soot.

Jim (*leaning forward*):
Damn, but what about you?

Middle Pass (*after a pause, looking up*):
I'm gone have a name,
a name a thousand free tell
to their free children
and them to their ten thousand children,
and them to their hundred thousand more.
And though I'll be as long gone as ash on a shore,

I'll be a name.
I'll be a name of hope.
And whatever trouble
comes ten years down
and ten of ten years more gone,
Middle Pass will mean hope
and hope will lead somebody home.
And all this flesh,
and the breath I speak
and the hands I work
and the stomp of my feet
and the shoulders that rumble
from my heart beat—
all that shall pass
to that from which it came.
But when my body is lain,
whether on high or in flame,
whether part of everything
or nothing at all,
my name,
not my slave name,
but the brand on my soul—Middle Pass—
will be the response to the call.
Middle Pass will mean hope
for all.

Jim had never considered such a sacrifice for someone other than his own kin. And as Jim listened, he began to grow a sense of hope, of seeds buried that might burst up to the sun, of rains that fall on the desert and flow, of days that rise from the darkest oblivion. And Jim, who'd known nothing but being a slave and being the son of a slave's son, began to see in this world, not in the heaven thereafter, a new day to come where his children would see peace as they made the most of freedom.

Jim thought of Sadie and of their children living in freedom. He thought of them running in freedom, just to feel their bodies run. He thought of them watching stars in freedom, just to see the light they brung. He thought of the songs they might sing in freedom, songs like a free bird sings. He thought of work in freedom, and through it what they could save if they were just paid the dignity of pay and could leave some treasure for future children in some future day. He thought of a tombstone in freedom, a tombstone with his name and of great-great grandchildren who might come to lay a wreath on this, his final fame.

Without meaning to, Jim thought of Huck and was certain he could not come. Huck's mind was made in a cave where men were slaves, and Jim's life, yet to come, would be made in the sun. Out of Jim and Huck, no twain could be strung.

Jim's mind jumped to the journey to come and to making preparation. If Huck returned he would ride with him as far as the last possible sun. But, at some point, there would have to be a separation.

Jim (*resolute*):
I need to get going.

Middle Pass (*curious*):
But the boy,
George, your master?
You planning to go on with him?

Jim (*with a curled lip*):
That boy ain't my master.
We both running.

Middle Pass (*as an offering of wisdom*):
Yeah, I saw that like I seen the day coming.
That's good cover for you,
a quick White boy like him.

That's a good cover.
Say, what your name?

Jim:
Jim.
And you right about him as good cover.
Can you let him know where I am?

Middle Pass:
I will do that.
You stay low to the land.
It might take a few days for me to get him here
without too much ruckus.
Understand?

And Jim did, so he made his way back to the raft to camp. And on the way he picked some berries to tamp down his stomach until he could find some prey. And as soon as he did, he feasted on a whole portion of roasted pigeon with no need to share with Huck. And thus he spent the days in wait, eating good, and spent his nights sitting up, ears open for a rustle in the wood.

179

Chapter 11
Jim Longs for Sadie

Love.
That is all.

****

Day and night, Jim's mind drifted while time sifted his thoughts and, in that time, his lonesomeness hardened. Soon, Jim began to dwell on his wife Sadie, a woman who had dug in him a garden. She had shucked the thick hide of his heart—had oiled the rust on the tin can it had been.[55] She'd bent back the lid and let herself in. And it wasn't without a struggle, no indeed. Sometimes she was a slippery eel to snag. Sometimes he was a snapping turtle to feed.

Jim thought back to the moment he met her.

It had been one of those days the enslaved knew well. When the hell that is a world of work meets the swell of human hopes lost. Jim had been calculating the cost of his days had he been paid for his labors, and it had come to more than he could count. And the weight of all the time that had been taken from him began to mount. Jim was surly as a burly grizzly bear as he walked a trail on a tear through the wood. Then he came across Sadie, inside a front door wide open, cleaning out an abandoned cabin.

At first he walked past. Jim wasn't one to pay a woman much mind. But then he caught a glance of something heavy at the base of her spine. She carried weight there like skins full of wine, rocking and sloshing on their way to a table divine—to a last supper. Jim about faced and walked past again to get a second look. Then walked past again for another.

On his fifth idiot pass, Sadie spoke.

> Sadie (*without turning around*):
> *Fool, do I look like an ass?*
> *Do you think I can't see you pass and pass and pass?*

She turned to face him.

> Sadie (*with a sly grin*):
> *How about you introduce yourself?*

---

[55] Shout-out *Beloved* again…

Jim (*embarrassed*):
I'm Jim.

Sadie (*grin fading*):
I know who you are.
Every woman round here done heard of Jim,
son of pretty Bill,
who got himself killed over a White woman.
Jim who never been married,
some say never will.

Jim (*hunching his brow*):
You don't know me.

Sadie (*one brow raised*):
Ugh. And maybe I don't want to.
You the looking head-ass one looking, fool.

Jim (*eyes rolling down, searching that truth*):
Well, I'm just trying to see what you up to.

Sadie (*cocking a hip*):
My business,
and I sure ain't sniffing my eyes
where they don't belong
like you.

Jim felt her a might intrusive and felt himself annoyed about a statement so conclusive. How'd she know he wasn't marveling at how she was as ugly as a bat? And no she wasn't anything near the universe of ugly, but how she know that? And he hadn't ever made up his mind about taking a woman's hand. And what kind of woman talks about marriage the first time she meets a man?

His head told him to walk away, but he couldn't move his body from mirroring hers heart-square and face to face.

182

Her skin was molasses dark, dark enough to fascinate the light. With teeth so white she looked like she'd suckled a cloud all night. Her cheeks were set high under deep, onyx eyes that shined and smoldered. And her neck was a crepe myrtle tree trunk that plunged into her shoulders, which were broad above sturdy arms that cupped the sides of her breasts as they hung free under a bodice with a waistcoat draped over. Her details startled Jim. He wasn't one to pay so much attention, and here he was tumbling down the gravity of her body like a loose boulder. And for a moment he'd forgotten all the fatigue and fury with being enslaved that had drove him to the wood in the first place.

Needless to say, he came back to see her many times and anyhow. Here are the things he remembered now:

How Sadie told Jim about a man she had loved and how her face went soft as she spoke of his loss, and how she looked like God after having given her one begotten son, and how it broke Jim's heart open and stuck in his head, and how Jim longed to raise her love from the dead.

How Sadie had these phrases she would say when Jim got into a funk, to remind him of the well of wisdom from which she must have sprung. How she'd say, *live your strength*. How she'd say, *let things come*. How she'd say, *walk your beautiful. talk your beautiful.* How she'd say, *you something else. thank the lord there's only one you.* How Jim's heart, now broken open, was filled with gratitude.

How Sadie was careful and stubborn and loved the way his attention savored her, and how all that made Jim want to work to keep her favor.

How the iron each of them became steel through heavy, laboring strokes that melted the hard greys of their limestone days till their night fuels cooled to coke.

How they'd made their mettle into a soon-to-be child through the fires they'd stoked.

How one day, Jim stood before Sadie gleaming with sweat, silently at the door of her ramshackle cabin. How the place was a beached shipwreck a sailor might trade for dry shoes. How Sadie still made it a lovely home through and through.

How that day, Jim stood at that door looking past her, unsure of what to do.

He perused the exacting order she'd kept this pile of boards in, everything in it its place—cast iron pots she'd restored hung from the ceiling here, the oak bed he'd built over there crowned with a nest of cotton stuffed with goose down and lined with the fur of hare. In front of the black stove pipe he'd dug up and cleaned were two cedar rocking chairs that smelled like live woods filled with wren—one room organized into a kitchen, a bedroom, a den.

Jim's arms felt heavy as he held picked flowers in a bunch. His belly growled in anticipation of lunch. They'd done this. They'd met here many times before, but not with Jim carrying this wish; he was there to ask Sadie to jump the broom. He stood at the door as a hungry man in whose heart Sadie had made room, a room that matched the one she'd made for herself and lit with fire and moon.

There was the kitchen, where Jim's belly would heat as his eyes swept over her flesh, flesh as full as rolling hills of daffodils and as soft as cotton woven into living mesh. There was the den where she would listen with the quiet of shadow and where she would speak with lips as lobed as mallow and where Jim would wind his mind around her words' every lull and peak. There was the bedroom where Jim finally found rest deep within himself, his chest a pillow for her cheek.

Jim had talked himself over the words over the whole walk there. Sadie was impatient for him to come in. But he stood, his breath lumbering, his lungs clenching everything the air could spare. Sadie, seeing the weird way he stood somehow understood. Her breath was split into halves of wood—would he, could he?

184

She'd loved another man once, a man she'd never had a chance to bury. That man had helped her make three babies she'd never had the chance to carry. Their love had never had the chance to root; toil had pulverized their soil. Their hope had never a chance to sprout for all the times it had been ripped, cut, and boiled. She'd loved a man once, a man she'd never had the chance to marry. And here was a another man with a bunch of pretty weeds in his hands about to ask her to tarry with him for life.

Jim spoke first.

Jim (*clearing his throat*):
Sadie,
it was a walk,
a long walk to meet you here
with a mind on the future.
But I drove my will like a steer
past the part of me that wanted to veer
rather than hold a woman's burden.
Lord knows it's heavier
than women be deserving.
But I just won't leave a woman
who has heard me
when I couldn't speak of the cracks of pain,
a woman who'll carry sacks of rain
for a man
who can't cry,
a woman who can think in why
but would rather figure how
and when and what then,
who, if she'd ever lied,
no man can tell when,
who'd rip and sever our ties
before she follow me to hell,
but who'd follow me through hell
if we could land on a root
and climb ourselves out.

So this I promise without a doubt:
If you keep my body warm,
I'll never search for new heat.
If you give my soul space,
I'll never retreat.
If you honor my gifts,
I will lay them at your feet.
If you'll have it all,
I'll give you all of me.

Sadie sucked a breath and covered her mouth. A tear broke loose. She wasn't an easy crying woman, but Jim had broke the knot that kept her emotions wrung. Her eyes curdled with water. Her hand shook with fear that she wasn't awake or was somehow flung into delirium. Could it be that she could have Jim as a husband?

Sadie:
If you think you have to…

Jim:
I don't.

Sadie:
You may want to leave
if this child isn't born.

Jim:
I won't.

Sadie:
Jim, I don't know what to say.

Jim:
Say you'll have me today.

Sadie:

186

You kmow I'll have you!

Jim:
Everyday?

Sadie:
Yes, everyday!

Jim:
Then what's done is done.

Sadie:
*We ain't done nothing
till we done jumped that broom.*

Jim:
*Well call preacher man.
Call the preacher to come.
But let me in first.
Let me in, woman.*

And she did.

And this wasn't the first time they had made love, though it felt that way. Most times they'd had to rush, gripping and ripping at clothes with only time enough to thrust through the must, flush with leery, weary lust. Between work—which had their minds spinning the loom of never-ending measure—and sleep—which was full with longing for a drop of a dollop of pleasure—they'd done a lot of humping against walls, a lot of grinding in the shadows of night fall.

But this time, they'd cautioned less and walked slowly to a stream. And once inside, soaking wet, her dress spread and fluttered slowly at the seams. And the rhythm of the water flow coaxed them to breathe and they made love out in the open sun—one with the water's motion—with birds, squirrels and bees bearing witness to the cooling of two bodies that seethed in the need to knead their want free.

187

Jim, back in his present, thought of their togetherness and felt the pangs of longing gripping in his fingertips. He was digging his nails into the ground and didn't even know it. His face had been mostly stoic or full of smiles bearing the wiles of a slave bound to a child. Now his face was twisted. He bit his lip till it almost ripped. He wanted Sadie so bad.

If he could have, he would have written a loving poem, a song even. If he had a writer's skill, he could pour his desire into a letter to give Sadie something to believe in. Now that he's getting free maybe he could learn to write, and even if Sadie couldn't read the words, he could read them to her under a tree next to a stream somewhere far away. And after she'd heard his words and felt what they'd say, she'd want him in a stream once more.

Jim wanted this woman so bad.

A rustle jarred Jim from the bustle unbuckling in his mind and his tightening middle muscle.

It was Middle Pass. Jim scrambled to settle himself.

Middle Pass:
Hey Jim.

Jim:
Oh, hey now Pass.

Middle Pass:
Why are you looking all full of frazz?
You're looking frazzed down.
What's wrong, brother?
Someone come around?

Jim:
Ha? No. I'm alright.

Middle Pass
No you're not.
You're all hunched and hiding in spirit.

188

What is it?

Jim:
I don't know man.

Middle Pass studied Jim and laughed.

Middle Pass:
I know.
I've seen that look.
I've had that look.

Jim:
What look?

Middle Pass:
Jim, freedom isn't free.
It need a purpose.
And love is the best purpose of all.

Jim:
Ain't nobody thinking 'bout no love.

Middle Pass:
Well you should.
Love'll pick you up
over every wall.

Jim:
I don't know nothing 'bout love...

Jim took a breath to study himself and the flat lie he just told. He knew love better than some people know their own souls. He had loved Sadie and loved their children like the gravity that keeps us all on hold from floating off into space. Jim knew love like he knew his daughter's miniature of Sadie's

face, like he knew the back of his hand, thick with the veins
that pumped the blood that kept him upright to stand.

  He took another breath and told the truth, as clear as
the air we all see through.

Jim:
I don't know much about love,
but I know my wife
the finest piece of earth
I could ever find myself in.
And if I could goddamn finish getting free
and get her with me,
I'd be in her
more than a bird be in the wind.

Middle Pass:
Shoot, Jim.
I hear you.
You don't have to call it love.
Just call it a reason
to keep keeping on,
to keep pushing push to shove.

Jim:
Yeah you right, bruh.

Middle Pass:
I know I'm right.
Now ask me how I know.
Look, freedom without purpose...
It's just another whip—
it's the whip of the wind.
It'll have you lost in the sauce
of whatever fate is cooking,
no idea what to do next.
Freedom needs a purpose
like a man needs sex.

Jim:
*I wouldn't know freedom
from a hole in the ground.*

Middle Pass:
*Well, let me tell you.
Freedom needs a purpose like a woman needs...*

Jack stopped and looked up, then down at the ground.
He kicked a rock into the bush.

Middle Pass:
*Well, I don't know what a woman needs
nor wants,
but I know freedom
needs a purpose.*

Jim:
Okay.

Middle Pass:
*Okay?
Look, some'll say money over love,
M.O.L.*

Jim:
Emo... what?

Middle Pass:
*M.O...,
Never mind.
Just promise me
when you get free
you will learn to read
and you will learn to write.*

Jim:
Alright.

Middle Pass:
Money over love
M.O.L.
just make you a mole
on the grind
for more money more
till you die
from all that work
with nothing to show
but some things,
which is something,
but mostly nothing
at all.

Jim:
Man, I don't know
what you talking 'bout.

Middle Pass:
Yeah, you don't.
But when you get free,
you'll certainly be shown.
As sure as you wear hair for a hat,
know a man can't live on bread alone.
No, a man can't live on bread alone.

Jim:
I hear you, bruh.

Middle Pass:
But no, you don't hear me though.
Brother, listen to this song.

Jim rolled his eyes at the thought of a song in the middle of a conversation, but Middle Pass was unfazed. He cleared his throat and began to sway and snap and tap his foot. He started to sing with soul as black as soot.

Middle Pass:
Man can't live on bread alone
Need some sauce in his life
Man can't live on bread alone
Need some sauce in his life

Bread don't butter itself no
Can't dip itself in gravy
Man so serious all day long
Need something to drive him crazy

Bread get toasted, bread get hot
bread get moist and tasty
But bread can get hard as a river rock
till it's dipped in gravy

Man can't live on bread alone
need some sauce in his life
Man can't live on bread alone
need some sauce in his life

Some men need a sweet lil' thing
Some men need a wife
Some men stay they whole life long
Some will stay a night

Some men keep a chicken coop
Some men build a throne
Some men travel 'round the world
Some men make a home
Some men ride the fastest horse
Some men right left right

But none can live on bread alone
He need some sauce in his life

And now Jim was humming and laughing with him, singing along too. He felt a bunch better about being so alone so far away from his brood. Quickly he was lifted into a better a mood from this little bit of soul food, until Middle Pass had to get on. Then Jim was once again alone with his thoughts and it didn't take long for stress to gong.

What if he never saw his children again? What if leaving was wrong? What if God meant for him to stay a slave to raise his children to be strong? What if God's plan was for him to raise them all along? And here he was running for freedom when he might never see them again before his life was gone.

Oh, the thoughts were heavy. They were spiraling gnats 'round his head. They pestered him. More than that, they sequestered him in a prison worse than any whip or chain. How does a man escape a prison in the brain—one that has no walls to tear down, no locks to pick, no floors to tunnel through? How does a man willy himself free when the lynching tree has his own conscience as its root? What do you do when you are caught between an ox and a wolf, when one is a yolk for life and the other will eat your guts as quick as deer can hoof?

Jim thought.

Jim:
Should I have left
or should I have stayed?
Should I have just lived my life
as a slave
and prayed for the day
that my children would be free?
Was it selfish of me
to just up and leave?

194

Now just think of that thought, friend. That there is even a question of whether he should stay a slave or try to get free is a deep reflection of the evil of slavery. Think of the daily, the perpetual hell of thinking one minute 'maybe my faith will pay' and then next 'I'm a fool if here I dwell' and the next 'I'm better off dead' and the next 'God will strike me down if I keep such a thought in my head.' Think of the anguish of it, the every day torture. The scorching fire burning slow as a tortoise, slow as hair grow. And here Jim was getting liberated, or supposed to be, with more trouble in mind than before.

Jim could do something about this kind of trouble in mind when he was close to his family. He could go to his wife for wisdom or just hold her for stability. He could go see his children and stare at their beauty, marvel at their ability, dream of the potential in them that one day might be free to meet opportunity.

If he worried about his children, he could go see about them. But here, now "free", he had no way to see about Sadie or their children—their well being, a mystery. Here, now "free", he had to roast in missing them, stew in his worry.

Well, if there's one thing a soul can learn from the slave's slow burn it is that unearned suffering is not redemptive; it is just more suffering on the world's ledger. There is no redemption in getting free when your people still aren't free. That ain't freedom, never. Freedom is a family thing; it don't exist unless we all have it. We are all tethered. If one brother or mother, sister or lover, if any father, if any child is a slave, then the world is a whole world tragic.

Freedom is a human-family thing; it don't exist unless we all have it. If even one is denied freedom, the world is a world tragic.

Chapter 12
Middle Pass Brings Jim to God

God is red.[56]

******

---

[56] *God is Red: A Native View of Religion* by Vine Deloria, Jr. is a complex book. There is too much to try to summarize here. But an idea that stuck from this book was the idea that Eurocentric concepts of time, science, and the cosmos are linear (think: Big Bang, evolution, and Biblical Creation). These linear notions are built on the presumption of progress. Alternately, in many indigenous civilizations, concepts of science, history, and the holy are tied to places like mountains, rivers, and forests. These places stay the same over spans of time longer than humans would ever matter in, but they also change with every season. This hybrid nature of being never-changing and ever-changing seems to be a most accurate and useful view of history and the cosmos. If you know that things never change and ever change, you are less inclined to rest in the illusion that humans have somehow progressed past some potential for self-destruction (war, slavery, genocide) and more inclined to be active on a daily basis to do something about the world that is within your immediate reach and leave everything else to God.

The length of Jim's sentence, swamp-stuck, seemed to be extending past what made sense. His mind was wandering through the muck he was in and whether running with Huck was luck or sin. He was choosing to wait for Huck, sitting like a duck, when he could choose to go. So what was it keeping him here? Fear? What was it holding him? Hope?

That was Jim's last thought before the sudden sound of a man's booming voice made him shiver. Its deep pitch peaked and quivered, then rode rhythms down like a river rides gravity. The voice kind of snapped into place in his mind and attached itself to his memory.

The voice moaned like Jim's Old Gran used to when she prayed. It rumbled like his father's when he was in a rage. It sounded like Middle Pass if Middle Pass was preaching. And it *was* him, in a nearby clearing, God-teaching. Jim followed the sound and crouched down near a prickly bush to peek in.

Middle Pass:
Now I know you done heard of that he-god
the kingly one
propped up on a throne.
He lays down law
and rules his universe alone.
This god is a manly god
people call him "He."
Powerful men made this god in their image,
but that god did not make me.

See, our God
is a good God
good and only good
a living God
a giving God
oh yes, our God is good

Yes you know that prideful man-god
who invented sin as a trap.

He'll tempt you
and then punish you
in a vengeful counter-attack.
To magnify his greatness
he had us little things made.
To prove his mercy,
he may spare you from his rage.
Now this god supposedly has everything,
but wants your soul all the same.
bishops, knights, and queens
serve as pawns in his game.
Wars from west to east
erupt in his names,
while the one true God promises peace
for both Abel and Cain.

That old man-god keeps a chosen few
ordained to hold the wealth of the world
and tithe it to you.
That god's unGodliness serves his priests
each and every need,
while he turns his cheek
to their wickedness and greed.
But I don't believe in that god
who is weak as a bird wing—
just a puppet
dancing on the rich man's string
to justify just about anything.

But our God is a good God
good and only good
a living God
a giving God
oh yes
our God is good

Some disbelieve and have faith in science.

Some worship math.
Some believe God is a walk—
an inner path.
Some pray to deities
of pain and sacrifice
who promise to exchange all earthly strife
for paradise in the afterlife.

But our God comes when we call out
because our God is already there.
Our God is a mystery with in We.
Our God is everywhere.
Our God is a dark power
shining through all that is seen and unseen.
Our God is love
whole, perfect, and complete.
Our God replenishes and restores
and never takes without giving.
Our God is peace in death
and breath for the living.
Now ask yourself if your God is that good,
because our God is good God,
good and only good.

    Then Middle Pass started to sing and humph and moan and grunt like he was possessed by something good-good. Then he called out: *Donny! Prince! Luther! Praise with me boys!* Then three angels seemed to join along with his voice.

    The sound went to bouncing up the trees to rain down all over the woods. And Jim was once again stuck in thought, thinking about all the truck he had bought about God being a White, man-god—that the sky was his blue eye watching and the clouds were his beard and 'whom shall we fear' since 'he had the whole world in his hands.' When Jim was young he'd thought it was no wonder so many leaked between his fingers into hell to be slaughtered, being that hands can't hold but so much water.

And where was the White, man-god standing to have such strong footing to hold the whole world?

And if the White, man-god held the world, then who was holding the sun? And considering this was the White, man-god, did he have his slaves hold the sun? Lord knows a White, man-god got more important things to do with his plantation of planets to run.

Was the black night sky actually some giant slaves holding the day—while the White, man-god slept hard—their poor, tired hands burnt and charred. Were the stars the giant tears those giant slaves wept? And worst of all, if that White, man-god was a thing, what had Black folks ever done to it to be so hatefully kept?

Preacher said the bible said that some Black boy saw a White man named Noah naked to the fat, and Jim figured since most White men naked wasn't much to look at that the White man was so embarrassed at his own lack, he went and prayed to the White, man-god to curse that boy and anybody else Black. Now Jim could believe a White man could curse this kind of willy-nilly cursing as a matter fact, but why would the White, man-god agree to something as dumb-mean and unnecessary as that?

And why the White, man-god make something he hate anyway? Why not stop making anybody Black much less a whole Black race? What kind of ignorant wickedness is that, to create a whole race of a thing that bothers you just so you can punish that whole race with the lash?

Jim, even when he was young, doubted that any god with any good in him would do that. But preacher said the bible said those who doubt the White, man-god are driven and tossed like waves in the wind. Jim thought now as he had way back then.

Jim:
I'd rather ride waves away
than stay and wait
to catch the burn of lash
for being Black

as if Black was born sin.

But all that young questioning left Jim as he aged as he just stopped thinking of God at all. If the White, man-god was a thing, he'd rather believe there was none. There was one certainty to which Jim had come: All the things he had seen done to his kin and anyone born Black had to be random. Couldn't no man plan such chaos and leave the world so madness-fraught. *Not even a White, man-god,* Jim had many times thought.

But here in the now, Jim had heard Middle Pass speaking of another God, one greater than the White, man-god—the one and great God of all. One that might be with Jim now and would be with Jim without stall or delay or wait because that God was beating in his heart.

Jim thought of this and took heart.

He sat for a second and put his hand on his chest. He felt the beat deep against his own hand. And he knew it was proof that there was something else that kept him alive and able to stand.

And then he breathed and he knew he didn't make the air. And he looked around at the trees and the leaves they bear.

He remembered the trees were once seeds, and that they just used what was around them in the soil's dark deep to be the biggest, longest living, givingest things the world ever seen.

Then he put his hand in the soil and said, *this is the seeds cradle*—fallen off the hooves of the workingest Ox and scratched off the dirtiest dog—this is the dust of a mountain that's been crumbling as it's been rising forever-long. He thought *dirt is the seeds cradle and the seed makes the tree that makes the seed and lays it in the cradle to grow on and on and on and on…*

Then he had a thought so powerful that he almost felt something pop loose in his mind, *if the one good God is in something as low as dirt, it's got to be in me and in anything I can find!*

And Jim began to walk back to his dry patch in the swamp and, as he walked, he looked around and Jim looked at the veins in his hands, and they looked like they were breathing as they pumped blood. Jim felt a tingle there.

Then he looked at his feet and saw his father's feet, the feet he used to stand on when his father tried to teach him to dance. Jim's heels bounced a bit in his stance.

Then he tasted a dollop of sweat that dripped on his lip and Jim remembered the taste of the tears he kissed from Old Gran's cheek the last time he held her hand.

> Old Gran (*in Jim's remembrance*):
> *Now don't give them my tears.*
> *Keep them to yourself.*
> *Let them think you got nothing inside.*
> *See, inside is where you keep yourself*
> *safe.*
> *Look at my face, babe.*
> *Rememorize it now.*
> *I'm going on,*
> *but I won't go nowhere;*
> *I'll be back anytime you call out*
> *on the inside.*
> *Say Old Gran name three times—*
> *Mary… Mary… Mary…*
> *and think of my face while you do,*
> *and baby James, I'll come to you.*
> *I'll come to you.*

She squeezed his fingers and swayed his arm back and forth before she turned with a bit of a buckle and walked out the door. Old Gran's back was bent as she walked on without turning back to look at him.

Jim remembered standing there for a long wait. He was waiting on Old Gran to climb in the back of the wagon that would take her away. He saw a White man help her into the wagon and wondered what would they make her do. Would she have to cook and clean? Would she have to keep some lady's dresses tightly sewn? Would she tend to that man's children like they were her own? Who would think to put her foot rocks in the sun to warm them up for her to press on her sore feet?

And that remembrance stopped Jim cold. It crumbled him to his knees. Jim eyes exploded in a cry and he whimpered and heaved. He fell flat—prostrate—and shivered. He shook so much that he ground his face into the ground. He hit his head against something hard and almost choked for what he had just found.

There in the ground—the cradle of the seed—Jim found a crown, not the crown of a king, but the crown of a skull. It was a small skull, the skull of a child.

That's when Jim really went wild.

He dug like a dog at the skull to free it from the earth and could tell that the child hadn't lived long after its birth. Someone else had once hid here. Someone had brought a child to this deep in the swamp to bury it, of all places, here. And Jim knew exactly the tree they hoped would sprout. The tree of freedom! The tree of by all means *GET OUT!* The tree of truth that can withstand any doubt—that, if even only in death, we all end up free, that even if only to be the dirt, the cradle of the next seed to grow into the next tree so tomorrow can have shade and fruit and shelter—we all end up free.

Jim got back up to his knees and bowed his head down and kept on crying because he felt he'd found the real God—not a White, man-god but the God of the seed and the tree and everything between.

That night, Jim cried himself to sleep, and in that sleep he had this dream:

It seemed he was in the same wood where he fell asleep, but the trees where bigger and broader and redder than a circle of Indian chiefs. He stretched his neck up to see if they had tops, and as far as he could tell they didn't. They didn't even seem to have leaves. Instead they were wearing headdresses that glittered like beads, and the colors were more than the greens you might expect. It seemed like the sunlight was screaming through to make them glow yellow and orange and purple and gold and some even glowed black, and if you've ever seen something glow black you know it can throw you back because when black glows it reflects every color at the same time, and something so strange and beautiful is enough to make a body bow to the ground. And before he knew it, that's just what Jim was doing.

He was on fours crawling like a beetle. The ground under his hands didn't feel like dirt, though. It felt like flesh. With every step it gave way the way skin would under a finger's press. And with every lift it sprung back like you'd expect the body's covering to do. There were even little curls of hair Jim found himself walking through.

That's it dawned on him like the dusk moon—he wasn't just crawling like a beetle, he was a beetle. He was crawling on his own skin! He was both the beetle and Jim, together feeling the same thing!

What a dream, he heard himself thinking. And just then he seemed to wake a little, because he was back in the big red woods, standing next to a stream that was babbling something good. It was speaking in the strangest tongues—in clicks and mumbles and coos—and Jim closed his eyes and sunk deep into the sound it made and maybe he fell deeper into his own dream, because soon he was inside the stream. But the stream wasn't flowing around him as if he were some hard rock. The stream was flowing right through his body as if he were one of its braids or knots—one of those places and times where the water bits eddy and swirl and curl and twist and lock and wind around each other, one of those spots where a little spittle of froth and bubble form as the water seems to be whipping a cream out of itself.

Jim was right there inside of that when the strange tongues began to make sense, and what had sounded like clicks and coos and mumbles became words. Jim could feel himself grin. At first they were words—he knew they were words—but they weren't words he knew. But slowly they started to become the language he spoke in his head, and this is what they said:

God is red.
God is red, friend.
This tree that we be
sheds leaves and limbs
twists, turns, and bends in winds
until it is fallen
and from the earth its roots turn up,
it roots to rise again.
God is red.
God is red, my friend.

And the next thing Jim realized he was sitting beside the stream looking at a stem of a fern brushing against his leg. It looked like a single green splash of water if a rock had been thrown in it. It was the way each little leaf was just a repeat of the whole stem itself, and the stem was just one version of the whole bunch of stems that made up the whole fern. It was curious to Jim that it all seemed like it was planned out so perfectly. And the questions that led him to sleep started once again coming… *Could this red God actually take the time to make these things in this exacting way?*

Or did the red God just speak a law
for all things to obey?
Did God have nothing to do with it, anyway?
Was everything just a thing
that is trying to understand itself,
and in so doing
keeps doing the same thing
over and over again
hoping one day it will understand
what in the hell it is doing?

That's when a splash of wind bent the fern back up against him, and Jim looked at it and looked at it and before he knew it, he fell. Jim's eyes fell to a zoom down inside the fern itself and, inside the fern, he witnessed what he didn't know to call a 'cell'. He thought it was clear bricks, little building bricks lit by rainbows around their edge, and inside them water seemed to be swirling and eddying and squirting in little green droplets. Then, just as quick as he fell into the thing, he was back out and into his own flesh, sitting by the creek, underneath the impossible-big red trees.

What a dream, Jim heard himself think, and woke up with a series of hard blinks and hard rubs of his hard fingers through his hard head kinks. *What a dream!*

Jim awoke before the sun come up and rolled himself up a smoke. And the smoke reminded him of Huck. *That's a dumb boy,* he thought, *but he can't help his luck.* He kept on.

Jim:
Huck actually pretty damn smart,
but he come from people that's dumb—
dumb to feeling
or seeing anything past their own pale skin.
They swear to god they own everything
and can't see no other folk as kin.
They think they kept going
and the rest of us stuck where we begin.
They can't see that they just as stuck
chasing and chasing their own tails
forever and ever chasing.
They don't see the trees for what they are—
the big chiefs of the earth.
They just see wood planks and logs.
That's all they think trees be worth.
They don't see nothing in the dirt
but something crummy and worthless
under they feet,
and they don't feel no need to give thanks
for the dirt—the cradle of the seed.
They can't tell water
from the bottom of a boat,
can't tell a bull from its flank.
Now don't that rank as backward as can be?
Then they call the most beautiful thing—a magic fern—
a weed.
Poor Huck was born into this dumb truck,
damn his damned luck.
Thank God that boy got me.

Chapter 13
Middle Pass Brings Huck to Jim

Loss is a bundle,
a sack we carry on our backs
that can never be filled.
We can pour a barrel of guilt into it.
We can stuff it with free will.
We can fill it flush with hard-earned wisdom.
We can pack it with unending grief.
But it will never be filled.
Loss is the bottom
of a bottomless bag.
Yet we must carry it,
no matter how heavy it gets,
and go on.

****

That next morning, Middle Pass arrived using his usual
tactic of announcing himself by whistling, but the whistling was
shaky. By the time Jim got a look at him, he know the man's
courage had gotten flaky. Middle Pass looked nervous, and he
didn't seem to be a man with nerves that were easily thinned.
Jim suspicioned some piss had done hit a stiff headwind. He
was right.

Middle Pass (*shaken almost to shook*):
Your boy Huck
might want to think about moving on.
There's two gangs of gentlefolk,
both with necks red with hate,
riding day to day
waiting for necks to break
over names dead and went on,
so much so
they can't even remember
what their families is bent on.

And mind you,
they go to church like this,
with shotguns slung,
praying with tongues righteous.
This is their day to day:
warfare over what,
they can't even say.
Usually its just a bunch of blust,
but now some real dust got kicked up.
And they got reason
over a treason in the highest regard.
The one family's daughter
and the other one's son,
done run off after their hearts.
The patriarchs don't know it yet.
But I suspect rifles
will soon come off some bullets.

And your boy Huck
will most certainly be mistaken
and struck on location
from gun turrets,
and left cold as a mullet,
dead and forsaken.
You best tell him
ain't no more wait to be taken.
Time to go.

Jim stood up. He thought of Huck shot up like a buck, mixed in some rich man's revenge. He imagined the poor boy's face covered in blood, his fleshed bubbled and singed. He could see Huck's body twisted on the bank of the river, dead as a dog dead. Jim shook himself free from the horrible vision with a hard shake of his head.

Jim (*huffed up and prickly*):
Get him.
Bring the boy to me
so we can get on quickly.

Middle Pass (*taken aback*):
It ain't so easy.

What was it between him and this boy that makes him hanker this way? Middle Pass thought this, but didn't say. *It's almost as if his use of the boy has become more than just a way, but a will rooted in affection.* Middle Pass balked at Jim's suggestion that he just grab the boy and bring him his direction.

Middle Pass (*huffed up and prickly*):
I can't go running
and yipping for the boy
like a wild fool.
What excuse would I have
for bringing him here to you?

I have business
beyond your need to be free,
I'm Middle Pass.
I'm a station to Galilee.

Jim (*assuredly, but still anxious*):
Look,
Huck ain't hard to pull into a scheme.
He's the spit-quickest boy I've ever seen.
He'll catch on in a split second
to a slit or sliver of a hustle's beckon.
I bet he'd decipher your code
with the tiniest crumbs you'll be done left.
Try him, you'll reckon.

Middle Pass (*unconvinced*):
Now, I don't know
what you and this boy been through,
but do you think you can trust him
to do right by you
if I lead him here?
It's not just you.
I'd be gambling my own rear,
and that work of why God brought me here.

Jim (*convincingly*):
I vouch for the boy.
I got no doubt in the boy.
He done come through again
and again.
I can't leave the boy to the winds
if there's bullets in them.
I won't leave him.
Please.
Get him.

Still unconvinced, but moved by Jim's deep-feeling insistency, Middle Pass started to think up a lure, to get Huck out the house for sure, to lead him to Jim and the both of them to free. It had to be something a boy might have interest in, but might also raise a hint, but only a hint of suspicion as to why he might be so insistent.

See, Middle Pass wasn't sure what mind state Huck was in. For all he knew, Huck could have decided to fall in and become conscripted into the Grangerfords, in which case he would likely turn Jim in to earn him and them a Bank of United States note and earn Jim a trip down to Old Orleans where he was bound to be sold. The irony of Jim's help hoofing him to hell would have been cold.

Middle Pass thought almost like a lawyer does or more like a politician-judge. He knew Jim could use Huck to make his way to Illinois disguised as the boy's slave. He knew the "once free, always free" rule of getting the enslaved to a free-state. He knew that in Illinois Jim might not be safe, but he might just have a case if he could find word of the situation to a lawyer Murdoch or legislator Bay.[57]

Middle Pass could see that the boy Huck might be Jim's best chance, and so he began to use that big brain—his greatest gift. He set his mind to find a way to rip Huck from the grips of the Grangerford family's rift. Middle Pass knew how bad it would soon get and that Jim and the boy Huck should slip as quick as a stolen kiss. But he couldn't be too obvious and wasn't sure how would he manage to cook these grits of wits.

---

[57] One of the travesties of American history is that the winners are remembered whether wrong or right, and the losers are remembered only if they are seen as victims of some unjust plight. That's why Dred Scott and Roger Taney are famous, while Francis B. Murdock and Samuel M. Bay are not. These two of the three lawyers who represented Dred Scott in the Supreme Court case that triggered the Civil War are generally not even footnotes of history. Imagine if America venerated those who fought for right even if they lost by replacing the monuments put up for those who fought for an unjust, lost cause.

Middle Pass needed a hint that something was strange, but only a hint. He knew he needed enough distance so as to attain plausible deniability in case anyone ascertained that he was leading Huck to Jim and the both of them free—out of slavery's rights, reach, and range. Middle Pass would have to use strategy to entice and entreat, but not explain in order to get Huck to Jim.

Now what can no boy resist? Middle Pass laughed as he thought back to his own youthful edicts.

> Middle Pass (*to himself*):
> *Critters are more curious,*
> *and thus more luxurious than crowns;*
> *Nothing flying the sky*
> *beats what's scuttling the ground;*
> *The more dangerous the deed,*
> *the better,*
> *especially if blood might be drawn;*
> *For a boy*
> *there is no use to a dawn*
> *without something wild for it to shine on.*

And the idea came through as quick as a cold turkey brings shakes. *No boy can resist snakes!*

> Middle Pass:
> *I got it, Jim.*
> *I know how to get him.*

With his plan set, Middle Pass gave Jim a handshake and talked him through his approach. He would mention moccasins to Huck in passing but wouldn't push or poach. He would sit back like a coach, studying the boy for a chance to lance his curiosity with another poke. And the next time Middle Pass would speak on snakes, Huck would be hooked, cheek to bait.

Middle Pass set about the web-weaving like Anansi at Nyame's gate.[58]

Meanwhile, Jim was hunting and gathering, replacing all he and Huck had lost when the raft was bust by that bullish river wrestler. Plus he'd caught bits of wounds and bruises and had to tend to it soon or it would fester. He ventured out among the Black folk and acquired all that was needed: Pots and pans, food and the healing herbs for which his body pleaded, along with one special order filled—a ridiculous old quill—for the writing Jim always wished he could do. He laughed at the silly hope but kept it true.

There was a life of thriving among these enslaved as if, away from Whites, they might even be free. They had builders and healers and teachers and dealers of goods, and cooks better than gay Paris. They were planters and smiths, seamstresses, preachers, and elders with rites and roots. And there were children, the young all around to whom the weary hopes of the old were bound due to the traces of joy found in their faces when together and away from slavery's disgraces. Jim thought *without all the work we spend on making White folk proud and rich, we right could have a nation, no doubt about it.*

While Jim was experiencing this taste of freedom, Middle Pass played Huck by the book. At dusk he approached Huck with an excited look. Huck was strife serious and cost conscious, like he had sensed the storm of imperious loss of life. How could he not with Buck's stories of casual killings and seeing the church rife with rifles and hoping they would stay cool, God willing. All this feud was new to him and renewed the fear he knew with Pap, that at any moment violence could strike with a whip's whistle and a fist's crack.

---

[58] If you don't know Anansi the Spider, go look him up and then wonder why you know Zeus, Mars, the Easter bunny and Santa Claus and don't know Horace, Oshun, St. Malo, or Yemaya.

Middle Pass saw the weight in his eyes and offered a distraction, certain that he could coffer Huck's attention and set it on to some traction.

Middle Pass (*as Jack*):
In trouble time,
I find that to see wild things
out in the free
make me feel braver
and safer than I be.
Come follow me
to see some moccasins.
Come follow see.

Huck had a curious look, thinking *this slave done said that before and he sure seems ready to pull me to the muck of some moor as if there was something much more in that moor to see.* He thought for another rip and decided that whatever it was that had Middle Pass flipped might be worth the trip.

O.K., proceed. Lead. Huck said half-curious, half-suspiciously. And Middle Pass led the way. And dropped alms in a siren song all the walk long.

Middle Pass (*as Jack*):
The world's honey drips
for boys as bears.
Those crusty clothes you wear
should be ripped to tears
by the prickly bush
through which you've swiftly pushed.
Rush to the wild, child.

Soon the swings
that adult trouble brings
will ring hard all around.
The wind will whistle
with thorny thistles.

The air will crack
like bones broke to gristle.
People will fall
to a war between the civil.
Their footsteps will fill with blood.
Rush to the wild, child, rush.

Come let me show you
a swarm of moccasins
that warn of the coming flood.
Come let me show you the moccasins
prophesizing the flood.
The world's coming to its end
sooner than sun can send light.
All those high and hell bent
will fall like day bows to night.
And all that will be left
will be what you came with.
Your own breath
and the raft of flesh your soul grips.
And maybe a friend,
if you lucky a friend
will come to cling to you.
Come let me show you a place
of danger right and true.
Come let me show you the face
of danger right and true.
Rush to the wild, child, rush.

Middle Pass led Huck to a marsh that was harsh to
trudge and hard to break. Forward he kept the boy trudging,
ankling deep in water, without telling him the way. Then he
paused and pointed—*it's right over there, there in that huddle of bush.*
Then Middle Pass (as Jack) stood and watched Huck go
forward for a look. Just before Huck reached a small clearing,
he looked back and saw nothing but empty air and open black.

216

Huck walked forward and saw a lump that resembled a man sleeping. He walked a bit closer and had to hold himself from leaping. It was Jim!

Jim, meanwhile, was deep in a rumbling, churning sleep. For the dream he kept, while he slept, was a hard seed to reap. With all the thinking he had done about escape, and a clean sweep away to Haiti with his family, he hadn't considered his sisters Yan and Ni Ni; he hadn't thought of his brother, T, now deceased. And that oversight tore through him as an insight that would ignite the oils of his slumbering mind into a nightmare, flared with doubt and a frightful regret for all those he will have left without: family and friends, all that he'd known, people who'd suffered, people as deserving as him to be freed away and out. All this began to bloom into a dream of doom in which his heart swooned as guilt crooned for loves lost before they saw freedom.

In his dream, Jim was peeking through a window into what looked like a storehouse. Inside a ripping, swirling wind of grey and red with flashes of white churned hay and wood shards in a wobbling tornado. Below a whirlpool of deep nothingness was circling. Up and down in the colorless, circling emptiness, he could see the breaching faces and arms and trunks of loved ones, long dead and gone, spinning as they rose and sunk. He even saw his own face once. He called out to himself as though outside of the spiraling grief in which he and they lay. He called from where he stood outside this window into his past, only steps from his new day.

His call from outside the window garnered a moaning response from the inside version of himself spiraling down. His outside voice pitched itself, almost to a preaching in a solemn, yet forceful way. Though his voice had taken this almost majestic tone, his words sought mostly solace from the painful yearning for his loved ones, for the bits and pieces of them, and of himself, that were, as they coiled ever down, passing away.

Jim (*dreaming, mourning*):
And when the weight of it all
finally came down,
it swept them from their bodies,
swallowed them down
into square black holes.
Are they now wandering stars,
far flung and spin-drunk?
Are they flecked ash, bits of dust,
crusted on the backs of bolls?

I see brother's decomposed face.
I hear mother's last words.
I feel father's swollen hands.
And all three had prayed.
They sweat blood, bled tears, cried with grace.
They breathed and heaved
their breath cleft, thin as webs.
And all three had prayed.

They prayed for me
more than themselves.
They prayed to survive
to see me well.
They'd prayed in songs—
echoes of dreams.
They prayed and died.
Their hopes, sunken swells.

Jim nearly cried as he slept, as he relived so many family deaths. Mourning crept and rung, and he'd become bereft: left with less joy for any joys yet to come, left with more mournings promised with every day yet done.

He felt the weight, weight that had pulled his people down in the first part of his dream, as he felt dirt fall on his cheek warm as steam. He saw light peering down at him, his back drenched in the earth's heat. He was in a grave and sensed his fate: to join them in death.

The heft of the realization piled as dirt on his chest. He looked up as he sunk and saw multitudes of faces hanging down in a cloud of grief. The faces lost any traces of individuality and begin to surge and cleave. The faces merged and weaved through and through each other until they all formed his mother, then his father, then his brother.

Jim began to cry as the familiar faces merged to form one he didn't recognize. It was a child. The child opened its mouth and the pall of Jim's dream was lifted by a call. It was as if the voices of suffering multitudes had been combined into that of this child—one from all. The child's voice didn't sound; it shone. Jim didn't hear it; he saw it. The voice was light.

The voice beaconed him with his name. It pitched high and bubbled down as a nestling shall. Jim tightened his body from its sleeping sprawl, and stretched open his eyes and saw a boy standing over him, his face lit with excitement. It was Huck calling him!

Huck (*frantic, half angry, and half sad*):
Jim!
Why didn't you send for me sooner?
I thought you was gone and dead
or gone and went on your way?
Did you think I was dead all these days?"

Jim, tears still in his eyes from the dream, pulled himself together to greet Huck, whom he was certainly happy to see.

Jim (*groggily*):
No I knew you wasn't dead;
I watched you come from under the boat.
But I couldn't catch up for being hurt

and I wasn't gon' call out
less I might be heard and roped.

Huck (*probing, a bit hurt*):
All these days
you been hiding in wait?
You knew where I was staying?

Jim (*unresponsive to Huck's hurt*):
Wait? Oh no, waiting a sin.
I been getting together
for ripping the river again.
Look at all this I been 'cumulatin'.

Huck (*softening, impressed*):
Woah, Jim.
You been busy.
But how will we fit all this on a canoe
and do we even have one
for us to push off into?

Jim (*smirking*):
I got the raft, Huck.
It took some doing
but I got some know how
and it took some time
to get it ready
and it's right ready now.

Huck was struck at how able was Jim. He felt that he could learn so much from him. How, with nothing, could he make all this preparation? How in the nation and the name of creation could a slave gather a vessel, utensils, kitchen and rations?

Jim saw Huck studying him and thought of how it was one of the most foolish qualities of White men, that they look at the excellence of the enslaved with utter amazement and disbelief. He thought he should teach Huck a lesson that he might be able to keep, to keep him from that pitfall. White folk think lowly of those kept low at the peril of their own downfall.

Jim:
Take this fact
forward into your life, Huck.
It's us with less things
that knows how to make luck
and build blessings.
That's you.
And even more,
that's me
and any slave that ever been.
Your world is as upside down
as calling the freedom of a child of God
a sin.

Huck studied Jim, then thought he should go back before they push off, just to see Buck one more time. Jim at first didn't think so, but then agreed he should so as not to whip up wondering and so and so. They set the next day to let loose the line and go. Huck went off and Jim sat, thought of his dream, and felt cold. He didn't want to go back to sleep, but figured he should. And this time his slumber was a peaceful and dreamless bit of driftwood.

Chapter 14
Jim and Huck Push Off Again

Pluck a string
and it will hum.
Pour water
and it will run.
Breathe deep
and calm will come.
Cause makes consequence come
sure as a pause
makes space for wisdom.

****

Jim woke the next morning and was ready to go when suddenly Huck came running like a gale tears and blows. Jim went to settle him, but Huck was frantic as a panicked deer's hind. He was ripping to go as if bullets were carving air behind his behind.

They boarded the raft and got to going, and not until a few miles down from town did Huck's words come flowing down. And down came the story of the Grangerfords and Shepherdsons mowing each other down. Huck broke the whole thing down and Jim was as captive to the story as a corpse is to its mound. The river rolled beneath them without a sound.

Huck (*eyes darting from bank to bank*):
Jim, it was hard to run and duck,
but that's what I did.
One of the dead was my friend Buck.
He laid right where I hid.
I covered him up and buckled.
Jim, I'd slept in his room,
seen the stock from which he suckled.
Them was doom good people got doomed.
His whole family was tight as nuts,
which is why I can't understand
how such a feud tore them up
by their own hands.
Col. Grangerford had a General look
that he carried with heavy pride.
He stood straight as a fishing line,
had deep caverns for eyes.
Mrs. Grangerford had warm arms
filled with sympathy.
They filled their clothes like royalty
with skin soft, toil free.
Their home was an acre on acres.
Buck knew words like the dickens.
They had so much pride,

so much for to stay alive;
I can't see why death
made them such easy pickings.
I'm done with it.
Done with any civilizing.
If the rich
that the poor wish they were
are so savage for blood
that they'd feud themselves into a curse
worse than a bible flood,
then they can all have it all.
I'll take the river
and you Jim.
I'd take the river and you.

Jim found this curious. What a strange story. Money was supposed to buy class and class was supposed to raise the savage in a man to the godly mold in which he was cast. Weren't it the rich who were all on the same team, bred and wed to encourage a reaching for the same dream? How could the rich be cannibals of death, shooting young flesh to feed the violence that vengeance expects. How could it be?

Huck was equally perplexed. Huck had to cover his friend Buck's dead eyes. He'd run from oblivion for his life, having seen these people of the highest station slaughter and sacrifice in the name of names and for no more than the greed of gripes. Huck wanted no part of civilized life.

For all that holy supreme that the civilized was supposed to be, Huck saw in the Grangerfords and Shepherdsons that they wasn't. For all the ways that White culture was supposedly raising the slave from backward and primitive, Huck could see in Jim that any of that would be redundant. Jim was already better than the best of them who, for all their money, was violent, ridiculous, and repugnant.

Huck *(quietly to Jim):*
Jim what do you know of White folks?

224

Are we all the things we seem?
There's so much
that we done, so The Widow told,
to make the world gleam
under the light of God.
But I look at the trouble I seen
along the river so far
and all I ain't seen yet,
and I wonder
if we got the whole thing upside down
and upset.

Jim looked at him, half-smiling and half-pissed. He had just said this to the boy and he was acting like he'd just thought of it. But he let that go. At least he knows.

Huck:
You a good man, Jim.
Better than most I've known.
Why should you be down in chains
and the men who killed Buck
free as a bird flown?

Jim (*warmly*):
Huck, some say
the White man is the devil,
but I don't believe such truck.
Give any man too much power
and he will take too much.
He'll keep a woman in prison
like a hen in a hutch.
He'll beat her and his children
to keep them shut up.
He'll take a life without a thought,
sweep it away like dust.
That's what any man will do
when his power is too much, Huck.

225

Huck (*resolute*):
Well I don't want that kind of power.
I just want to be free.
And if I need that kind of power
to get what I want or what I need,
I'll do without.
If being White means
slaving a father from his children
and killing a child for a feud,
if White means thinking you better,
no matter what evil you do,
if being White means being civilized
and this is what being civilized be,
then I ain't being White,
and nobody can make me.

Jim (*holding chuckles in, and with a bit of pride*):
Well that's because you are you, Huck.
You ain't White like White folks.
You are White like you.
You are White like cream all shook up
in the butter churn,
not White like dead ash
leftover when you done burned
everything there is to burn.
You White like a frothed up water
rushing when the river rips,
not White like slobber from a mule
that you done forced to bite a bit.
You are White like clear eyes,
not like the puss of a wound's drool,
that infection of revenge that led
to the Grangerford and Shepherdson duel.
You are White like you,
not White like they tell you to be.
So you be you

226

and you can make being White
a righteous way to be.
Being White is like a blank page
and you can write right?
You can make the story of White
whatever you like.
Just make it be good, Huck,
and make it true.
Don't make it an excuse
for doing whatever you want to do
to whoever you want to do it to.

And these words struck Huck as almost too friendly, friendly in a way he had never known. For here was Jim showing him a mercy he himself had never been shown. There were White men everywhere who would burn Jim as quick as they'd have a picnic. There were White men who would steal him and sell him for a dime if they could get it. And there were White men that wrote the law of slavery and White men would get all the benefit of all Jim's work till the day he was bones in a pit. And still Jim looked at Huck and saw in him something worth it, worth the trouble.

And the words struck Jim too, at how easy they'd come. For a many times he'd wished all White men burn in hell for all the evil they'd done. He'd seen White men and their women and children and thought them walking dead, soulless bodies made of nothing but pig-pink meat waiting for hot led. He'd day dreamed of snatching them by the throat and bashing their soft heads. He'd night dreamed of a world in which they had been eradicated.

And yet, when Huck questioned his own worth in light of being White, Jim couldn't help but encourage him this night. For Huck, he thought, just might be different. Maybe Huck was the one out of a million who could resist it, the power that had corrupted the rest.

Maybe Huck had come to show Jim what might be next for the White man—a new way to be. And maybe him and Huck might be on a journey to carry the world to this possibility. Just maybe. This thought, as warm as it was, was followed by a flood of worry.

Jim thought of Middle Pass. How was he making it in the feud? Was he caught in the middle of the gun blasts, left in a puddle of his own blood pooled in the morning dew? Jim took a breath.

Did you see what happened to Jack? Jim asked sheepishly, certainly only one answer would keep him from spending the rest of his days guilty for not having helped that good get man out. *If Middle Pass didn't make it,* Jim thought, *ain't no god worth a shout.*

That Jack was some sharp, Huck started, then finished with just what Jim needed to hear.

Huck (*with admiration*):
He'd told me what was coming,
and that I should run and keep running
like he was running.
He said he was going to grab a gun
like he was joining the feud
then would gather up his family
and do what he had to do.
I wasn't sure why he told me,
but I suspect he wanted me to tell you.

Jim knew that was true, and he felt thankful that Middle Pass had taken the risk to make sure he knew.

Jim (*warm with honoring*):
His real name was Middle Pass,
and he was the best man I ever known.
He was a blessing come, and I'm glad he gone.

The last bit of sun shone its last swell as Jim thought, *all might just be just about well.*

Chapter 16
Jim and Huck meet the Jack and the Joker

Friendship is an organism
It lives, breathes, grows, and molts

****

Two or three more days met nights at their ends. Jim and Huck ran the raft night-long then laid up and hid when eve would bend to let the light in. Daytime, they cut brush to cover the raft, set fishing lines and sometimes slid into the river to swim, to fresh and cool away the time.

There is no more refreshing a blessing than being sunk body-long into water—when the water cups your body like the hand of God to carry you from the constant slaughter of gravity pulling you to your grave. That water kind of snug—the swallowing hug of water—is what it must have felt like to be a babe in the womb before we were all born into the living doom we call life, the perpetual death we call living. Water, when it slides around you—shimmies between your every split and cranny—licks you fresh like a mama goat cleans her little billy. Water—even the nut-brown, gumbo-green, moss-grey water of the Mississippi—satisfies something deep and holy.

In the water and in those hours, the songbirds would just go it a full choir for the woods and flowers, as the mist curled up off the river to mix with a steamboat coughing its power, its guts heavy with deliverance. At times like this, a little smoke wouldn't be noticed, so Jim and Huck would cook up some hot sustenance then lazy off to sleep under the speckled shade of passing clouds and reaching trees, loud with cicada-locusts. And the whining machinery inside those little beasts, was enough to make one believe in hocus-pocus. Once, Jim said the voices they heard cussing and laughing in the distance were spirits as sure as a tree is a future log. Huck retorted that spirits wouldn't say *damn the damn fog*.

In the cover of night, they shoved off, out into the middle of the river, at some places a mile and a half wide, and it was as if they were two fleas on the river's hide. They were damn near naked whenever the mosquitoes would let them be. The heat and the beat of the river's bucking made clothes ripe and ready for the shucking. And as raw as they could be, they laid face up on the raft to face infinity.

There was a peace to this time, this time away from society. The two of them shirtless and the same kind of dirty, with no regard for propriety.

Unbeknownst to them, soon would come a break in their affinity, cracked open by two of the most dastardly bastards ever thought up in memory. It was cold-blooded enmity that these walking maladies came to conjure, and the bond between Jim and Huck would soon be injured.

One morning, about daybreak, Huck found a canoe and left Jim to go snatch that as just the thing they needed to get back on track. Just as he got to the canoe, he saw a couple of dudes, tearing down a path, almost outrunning their shoes. They yelled that dogs were coming and begged to jump in Huck and Jim's new canoe.

Huck must have still been shook unsure by the horrors of the Grangerford feud, because, without thinking, he yelled for them to get in the water to wash off their scents, and to wade in the water over to him so he could let them in. Soon the boy would learn what a mistake this had been, a fact that was immediately clear to Jim. As he saw the two of them—one old and one young—he went to checking his pockets for his rusty blade in case he needed to shank one or both of the rapscallions.

The young one was rail thin with a nose to match. He had grimy, slick hair as flapping wild as a flock of bats. His eyebrows were ruffled as crow's wings after a powerful hard wind. He didn't have a chin, but a sort of knee bent at the bottom of his face, which seemed to narrow down from a bulbous balding forehead at a rapid pace. He resembled a sock puppet with a tear for a mouth, stains for lips, and eyes the color of shattered beer bottle shards. He looked as if the Lord, in a fit of laziness or a drunken haziness, threw him together out of broken parts.

The old one was orange as caked on clay, with an easy meanness shaping his mouth. His eyes were grey-blue as crabs and they carried bags so heavy they seemed to pout. His forehead sloped into a cliff at his brows, which were greyed red and fat as grazing cows. His face seemed to jump forward due to a thick, heavy nose and the ripples of fat turkey-neck jiggling under his chin up from under his clothes.

Neither was a nice to look at and both were an unwelcome sight. Jim saw in the two of them a familiar spite. They looked at him with the look of men who wished for slaves that fate hadn't allowed. They had the look of men who saw in Jim some lost past opportunity boomeranging back now.

Jim (*to himself*):
What is this trash that Huck done dragged on the raft?
They look, smell, and probably act like his own bastard Pap.
There's no place on our path for scabby alley cats like that.
Before long they'll be ransoming me for whatever reward they can scratch.
Huck ain't shown this level of foolishness yet.
Can't fathom what he was thinking
putting us in this kind of debt.
Now, in exchange for their silence,
we will owe these catfish.
And ain't no telling
what violence they might wish and demand
to keep from calling out
to every man-hunting, patter roller
prowling the land.

And what they would demand became quickly clear, as the two lying, low-down, filthy frauds began to be prickly for reverence and fear. *Fetch this* and *fetch that* they started off the bat. *Boy, now* and *now, boy* they threw at Huck and Jim the same as if they couldn't see that Jim was grown and game enough to snatch both their souls out their frames.

The young one claimed he was the Knight of Stagwater, at least that's what he told Huck. Jim thought to himself, *this walking calamity of vanity looks more like the puke of a duck.* Jim began to think in Spades[59] and luck.

---

[59] Now we should pause for a breath. The life-blood of the story has been tapped and the sap is a sticky mess. And the next turn of the story is a gnarly river twist. I'm not completely sure why Big Mama even told me this part, but she did drop a bit of a gist.

My four times great (4G) grandfather, Jim, and his young companion Huckleberry are about to get captured by two conniving thieves who intended to ensnarl both my ancestor and the boy as servants to their dastardly deeds. The whole string of sins hinged on the thieves personal mythologies of being descended from royalty, but trapped in a steady descent into poverty.

Now neither my 4G grandfather, Jim, nor his boy companion, Huckleberry, believed a word the two liars said about their backgrounds. However, in their precarious state of being runaways, trapped by thieves was better than being dead underground or back in slavery or back in the savagery of a slave society. So my 4G grandfather Jim and Huck rode the raft through these two, a rock and a hard place, to the next opportunity.

Big Mama called these two thieves the Lil' Joker and the Jack of Spades. I think she gave them these names so I could relate the story to the card game we often played—Spades, the rules of which are relatively straight-forward and interesting enough to tell. One could veer into many metaphors sprung from this game, but the magic is in the playing and the strategy required to play well.

In Spades, you don't have to win every hand or even win every game. You just need to plan and negotiate to maintain the rhythm of team-playing. Sometimes you set your partner up for a win. Sometimes you win it yourself. But you always keep count of what you and your teammate have bid, as this, in the end, will be your shared wealth. As the game gets closer to the end, even long-held low value cards can cut high-value cards if the team has played as a team and played to win.

In Spades, Big Mama gave me the perfect analogy for the negotiated space of enslavement. It isn't popular to think it, and certainly unacceptable to say it, but I will write the truth here. And maybe the truth will fall on fertile soil if you read the words to your own inner ear. There was affinity between the enslavers and the enslaved. I repeat. Anywhere humans are engaged in endeavor, there is the potential for affinity no matter how unhealthy. But more important than this fact is what is ultimately revealed by acknowledging this affinity: Power.

If the raft were a game of Spades, the young "Knight of Stagwater" might be the Jack of the trump with no power but the make of his suit—a card only good enough for cutting. The old one, not to be outdone, claimed to be part of a royal family—kin to a King of France—who could accept no less than the concomitant respect and deference that royalty commands lest one have a guillotine land on their neck. In Spades, you might call him the lil' Joker of a deck—another trump hiding behind his colorless flesh. Jim, with plenty Spades under his belt, heard his game clear and without doubt. Jim had to stay quiet, but said thought-loud, *to this foul orange cloud I will never bow.* Yet, Jim knew that wasn't true.

On cue, these hellions demanded service hand and foot, and both Jim and Huck knew they had to swallow their soot. They started asking questions about Jim as sure as sin, and Huck had to make up a narrative to convince them Jim was a slave his dead father had left him. Convinced or not, the two knew they had a boy and a slave by the draws and, predictably, they took advantage without pause or sympathy.

———————————

Now I will share the real sacrilege against history often overlooked in our consideration of slavery. The enslaved had power the whole time they were enslaved. I repeat. The enslaved had power before they were free.

Their power was in the *resilience* to live through physical violence and psychological terror to give their children life, and plant in those children the seeds of resilience that would flower in some future sunlight.

Their power was in the *resistance* to the stripping of their humanity, and whether they resisted this by cutting off an overseer's head or by showing her children mercy, they kept themselves human despite being treated as cattle and held their human souls above the whips and shackles.

Their power was in the *rising up* at every chance they got, whether following Nat Turner or St. Malo, whether they were hung, burned, or shot. The spirit of rebellion is often maligned on its own, but when rebellion is aligned with great philosophy or great art it becomes Dr. King or Nina Simone.

Slavery was a negotiated space. And men like my 4G grandfather Jim played the game masterfully, even during turns like the one we are about to take that, on their face, seem like tragedy.

The Jack of Spades (*studying Jim*):
He quite a sturdy buck.
He might be worth a buck.
I can see why your Paw left him to you, Huck.
But how're 'sposed to control him
should he get the urge to sin,
and get in the wind to test his luck?
There's a lot of that going around.

The Lil' Joker (*studying Huck*):
Aw, this boy's got that part down.
He wise enough to know
mind control is the crown.
This buck'd be long gone otherwise.
He'd be done cut you up, Huck,
if he wasn't White-hypnotized.

The Jack:
Malarkey!
You got to keep a darkie chained up
with whips on your hip
and a shotgun racked up.
Force is the only course with them
lesson you set yourself up for a tussle
when slavin' gives them the muscle of ten men.

The Joker:
And what do you know?
You ain't never owned a slave.
You ain't never learned the psychology
of keeping a savage in their cave.
You was an overseer.
You a simple cracker, son.
I got the strategy of chess.
I'm just made master stock, I reckon.

235

The Jack:
And who do you call when consequence come?
When their conspiracies take root
and they come for you with your own gun?
You call me and mine
to be your spine
when they done psyched your mind
into thinking they dumb as pines.

The Joker:
Naw, they ain't dumb,
but they are bred for submission.
And long as you act like their White king,
their will will succumb.

The Jack:
Look my style is my way
or the die way.
I keep it simple for a slave.
I lay it out clear as a bell,
no games played.

The Joker:
It's all a game.
Call it politics.
The whole world is my plantation.
Yours only stretch as far as your fist.

The Jack:
You a thespian.
I'm a thug.
I'm a slap.
You a hug.
Add one to the other
and the cage is snug
keeping the slave in his place.
You get that, Huck?

And all this right in front of Jim, and all really for Huck, and Huck taking it all in, and seeming to get bucked up. Jim could see Huck's mind considering all this stuff and probably thinking he needed this class in keeping a slave cuffed. But whatever he was learning about how to rule the enslaved, he was learning it even more from how the Jack and Joker ruled him every day. The Jack was like Pap on him, ready to crack on him. The Joker was like the Widow, trying to change his mind. Both where like-wise trying to shackle him and put him in their binds, two parties of the same politics set up to keep him in line.

As time with the Jack and the Joker went on, one thing became as stinging open as a cut: they came to conquer the raft and use Huck and Jim up. The two runaways would have to do whatever the two required and had to play from the script of the two liars. Huck knew their type of people and that type needed pacifiers; one must let them have their way or a situation could quickly turn dire.

In Jim's wisdom, he knew the truer truth that, on a raft, no unfriendliness will do. For what you want, above all things on a raft, is every person to have as much as they see fit. If one is more loaded down with stuff than they can manage, the raft will tip. If the other doesn't have enough to balance the first, the whole thing will flip. There must, at all times, be a connection between each corner—a middle, where all intentions lie. There is a utility to affection on a ship of confluence when folk glide the river and its thin divisions between those who live and those who die. Society itself rides such useful affections between circumstantial friends, and the raggedy raft that is a slave society is certainly no different.

So Jim figured these two were the best option he could have, since Middle Pass was way back and freedom was still a kite in the wind. And at least Huck was still, for the time-being, a friend.

But then what kind of friend would demand that you contort yourself, that you comport yourself as bent? What affection would command a friend to mold themselves, to fold themself into an abject wretch for long stints of pretense? None but the twisted and wicked, conflicted, parasitic, slick with degenerate paternalistic iniquitousness, pure abomination of avaricious codependence that is the relation between master and slave, which is made more of an outrage when they share the same small space.

We must digress.

Those enslaved to an enslaver's house knew, particularly well, what torture a proximity to a master wrung. The field slave—though made to burn their life's labor through long, hard days under the lash and under the gun without a whiff of shade and no promise but more work to come—the field slave at least had some space between themselves and the wretched demon that is the spirit of an enslaver. The house slave spent every day in a mental cage where their will was raped until spent and splayed, where they were forced to suck it up and raise the enslavers little succubus while their own children were sold away or kept for lust and bloodlust.

Just imagine the must of incubus in the stale-liquor breath of some enslaving manslut. Imagine the violence he done done to enslaved women's guts. Imagine him demanding she pretend pleasure or raise the volume of her pain, knowing she either has to keep this torment in trust or hear it bragged about to her father or brother while they bit rips into their lips with shame. Imagine his zealous expressions of disgust at the suggestion that he was lascivious when his wife got jealous. Imagine how he would use enslaved women to prove his power. Imagine him slapping her behind to show off while her husband or chosen lover covered their glower. Imagine the enslaver father and his enslaver son, and the holy hell they wrought when they came stumbling, filthy and sour. You should shiver when you think of the cold rot in their souls— lust and violence powered. You should shudder when you think of their stink.

238

And though this is a horrible, sorrowful digression, it is mandatory for understanding this part of the story. For though Jim didn't have to bear anything as foul as what an enslaved woman had on her back, his raft-mates kept him in a perpetually humiliated state meant to degrade him inside and out, front to back. And like one enslaved to the house, Jim was now enslaved to the raft, so he had to do what his raft-mates said, no matter how daft, and do it all while holding his true feelings inside. For the two liars *and* Huck (to Jim's utter disgust) teamed up to think up ways to hide Jim from the man-hunters, in plain sight. And the ideas that came marked a twain[60] of perfidy and spite in the minstrel-loving mind of whatever god made them White.

The Jack:
Well we could tie one arm and shoulder
to the edge of the raft
to keep his head above river.
That way we wouldn't have to worry about him
gutting us in our sleep with a shiver.

Huck:
But wouldn't that hurt?
And couldn't he die?

The Jack:
Surely you don't think he feels pain?
Much as he been beat in his life,
he's likely to enjoy the ride.

---

[60] Everything a character does comes out of the mind of its author. All that is about to be described comes from the mind of Twain, who, according to *Huck Finn's America* by scholar Andrew Levy, loved minstrelsy as much as he loved his own pen name. If anyone is to blame for the shame heaped on the character Jim in *Adventures of Huckleberry Finn*, it is him in his perfidy: Twain.

Huck:
But sir, Jim wouldn't try to take our lives.
I've been river riding with him
for weeks and weeks
and he ain't done nothing
but help me.

The Joker:
Ah, a young soul of charity.
That's a good trait with good use Huck,
but you must keep clarity.
Slaves don't feel for children.
They done seen too many of them sold.
They don't have human sympathy anymore.
We bred that out of them
so they wouldn't feel for themselves
and think they deserve something more
than just to do what they told.

The Jack:
Boy, if the urge comes into him
he'd gut you head to sole.
Didn't you hear about the runaway
that murdered a boy about your age up river?
Why any slave would deliver a shiver to your throat.

Huck:
Excuse me sir,
but not Jim.
I know him.

The Joker:
I see what this is, Jack.
Those of us who done owned know this well.
This is the natural affection
between master and slave

240

sure as a turtle has a shell.
And a kid his age should keep that innocence
as long as he can.
But one day he'll have to grow up and be a man.
He'll have to learn that White must dominate Black
or all society will go to hell.

The Jack:
Yes, Huck.
this Lil' Joker and I
take different tacks,
but we both agree
on the bottom line facts.
I think every slave needs a cage,
a whip,
or a shotgun in his ribcage.
He thinks you can whip a slave's mind into shape.
Either way, we agree.
They must stay in a slave's place
if WE are to be free.

The Joker:
See, I need this Jack,
and his ass needs me.
Alone, he'd work them all to death
and waste all his investment of time and money.
Alone, I might screw around and sire
a whole tribe of mulatto squires
and that's a trouble society don't need.
Jack would just as soon form a damn army
and attack the North to keep slavery.
But me, I'd confederate a clan
—a secret society—
to remind the White men of the North
who they been
and who they must be:
the bearers of the light of civilization for all humanity.

241

Huck:
What you're saying makes sense, sir.
It rhymes with all I've been taught
as far as I can see.
But what do we do with Jim now
to keep him
as my rightful property.

The Joker:
Now this here's a focused boy,
a smart boy, Jack.
He been bred to own and keep.
Let's come up with some good ideas
to protect his inheritance
from thieves.

The Jack:
Oh yes, we must protect the boy's property
from all the river thieves.

Huck:
Yes, please,
and thank you, too.
So what should we do?

And they had this whole conversation in front of Jim, as if he were too dumb to understand the evil ends of their wicked intentions. Once they started puking ideas, Jim knew they had it out for him. They were shucking Huck of the burden of being Jim's friend. They were trying to make Jim look like an animal to reduce Huck's opinion of him.

The first idea was less a study in stupidity than the spawn of a tendency toward callous indignity. The two liars, and Huck *as well*, factored a way to keep Jim from recapture. The Jack reasoned, with seasoned indifference, that this was the way Jim should stay all day: Jim was to lie on his belly, his wrists tied behind him, his ankles tied, his knees bent back, his wrists tied to his ankles, his shoulders and elbows jacked to reduce rope slack, his face flush to the raft so that the must of the wet logs were thrust up his nose such that he would cough and hack, his coughing and hacking causing his stomach to convulse, and that convulsion battering his ribs till they felt as if they might crack.

And when the raft would waft atop some corrugation thrown by something as small as a passing bullfrog, he'd damn near drown from the undulation of his face in and out of the streams of river water squeezed between logs.

Water, which can be as fresh as breath itself, became a torture, teasing death. And this is how the two liars, and Huck *along with them*, thought to keep him, to keep Jim all day. And as he was enslaved to the raft, and at the mercy of his raft-mates, there wasn't anything Jim could say. The two liars, and Huck *agreed*, reasoned this would keep Jim safe.

So Jim submitted to a treason against himself, to be disgraced, laid on his face in order to be in stealth. But, nevertheless, Jim was still a man. So the hair on Jim's chest jumped to a stand as soon as the two liars, and Huck *with them*, left him perchance.

As soon as the three of them were out of sight and Jim was out of their minds, Jim's body shook off its rankles. It shook with rage under the wet rope, taut and hard, that manacled his wrists and ankles. First his blood hopped like a fire in a stiff breeze. Next his bones trembled like drumheads tapped with sticks for war beats. Then his sinews sizzled with steady heat. Even his fat, and he didn't have much of that, clung to his muscle under his skin, which almost bubbled as Jim boiled down to the corpuscle.

243

And the boiling built up steam. And the steam churned in Jim and balled into his fists. And Jim pulled his wrists apart with a force of ferocious sorcery, ripping the rope from him as if it had been gnawed by Brer Rabbit or cut by Staggalee. Through a twine an two inches thick—robust enough to hold a skiff in a hurricane, tough enough to hold a horse tight, heavy enough to a hang a tug boat rudder frame, strong enough to fly a gator like a kite—through a twine two inches thick, Jim ripped himself free, and Jim was amazed at himself for doing it.

Though he had certainly swung a hammer harder than many a mortal man, and he had held a bale on his shoulders longer than any man the earth's atlas over, and he had taken pain beating through his back, holding himself square as hardtack without showing one crack, thus far, he had never ripped rope in half. He had to laugh at the magic of that. He laughed until the sting of the rope burns began to whip and whap.

Jim was badly bruised by the act of freeing himself. He had to sit for a while, rubbing his wrists as they swelled into whelps. And once he was able, he had to weave the rope back into shape in case the two liars, and *Huck* along with them, came back and saw the lengths of Jim's strength. No, that would not do. White men get to panicking if they think their deepest fears about Jim's race were true—that Black is strong beyond White measures and could tear them a new hole or two for spite or for pleasure.

Once he'd freed himself and rubbed himself through some of the ripped skin and bruising, Jim began to feel a new type of wound torn by Huck choosing to participate in all these miserable, despicable doings. How could he? Why *would* he?

Jim's mind wandered over the alternate ways he could have been kept safe, and he remembered all the slick things Huck had thought up as quick as a quake. Why hadn't he thought up anything different *this* time?

He thought of the empty look on Huck's face as Jim's ropes were laced, and he remembered when they were separated by the fog and how the boy frantically cried *Jim! Jim!* and banged pots to send a message to him. Where was all that feeling for Jim *today*?

Then Jim hardened on this fact: to Huck, he might always be a slave. Even if he escaped, he would be an *escaped* slave, a slave freed by Christian charity, but still a *freed* slave till his last day, just a law or a lynching away from being placed back in a slave state.

It is in moments like these—where the enormity of the deformity that is slavery becomes crystal clear and trust true—that a stillness settled into Jim, and, in that stillness, a seed of poisonous shame would split its skin to root. And that shame would quickly unfurl into a sapling shoot. And that shoot would, over generations, thicken into a tree. And that tree would bear a poison fruit bearing poison seeds.

And those seeds would never know their roots or the shame upon which they feed. And the shame would cocoon into a blossom and shine above the dirt of indignity. And that flower of shame will call the world to its fruit. Then the poison will be sweet to go down easy and do what it was meant to do: destroy its maker.

But again, we digress.

Jim kept the ropes near, so that if he heard the liars and Huck coming back, he would reattach them behind his back. And this act, as much as he saw it as needed, was more of the same self-treason that was required for his freedom. But Jim did it as it needed to be done.

When the time came for Jim to be released from his binds to take night watch, as their royal pains required he and Huck do, he let Huck sleep through a storm even as the river hopped the raft in waves over and through. Jim let Huck sleep in the comfort of his dream while the water came creeping, almost sweeping Huck into the river's froth and cream. Jim had one urge to wake the boy and another to let him drown along with the puke of duck Jack of Spades and that glass Lil' Joker with his cretin crown.

Jim (*to himself*):
And what of it
if I let their bodies sink,
let their dreaming bodies flood with water
and rot 'til they stink?
What harm would it do the world
to have three less Paps cursing life,
three less White men
willing to twist shame into a Black man like a knife,
three less White men
to twist pain around my arms and legs,
to keep me a slave,
to twist rope around my flesh
so quick and willingly,
then to sleep so sound,
so sure I'd protect them willingly?
I'm more willing to let them die than they know.
Only for Huck, so young,
do I carry even a bit of pity in tow.
He has saved me more than once
and not just for show.
And the man that he could be seems good soil to sow.
But maybe a little baptizing in the fact that he needs me
might help him understand the righteousness of setting me free.
Yes, I'll let the boy tumble into the river deep
and save him with a hearty laugh
that he might come to appreciate me.

And that is what Jim did next time he was on guard. He let a wave sweep Huck away a few yards. A brief creep of worry troubled Jim, but when Huck come up from under the water all he could see was Jim's laughing face. What he had been dreaming, Jim would never know, but the look on Huck's face was a story told. He'd been dunked in salvation as a babe being christened, then returned to damnation by Jim's laughing and whistling. Huck had to laugh too when he realized Jim had got him good, through and through.

And that night rode on as if the moment was a tick, stuck on a running dog, as a flicker bouncing off a burning wick lit behind a wall of fog. And the morning would fall, bearing the rope that would strap Jim into a bundle to be carried deeper into Dixie on the river's tumbling trundle, until Jim ripped himself free. And it went on this way, through quite a few cool blue nights and white hot days as the Lil' Joker and the Jack of Spades engaged Huck and enslaved Jim as accomplices in every scummy scheme they could dream to dummy ducats out of leaden-headed, hoe-heaving river town pauper's coffers, and get away clean.

Jim and Huck shook spears on stage and shed tears under tents. They pretended penitent piracy to preachers and sold sucker subscriptions to gents. The Joker broke into a printer's office to make a bill of reward for Jim's capture, worth $200 to a man in Orleans city, and said this might just be the key to travelling days without worry of Huck losing Jim as his rightful property, and leave no more need for ropes.

Though this new approach raised Huck's hopes, Jim was shook at the look of it, a paper they told him would hold him safe and, at the same time, advertised him as a runaway slave. Now he was locked into a descent deep down south with a piece of paper calling for capture as his only route out. The irony wasn't lost on a man as wise as Jim.

That evening ended as most evenings on a raft do, with each finding his balance and settling into a nook in which to snooze. And the two liars, woozy under a doozy of booze, went out like lights. And Huck went down quick too despite the chance that Jim might get him again, let the water baptize him in fright, like he'd done that other night. Jim still felt a torn rip at how easily Huck had joined in the oppression of him, at how quickly Huck fell in with the worst of the Whites.

And when the day came and the three left, when Jim ripped the ropes to get himself free, sometimes Jim rode the raft quietly, kept by his circumstance and its absurdity. Sometimes Jim took some time to himself and left the raft to do what he pleased, despite all the dangers and in the face of fear. And in this time to himself Jim worked to get his mind clear.

Chapter 17
Jim Looks for Clarity and None is Found

Freedom got a shotgun.
Freedom gon shoot it.
Freedom got a shotgun,
and ain't afraid to use it.

****

Jim's body had to walk. He couldn't sit still. He needed to straighten and stride, to redistribute the weight of the thoughts churning inside. So he disembarked the raft to snatch himself up a bank and moved toward the town, where he might disappear as backfill in a crowd.

As he approached the road, he sensed some tension and slowed his walk to bend his back with apprehension. This is an instinct the enslaved must perfect, lest he walk too erect and expose his neck for breaking. For when White men were tense, they were quick with blame and hurried to judge the first men they could find who bore no name or rank or money or fire arms as defense. And the enslaved always fit the bill for the collective will to do easy harm to those who could put up little resistance.

Sudden cracks popped in the distance, ripping through Jim's nerves. He was sure of what he'd heard and so scrambled down, looking for any tip of any rifle. It would be a trifle for a White man to potshot a Black man as he would a waddling duck, just to see the reach of his power in order buck himself up.

Around a bend, Jim saw a crowd gather, a terror of a sight to look at. He looked at the long open road back to the raft, and judged it rather daft to walk back. So he slid to one side of the rapidly formed crowd that was growing rambunctious and loud. Then Jim heard the word that would make a Black man cinch himself into a clench, and buckle and flinch for the horrors that could become of him.

Jim heard rabble-rousing, 'lynch him!' Rattle tattle, 'Lynch Him!' Grumble rumble, 'lynch him! Lynch Him! LYNCH HIM!'

Jim's feet collapsed in their tracks as a whole body full of fear dumped into his legs. He held his breath and felt heavy as ten kegs. His breath broke in half as he slowly backed-back, keeping his eyes forward at the mob so as to be sure to catch the moment that mob might tack his way. As soon as he was able to tell the crowd wasn't coming at him, he twirled like wind and dashed to the raft again.

Jim's hands shook. His eyes jumped around like a wet cat. He unwrapped the anchor tie and whispered *forget that, I'm gone*. He was in the midst of shoving off with a rough stab at the riverbank with his staff when Huck came running. Without a word, the boy hopped on the raft. And as they pushed off again, Jim, needing to know, had to ask.

Jim:
Huck what happened?
I heard shots,
saw a crowd gatherin'.
The mass was shouting 'bout a lynching,
and that was enough
to keep me from inching in.
I was a ghost.

Huck:
Jim, it was the wildest scene I've seen.
One man with no team
shouted a whole town down
by just baring his teeth.
He'd shot the town drunk.
I think I seen that drunk
on that barge a bit back.
He'd thunk he could punk the other man
by talking drunk junk,
but that was not a fact.
In fact, the old clown got shot,
dead down on the spot.
Where he had fixed his lips to spit

251

something slick and hot
'bout being tougher than tough
'bout being rougher than rough
'bout making the devil swallow his snuff.
That's what I saw of it
before I got up to get.
Oh, I could've stayed
but I just didn't feel like it.

Jim could tell the boy was afraid and covering up his
fear. For a second Jim thought to draw out the jelly in his belly
by striking at his pretense with a word-spear. Huck deserved as
much, for all that truck about tying Jim up. But then Jim
thought back to the boy Buck that Huck had watched die, shot
and bleeding in the muck. He decided to let Huck lie a little to
cover his fear up.

Huck recalled the lynch scene where the drunkard
Boggs spoke mean to another man who stood a menace quiet.
Huck could tell, where Boggs couldn't, the other was a one-
man riot. Huck said it went like this.

Boggs (*drunk*):
I'm the original iron jaw.
A brass-mounted,
corpse-maker
outta Arkansas.
I'm sudden death
married to a great earthquake,
born to a hurricane,
brother to the plague
suck the bones of a gator
as if it was cane,
snack on a bag of rattle snakes,
drink the blood of a bear,
make a wig out a lion's mane.
My favorite bit of lullabying
is the pitch and wail of the dying.

I split rocks and squelch thunder,
leave lightening crying,
bottom out ten bottle of whisky
if I want get tipsy.
Bullets fly to come get me,
but them bullets they miss me.
You better beg a truce
for I'm about to let loose.
My heart is fossil,
sharper than a shark tooth.
I put my hand on the sun
to turn the day dark
bring winter 'pon us.
I massacre isolated communities
in the pastime of my idle moments.
The destruction of nationalities is my business,
and I own it.
I reach and suck a cloud dry as a crumb,
and piss the Mississipp
when the day is done.
Now calamity done come.
And the beast in me
bout to release on you son.

Huck (*recalling the scene*):
Then the other man raised his gun
without a word to swap,
tugged his trigger
and the thing went POP!
And then POP again,
and then Boggs dropped.
Oh, the town gasped and yelped.
And somebody called out for a hanging.
The man,
his name ended up being Sheburn,
turned from all the yells.
He walked slowly in an inn,

253

then went up to the top balcony
to face the mob looking for a lynchin',
A shotgun clenched in his hands,
and not a hintin' of flinchin'.

Sheburn (*from the balcony*):
Ain't but half a man among you.
None enough to face a man, matter fact.
Better go get your hoods
and come at night
so you can hide
and shoot me in the back in the black.
You ain't got three fifths[61] the heart of a slave.
Ain't got a fifth the bite of a swallow.
You're average the whole lot over,
and the average man will follow.
He'll ride the mob
in a wave of cowards,
rushing up,
roaring on the crowd's power to trod.
He'll acquit the lynchman because he's scared.
He'll yell out all about, his nostrils flared
like the mule he is, like a runt bitch.

---

[61] The Three-Fifths Compromise, agreed to by the Framers of the U.S. Constitution during the 1787 Constitutional Convention, counted three out of every five enslaved people to determine state representation in the House of Representatives (Congress). They did this to give the lesser White populations of the South more political power at the birth of the nation. Not only did this compromise extend the life of slavery by giving the Slave-Society states of the South disproportionate power, but it codified, in the U.S. Constitution, this mathematical formula of White Supremacy and Anti-Blackness: Black folks would be 3/5ths of a human citizen in America. Here, Sheburn calls out this compromise as the complicity of all ruling class (voting) White men (North or South, slave owners or not) as the political lynch mob that institutionalized slavery as an essential ingredient of U.S. representative democracy.

Huck (*recalling*):
Then he swings his shotgun over his hand
and cocks it.

Sheburn (*almost growling*):
Ain't a man out here to clear my fog,
you old dogs on chains.
You ain't a got no name,
you a bunch of pawns in the game.[62]
First bastard
take one goddamn step my way
get sent to flames.

Huck:
And people start a tearing
and ripping every which a way
I could have stayed if I wanted,
but I didn't want to stay.
It ain't that I was afraid.

And Jim let that sit, let the boy have his pride. He
thought about how many times he had lied to himself about
being brave knowing that inside his gizzards were shaking in
waves, twisted every which way while he fought to keep a
straight face. *Boys become men and nothing changes*, thought Jim.

Jim (*thinking*):
The young boy
with the biggest stick
gets the ball.
The grown man
with the longest gun
walks tall.
Freedom ain't such a complicated thing

---

[62] Shout out to Bob Dylan's song "Only a Pawn in Their Game."

when all is said and done.
Freedom might be the best feeling in the world,
but in the end,
freedom ain't got a thing
unless freedom got a shotgun
and is willing to let that shotgun ring.
Freedom can't be earned
and it can't be given.
It can't be granted
and it ain't got a thing to do
with how rich a body is living.
Freedom can't be bought in a store,
can't be raised in a flag,
or written into a rule.
Freedom has two laws:
keep a shotgun
and keep it heavy
and ready to boom.
In this world,
freedom is kill or be killed.
Freedom is doom or be doomed.

As Jim's thoughts trailed off, Huck sat still. Jim seemed struck numb. He hadn't hardly remembered crying, not a day in his life, old or young. He wasn't sure he would know how to cry if his soul was to be strife-wrung. But something phlegmed up in his throat and lit hot in his nose. Then something began to sting in his eyes so bad they were forced to close. And sweat came dripping from his brain like it was working too hard, and drops came slipping through his eyes in streaks and shards.

See Jim hadn't really faced one fact along the whole journey: that he might never really be free, that even if he got his family to Haiti, without a way to protect them, he would never see a day of peace. He would always worry about how they would eat. He would always wonder if there was some hound around a corner foaming at the mouth with villainy. Without a gun, without a pistol, without a way to quickly take a life, what could he do to stop a White man from coming to take his wife or his children?

Jim looked at Huck, nothing but a scared little pup, and felt nothing but contempt. Huck had a widow hunting after him. Huck could run West to wild off his childhood in the wind. Huck could pretend to be a girl and pretend to be rich and he could pretend he ain't ever afraid. He could pretend anything he wished and wish anything he could imagine in the day. Jim curled his lip in disgust with the injustice of the way of the White man's world.

Meanwhile Huck had noticed Jim wipe his face and had sensed Jim coming certain of his own fear. Huck figured the story of Sheburn and Boggs had left Jim thinking of all the danger near. Huck's heart sunk at the thought, just an inkling of a hint, that Jim was in big danger everywhere he and Jim veered. Huck knew he had seen some rough—some belly-bubbling horrible stuff, had been beat cap to cuff, had watched a friend cough up the bloody muck of a last breath, had watched his poor Ma beaten to death—and yet he knew that if he survived being a child, being a free man would come next. What did Jim have to look forward to but being on the run till his last step?

And Huck had no idea of what to say, or what words could do to change the situation in any way. Jim was a slave, and always would be. Jim might never be more than an *escaped* slave, a fugitive in a slave society. The thought left Huck's heart heavy.

And there was silence between them, Huck and Jim – a silence that followed them for the rest of their fits and starts. Even when they spoke, even when they were apart, from then on Huck and Jim shared a canyon of silence between their heavy hearts.

And the ride got long then and quick at the same time. Such is the mind when it is confined by thoughts that can't be rhymed with words or sung with feelings. Such is time when it can only be waited out and thought through, and the pent up nature of such trouble is enough to weigh a boy down in his boots, enough to make Huck frightful of words for what those words might let loose.

And, at the same moment, Jim was feeling no different. And though, like Huck, Jim was feeling much trepidation about a nation of threats of capture, Jim was most afraid of his own thoughts and what hellish rapture all this time to think might sink him to knowing that, even if he got free, what exactly was he going to do?

Chapter 18
Jim's Longs for His Children

Children don't belong to their fathers,
and their fathers know it well.
They belong to the heaven they come from,
and to all the oncoming hell.

******

Most nights Jim let Huck sleep to give himself space to think. Jim's head was heavy with so many shots of ideas to sip from, so many gulps of thoughts to drink. Escaping had been no crystal stair, but most nights he felt a feather lucky for even an inch of space to dare.

But this time he counted a care he wasn't ready to bear. It was Sadie, and the memory of her hands that weighed on his shoulders. And it was thoughts of his children in particular, and a particular moment that was knocking him over. Bowed, he sunk between his knees, his head willowed down toward his feet. He was bent, as a wind weary sapling grown too steep for its roots. His heart was wrenched with brooding for the warmth of his brood.

Would he ever see them again? Was this escaping foolishness nothing but the sin of impatience taking him into the lion's den? Should he have stayed and raised his children, even if they were raised as slaves? What if he never made it home to see them another day? What if his wife thought he ran off without them? How would he get them word? How many nights might she curse his name for leaving her in slavery's curse? His Sadie, his Marcus, his Elizabeth, his little loves might never recover from the loss of him. Them being his reason for leaving might never come across to them. Would they feel abandoned? Would they feel they had no worth? Would they feel their daddy didn't see in them enough reason to stay to make it work?

He moaned and mourned to himself like a man half-broke. The questions were crowing and cawing, like a cock croaks. Half-awake from staying up so late, Jim spoke.

Jim (*groggily*):
Little 'Lizabeth, girl. No.
Little Marcus, No.
I expect I'll see you no more.
Nevermore.
It's lightening hard and mountain rough.
Mountain hard and lightening rough,

Just as tears began to crack Jim's dam again, Huck awoke. Huck had been squirming through a nightmare of his own and needed him a toke. Just as Huck reached to pack his pipe to smoke it for a span, Jim reached for the boy's listening as a drowning man reaches for a hand.

Jim:
What's got me so bad this time Huck,
and I know I done bothered you with it before,
but right now I'm stuck,
stuck like barge run ashore.
I heard something like a whack or a slam
on the bank a while ago
and a memory was borne to me.
One time I treated my little girl so ornery.
She was only 'bout four,
and took sick with the scarlet fever.
It was a powerful terrible spell,
but she made me a believer
when she got well.
I thanked the Lord when she got well.

Well, one day she was standing 'round
and I say to her,
'Shut the door'.
And she just look up at me smiling,
and never done what I call her for.
'Don't you hear me, girl,'' I say.
'Shut the door.'
And she just stood the same way,
kind of smiling up.
And I'll be damned
if I wasn't riling up with rage.

See, that very day I'd been walking in the notion

261

that we might runaway,
that I'd hate for my children
to live they whole life as slaves.
And I had just been thinking,
if we run off,
I'd have to trust
that the children would need to heed
and obey every word I say.
Couldn't be no wait.
If I say hide! Stay!
They need to stay.
If we on the move and I tell them go.
they need to go.
Couldn't be no wait
once I tell them which way.

"Shut the door, girl!" I'm screaming now.
And she just standing there
not hopping to it, somehow.
And I'm thinking about running away, Huck,
and how she would need to heed
every single word I say.
So I figure now is the time
for the rod I must teach.
But one should always spare the rod,
when in the midst of fear or fury.
But I didn't, Huck.
I didn't spare the rod.

Now I'm yelling
loud enough to wake the dead.
Then I slap my child on the side of her head,
and send my child sprawling.
I hit her so hard
she can't even catch herself from falling.

Jim sucked his teeth at the memory. He took a few deep breaths to get himself steady, then continued to speak haltingly.

Jim:
She crawling away,
and I went on after her too,
and just then a hard wind came
and slammed the door with a bang
loud enough to spook a moose.
It was probably the ghost of my Old gran!
But little 'Lizabeth, she didn't even move.
Huck, she didn't even move a tooth
at the sound of the slam.

I lost my breath and didn't know what to do.
I had a thought
and tested it for truth.
Later, I crept up behind her and shout Pow!
And she...
Huck she never budge
as if I had only moved my mouth!
I bust out crying, Huck,
and grab her up something fearsome.
O my child, Lord Almighty,
my child is plumb deaf and dumb,
and I done swatted her to the ground
like a fly off a dinner crumb.
Huck, my child, Huck...

Jim mumbled and covered his mouth, still sucking deep breaths. He was wrecked at the thought of this trouble he kept. He rubbed his head hard as if he was trying to grind down the thoughts, to forget.

Jim:
It wasn't all bad, though, Huck.

Later on, when she was sleepy,
I held her close to me,
and sang her my Old Gran's song—
Oh Baby Babe.
And even though I knew she couldn't hear me,
I hoped she could feel how the song made my body shake.

And Jim begin to sing and his body did shake as the words made their way from his soul out his face.

Oh baby, babe.
It's time for you to sleep, babe.
Oh baby, babe.
It's time for you to sleep.
And when you sleep,
the world will calm around you.
And in the calm,
you'll dream the night away.
And when you wake,
the sun will come to greet you.
And when you wake,
the moon will wave goodbye.
And I'll be here
to hold you so close to me.
Oh baby, babe.
Oh baby, babe.
I love you so.

Huck was dumbfounded. He could barely understand. Here was a grown man wailing about having raised his hand against his child. Shoot, Pap had raised hand and fist and foot, stick and knife against him, and Pap hadn't felt the shame of a nit when he done it. And here was Jim in tears, crying and singing over giving his daughter one hit!

It was something in the moment, something that came over Huck. Before this time he'd thought Jim a good man, a good friend and such and such. But he'd never thought him a father, never seen in him a paw. And seeing Jim crying over his daughter was the heart-breakingest thing Huck ever saw.

And Huck's heart broke open too. And tears welled up in him, though he fought them back from coming through. And he thought he was hiding it from Jim, but Jim saw, and Huck couldn't hide it from himself. Jim was the best man Huck'd ever met and the best he'd ever meet, he bet.

It was right then, right in that moment that Huck must have made up his mind. He would never allow Jim to be a slave in this lifetime. He would see Jim free no mater what it took. And as Huck swallowed his tears, you could see the resolution in his look.

But Huck didn't see the test that would come next. Jim would soon face his fears in full breadth and banged bell, and Huck would have to decide if he would stand by or ally with Jim in the part of the story left to tell.

Ch. 19

How Jim was named "black"
(reader discretion advised)

Other than "White,"
"black"
is the most powerful magic
the White man ever made

****

The day was thick with the sticky grip of the slip of muddy air that covers the hips of the Mississippi. The wind was still, and in still humidity, the gnats, stinks, mosquitoes, horseflies, and ephydridae swarm slovenly, heavy with the dirty dew of the haze everything moves through. The glare of the sun might trick you to sleep as it refracts and crackles in your eyes and ears to bend sight and crumble sound as if your senses were drowned in tears. The slow scratch of a phonograph, the drag of a needle through a groove, the quiet rattle of time itself are the closest things to the field of sweat that envelops you on a day like this.

It was a perfect day for a fall from grace.

Thus far, for Jim, grace had been a fickle queen coming and going as she pleased, one moment begging to be pet—purring up a tease, grinding her fur through his hair (and sharing her fleas)—claws out the next, hissing and humping herself into a flex, ready to rip up your veins and tear any spurt of hope out your neck. For Jim, grace was an alley cat or a galley bat or a big daddy rat with nothing to offer him but pain. So he wasn't surprised when she crawled in the lap of the two liars, the Jack and the Joker (yep they were still around), whose whim for sin formed his most recent prison and shame.

The two liars have been described, physically. But to understand how deeply any human decency in them had been compromised by slave society, you need to get a glimpse into their hearts—if that's what you can call the moldy maggot infested masses of meat rallying to the drumbeat of vainglorious savagery that have plagued humanity since the invention of slavery. Here are a few of things they had schemed to do most recently.

The Jack and Joker had blasphemed a holy roller revival to mock God and cried about their sins to lie a whole county in the trap of giving dividends as spiritual penance for their individual share of the world's putrescence. They'd pilloried young women's bodies, after tapping the molasses of lust that can crust under the belts of those kept under public suspicion of being sluts in small towns, and who thus thrust themselves at passing strangers to let some of their young sap flow from under their chastened gowns. They'd stolen an inheritance from the brethren of the dead–dumb with grief—to show no mercy for the dead weight of regret that the grieving carry. The two liars had done these three of the seven deadlies and so much more.

Jim watched these two liars come and go from the raft, and heard the stories told with the giddy guiltlessness of those for whom pure evil was pure gold. Huck would sit there and listen, soaking in the venom the two snakes were spitting. They were training the boy in the principles of flipping society's guilt into grifting.

Sometimes Jim felt bad for the victims. Other times he would see that this was the evil they'd brought on themselves. If you allow the heathenry of slavery—public inspection of naked children to sell, public hangings of innocent men for lies a whole town will tell, rape of women made public by children made in the image of their popular rapists' thin veil—then you've willingly nestled into the lower bottoms of hell, and hell hath no fury like the scorn of the self.

Jim thought, *these people can't be this dumb. Somewhere inside they must hate themselves for the wickedness they sprung.*

Jim knew that these fools had built a society built on enslavement, and all the debased waste of God's creation that enslavement wrung. So Jim saved his mercy too, and didn't follow the urge to turn the two liars in for the evil they did to stop the evil they might do. White folk wouldn't likely take his witness anyway, so loss of Black wisdom about White mistakes is a price White folks are bound to pay.

Jim slept easy with that—holding his wisdom back. He kept his mercy and concern for himself and his own, for what he expected might at any moment fall splat—that the two liars would cash him in at the first game of craps that opportunity shat.

Let's backtrack a bit to get reacquainted with what the two heathens had been instigating. First they hog-tied Jim, which we have already had to recount, but this was to allow them to go off with Huck and dream schemes to get as much loot as they could count.

A second plan left unmentioned earlier because it was a particularly putrid fart of stupidity, was them thinking better than having Jim hog-tied like a calf waiting to be skinned was for him to paint himself blue because, in the endless shades of the fears of White men, this would do to keep them at bay and afraid. Jim was to act a fool, like a mad man on the loose, monkeying behind a sign that said *Harmless Arab*[63] as a ruse meant to confound and confuse.

And, as this was the way for days, Jim had to laugh at his plight, but he laughed harder at the White folks for whom this costume was enough to hide him in plain sight. *Is this all it's taking to set them to chasing safety down river?* Jim asked with a smile inside.

If a deranged Muslim is their biggest scare, than a mad Muslim I'll be, and watch the terror in their eyes turn into the taste of dry heat between their teeth and fall into a haste in their feet as they buck and jump to get away from me.

---

[63] Who could make this up? Mark Twain could, and he did in *Adventures of Huckleberry Finn*. It seems as if the irrational fear of the "Arab", which Shakespeare (in *Othello*) wrote about in the 1500s, has been a European and European-descendant mental illness since Moors ran roughshod through Europe spreading algebra, architecture, astronomy, macroeconomics, medicine, music and language like Europeans spread the black plague. Racism is diehard, ask your unfriendly neighborhood Islamophobe.

Jim (*thinking a singing*):
They ain't scared of shark skins,
and ain't scared of lions neither,
but show them colored skin
and they screaming grim reaper.

They can climb a mountain down,
probably one day try to fly,
but if I look like a man, but brown
they run under hoods and hide.

They'll stare down bulls with swords,
build bridges and tall buildings,
but a Black man's deep vocal chords
turn they guts into chitterlings.

Of all the things the White man
done got himself to do,
he still can't seem to understand
that all men have a hue.

All us have a hue.
All us have a hue—
Mahogany, onyx, cinnamon, peach, gold
and pink too.

All us have a hue.
All us have a hue.
Ain't nothing white 'cept fog and snow.
Ain't nothing pure that's true.

He sees himself on pages
as the white between the ink.
He sees himself as the light of day—
to take all the space between blinks.

He thinks his skin is see through.

270

No color to hide evil.
He thinks his eyes must be blue
because the sky is his only equal.

In his color-struck mind,
his blonde hair is a golden beach.
His red hair is the fire's shine.
His green eyes—jewelry.
But, by Jesus,
it's hard to understand
why they hate color on me.

All us have a hue.
All us have a hue—
Caramel, redwood, indigo, corn, bronze
and birchwood too.

All us have a hue.
All us have a hue.
Ain't nothing white 'cept froth and lies.
Ain't nothing pure that's true.

And as you can clearly see, the blue hue plan was just as dumb as it seems. So, recall, they thought up a colorblind scheme to keep Jim "free" amidst the pursuit of man-hunting teams. They printed a man-hunters's bill, an IOU for $200, in accordance with the Fugitive Slave Act. They were to pretend that they were returning Jim to his rightful White owner, that he was indeed accounted for, his paperwork in tact. And this, they reasoned to Huck, would keep Jim from being stolen, on man-hunter's honor, from their guard. Jim knew better, and he was clear that sooner than later this paper thin construction would be the two liars get out of jail free card.

As soon as they said the new plan, Jim began to prepare his next move. He planned to dip while they were asleep and get gone with the canoe. But he kept being stuck with stall. The idea of leaving Huck in the claws of these two human hogs kept gnawing at Jim's gall.

Jim knew what he had to do, but he couldn't reconcile himself with how that would leave Huck slave to these two demons' criminal use. His conscience felt like the hangman's noose. He thought, *damnit, this boy's going to make me lose the last chance I got to lose.*

And almost as if on cue, what Jim had expected came true. The Joker arrived with the news that he was to sell Jim for enough bucks to pay for a drink or twenty-two. And that's all Jim was worth to them, that's all Jim might be, a piece of forty-five year old cured meat to toss to the ravenous beasts of greed run amok and set free by the Fugitive Slave industry.

The Joker came, already a drunk, stumbling, coughing hack. He came aboard the raft grumbling and stinking of sin. Jim felt no pity for him, no empathy at all, for this is what a man will fall to when he puts himself above all. He loses his senses, any pride he might have had, he loses his wisdom, and his soul becomes a tattered rag. And even if he gets rich and high on a split of his take, his euphoria never nourishes him, but soaks up his hopes like a man-sized hoecake.

So here he came, doing what he was bound to doing—to trade a man for just enough money to bring himself to ruin. But that wasn't enough of a shame for the Joker to comprehend, he had to heap a mound more odium atop the mount of degradation underneath his desperation to feed his addiction. He almost fell once he took a look at Jim. Something in the sight of him upended his gut which was churning with rotgut liquor's malediction.

The Joker fell to his knees and crawled to a corner of the raft to vomit like he had to puke for his life. He upchucked and chucked up so much he sounded like he might die. He was belching and farting and heaving and even started to cry. Jim sat on the other half of the raft and tried to keep his ears dry of the sound of it all and the smell of it all too. The joker then dunked his face in the river to get himself come to.

After while, the Joker turned and started to speak, first as a mumble, then his volume picked up. At first his words slurred and bent, then they stiffened rough. His face was twisted with sickness, but as he got the bearings of his witness he settled himself with some snuff. He stuffed it up one nostril and snorted. He stuffed the other, then pulled a pinch of tobacco from his pocket to suck. Jim still wasn't looking, but could hear the sounds of it all, and writhed a bit with disgust.

Without looking, Jim could see the truth clear as dust on a white suit. *This is what it comes to. Sin-hollowed men must stuff themselves with muck to buck up for the evil they do.*

This was a man ashamed, grinding his guilt in an empty tin of a bin he had built to catch all the muck that he'd raked up over a life of sin. In order to live with himself for this next bit of corruption, he took his hatred of himself and put the blame on Jim. He put all his hate in that name, that stain, that self-fulfilling prophesy of hypocrisy, that invisibility cloak.

The Joker trumpeted that trumped-up perpetual scapegoat.

He gorged on that stigma and figment heaped on a human cousin's God-given pigment.

He carved that stone gargoyle of White mythology, that hangman's lever, that bossman's tether, that incantation of those who invented Whiteness with a wizard's alchemy.

The Joker dropped that word cursed to the nth power.

He spit that verbal scour used the world over from churches to ivory halls to prison towers.

He planted that staple crop of the iron harvest, that spitfire rip for the rotgut swigger.

He dug up that unexploded ordnance and rotting shell of English language artillery.

The Joker spoke that formless mystery and zombie of history, that sniper's trigger—the radioactive n-bomb: N*gger.[64]

The Joker spoke to Jim in vulgar monologue—a soliloquy to his own soul—to carve a hamlet of justification for the injustice of his act in the fashion of a true rogue.

> The Joker (*to Jim, as matter-of-fact*):
> *Well some part of me hates to do this, Jim.*
> *You been the finest boy I know.*
> *Yes, the finest picker since Curtis Loew*
> *you been.*
>
> *There's just a natural order to things, you see.*
> *There's mules and there's men.*

---

[64](6) And there it is. You must have been wondering when or if it might show up. One can't engage with Twain's great muse on race without encountering this conundrum. And though no one should throw this word to page 217 times like Twain did, it would be a sin to run away from facing the gorilla in the room. This word only appears here in this book. And that is for a reason. It bears the deepest treason to the notion of freedom. It carries the secret fear and shame and rage of every descendent of the enslaved, that, no matter what may change, the majority in this country will always see us as slave—escaped slave, freed slave, or descendant of slave. In the richest corporation, in the most powerful government role, in science, in the entertainment industry, there are supremely gifted and intelligent Black folk waiting for it to slip from a tongue, waiting for the implication to bare its fangs in a contract negotiation, listening for it drip effortlessly from the tongue of a friend, or to whistle from the barrel of a police gun to summon a bitter end. This word can't be erased by overuse. It's bind can't be undone. So why it appears here is to underscore America's most despicable treason against freedom: that a government would empower and pay poor White folk to return an escaped human to slavery. And the demon that possessed White minds to carry out this atrocity, was this monstrosity of an imagined fiend, a curse, a one-word call to arms for a final solution that could have come from Hitler or any of Hitler's many inspirations in America, a psychic dirty bomb, strapped to a hair trigger, that will radiate hate for all time. You can use your own mind to complete the rhyme—******. P.S. the "I" is removed because that word ain't got nothing to do with me.

There's you and there's me.
Jim, all that you will ever be
is a n*gger,
whether slave or free.

I been all over the world
and that's just how it must be.
There's Chinese n*ggers over in the far east.
There's sand n*ggers
Muslim and Jew.
There's Indian n*ggers,
Irish n*ggers, Italian n*ggers,
and Spanish n*ggers too.

N*gger is like a title
of a book we wrote
to tell the story of the proper order
on the world's totem pole.
And Jim,
you and I both know
all them other n*ggers
get to look down
on the black n*gger
who ain't on the bottom
so much as he's in a hole.

Unfortunately for you,
being a n*gger
it's built into your skin.
That darkness that you walk with
is a stain, came from Cain's sin.
Now I know you been good,
a mighty good boy true,
And it's sure a bitter truth.
You are a n*gger
and a White man can't treat you no better than he's bound to.

See some Whites are too nice to n*ggers—
make them think they have rights,
make them set sights on unreachable heights.
It will just come to break
a poor n*gger's heart
when he sees that liberty
was never meant for him from the start.
It's better this way Jim.
It keeps things certain,
and believe me, Jim,
you don't want the White man's burden.

The White man's got the world on his back, Jim.
Like old Atlas, he can't even shrug
without the whole foundation cracking.
Jim, it's like when you raise a town hall.
You got to dig a hole for the foundation
or the whole damned thing would fall.
Jim, the black n*gger is the foundation
that keeps the White man's world stable.
That's why the White man must always keep
the black man in his stable.
That's why a collared n*gger
will always be a dollar made.
That's why he'll always be
either a commodity,
a ridiculous oddity,
a timely scapegoat,
or an ode to White Christian generosity.

Oh, Jim, I know it don't seem fair,
but you know how y'all n*ggers are
when left to your own devices.
You'll steal, murder, and rape
and revel in all kinds of vices.
Its not your fault, Jim.
It's the way you was made.

That's why you should always
aspire to stay in your place
as a slave.
Yes it is bitter
But it is true.
You are a n*gger,
so a White man can't treat you no better than he's bound to.

Yes, the White man needs his n*ggers
to feel like himself.
Without a n*gger to look down on
we lose our sense of mental health.
We get dizzy
all out of sorts,
unsure of where we stand.
Without a n*gger to use
the devil get's hold of our idle hands
and we put them on our women,
and our neighbor's,
and on our poor children.
Without the n*gger to abuse
we feud and war with our own kinsmen.
So see god gave us you n*ggers
like he gave us to himself,
so we could live in his image
and you could work
for our glory and wealth.
So Jim, this is for your own good
and I think inside you believe it too
as your own bitter truth.
You are a n*gger,
and a White man can't treat you no better than he's bound to.

Jim, here's the story:
I got to short sale you.
I got to cash you in.
It's time to move,

277

and that's just what I need to begin.
And here they come right here.
You go easy, you hear?
I'd hate to see a good n*gger like you
lose a limb or an ear.
Just keep being the good you been,
and one day when you die
the big White man in the sky
might let you work the fields
or paint the pearly gates up high.
He might even let you inside
to prepare the milk and honey
and keep the angels' robes white.
Just keep good behavior
and the reward is sure.
You can be the black that holds up the light
of the stars, white and pure.

Goodbye, Jim.
I do wish you the easy way
promised to you
if you do your best to do
good for a White man
as a credit to your race, true.
But remember,
no matter how bitter a truth.
A White man will never treat you no better than he's bound to.[65]

Then the Joker turned to face the man-hunters and yelled, *I got him right here for you!*

---

[65] This monologue will cause much consternation for some, and maybe some pain. Like "n*gger", this monologue was designed to cause pain. This word needed to be used the way it was used on me—and my mother, and my father, and countless numbers of my ancestors—in order to shame the devil who possessed the people who used it. If you want the word gone, exorcise it.

Jim felt heavy as a barge fully freighted as the man-hunters paddled their canoe to the raft, guns slung over shoulders, clay caked on their faces, clothes soiled as steamer trash. Their eyes were masked in shadow under wide-brimmed beaver hats. Their hands were skin on marrow, lips split and cracked. One spoke and the stink of bubbled up rotgut belched with his breath.

Jim saw them coming and started running options. Between these two—armed with shotguns—and the Joker, any resistance would trigger a violence that would leave him swole up and throbbing his whole body over. But they wouldn't kill him and lose their bounty, and crackers as dung poor as these would need to move him by the power of his own feet. So though he would catch a rotten beating, he would survive enough to walk. Maybe the pain would be worth it just to duke them a few in their blue eyes, shuck them a few pounds of flesh from their corn stalks.

He could dive in the water and try to hit a current in a seam swell. They would for sure catch him with that canoe, but he could pull one in the river, then the other and hold them under to deliver them both to hell. They'd have a better chance of drowning him, but at the bare bottom least, he'd die unwillingly.

He could try to force one to pull his shotgun and wrestle it from him to make the whole scrap one on one. Then it would be the luck of the draw and, if he popped one, the other one and the Joker would hit the wind quicker than cat's paw. This actually seemed like a plan, and so he started to eye the thickness of each man's arms to see which would be the easiest to disarm. That's when he noticed something of a swarm.

There were men lined along the bank, ten or fifteen or twenty, each with a shotgun and boots on their feet. They had rallied troops, each as playful to shoot as a kid skipping rocks from a beach. *White men always run in packs*, Jim thought. *If I attack, they'll riddle me.*

279

And then the canoe was right up on the raft. One of the man-hunter crackers said something and spit. The Joker laughed. The other cracked a rotten yellow-greyed smile, his bottom lip half-eaten by fist beaten teeth. They boarded the raft and now Jim had three feet between him and destiny.

That first man-hunter said something directly to Jim and wrapped rope around his fists. The other began to flank Jim and drew his shotgun. He put the barrel, trained on Jim, at rest on his forearm and wrist.

The first man-hunter spoke again, and though Jim didn't hear a word he said, he could feel that he had no options left. He bowed his head and set his eyes at their inching forward footsteps. Jim closed his eyes and saw a memory of Sadie standing in her doorway. His heart leapt. He saw another one of his son clumb up high in a tree, and Jim quietly wept. Last, he saw his daughter's smile and into sobbing he was swept. He felt the blast of the back end of a shotgun on his neck and fell deaf.

Ch. 20

Jim's Long Walk Back

Before Jim knew it,
he was worshipping a massive stump,
his body bent over its jagged flats
atop its new bottom,
his knees dug between the knees of its roots.
And his prayer,
which the enslaved call worship,
was to know how it was
that a dead thing could keep growing.
How could a thing grow after death?
And as the answer came,
which the enslaved call catching
the holy ghost,
he watched his skin,
once a taut maroon auburn,
grow loose and mossy brown.
He heard his voice,
as if he were watching himself
mumbling.

****

Jim didn't hear the rattle of the chains or the thumping plod of hooves. He didn't notice the spurs on their boots spin and clink as they shook. He wasn't aware of the dogs panting heat or the horses tossing tails or the stink they heaved back at him as he wheezed. Jim was only aware of the flecks of light that slipped through the leaves to ignite the dust kicked up from his bare feet.

Jim only looked down, where a deep mob of thoughts wrought Jim to a bowed walk. There was his wife, whom he'd rejoined in memory and his children, whose faces set his heart to frenzy. There was his wonder of how he would fare in the bottom of the south. There was the taste of dust-thick sweat, hardening in his mouth.

When low and in chains, dwelling will break a man. Jim knew this well. He could feel the weight of his fear for his family swell like tides of hell. What could he do about it now? What would thinking about the loss conjure, but more certainty that hurt would be the plight of his future? And Jim, walking now with his spirit cowed, could feel the thoughts of his family turn from forlorn to foul. *I hope they die young. Let them die rather than live this way. So we can meet, heaven or hell, a sooner day.*

Then there was a passing thought of Huck, now on his own, and Jim's worry of what the South will have made of him by the time he was grown. And it was with thoughts of Huck that Jim stayed for much of this march as it was a place to depart from the heartbreak over his family. It was a sort of relief for Jim, this philosophical pursuit of scouring his times with Huck to predict the boy's future from his purview.

> Jim (*in his mind*):
> *He's got it in him,*
> *that ounce of good over power.*
> *I can't see him whipping a woman*
> *while she trembles and cowers.*
> *Can't see him selling a child*
> *away from his mother.*
> *Can't see him hanging one man*

to terrorize another.
Can't see him become
all the things he sees men do.

But seeing is believing,
and believing is truth,
and truth is the place
where action is born.
So how long
before his nature
is overcome by his form?

But Huck,
he's got some heart,
smarts.
He's got so much life left.
He's right as his start.
And his talent,
as far as he shows,
is to see situations
right on the nose,
and with a little bit of judgment,
he's steady she goes
to the right thing to do.
He just seems to know.

But
seeming ain't being
and being is what we do,
and will he do
what the world tells him to?
Will he set
his clock by the light?
Or will he face
the night sky beyond the white?

And Jim's wondering on Huck came to a sharp end as the man-hunters drug Jim to their destination. The catchers were leading Jim to a farm, bucolic and warm with charm, beyond a simple white two-story coop. A porch wrapped around its front, thin wood columns held its roof; each railing between each pillar looked like a thin, blunt tooth. The porch was being swept by an enslaved yellow gal in a dress and, as she looked up at Jim, a voice leapt through the open door to protest.

Keep sweeping, you hussy! Don't you eyeball no men. Mind your business, Mrs. Sally Phelps, a thin white woman in a bonnet, said with viciousness.

Then her tone turned soft as a daisy petal's touch. *You men come on 'round the back, we'll chain him in the shack next to the tool hutch.*

Jim shuffled, making a rhythmic clinking with the chains that happened to keep beat with the shushing broom-pushing the yellow wench maintained. She dared not look at him, but could sense his attention under the piercing eye of Mrs. Sally Phelps and the hungry stares of the man-hunters who perused her shapely body where it flared. Mrs. Phelps's anger again squared on the yellow wench though this time she whispered to build up to a yell.

Mrs. Sally Phelps:
Go inside,
you ugly devil's daughter,
'fore I get a switch and split you.
Quick!
No slack,
'fore I tear a rip into your back!

Jim heard her, and it jarred him, but he had heard worse. It sounded to him like the empty curse a White woman keep tucked in her purse to spur a spurt of work and spice themselves up in a White man's eyes. But the way the yellow gal hopped to it, made him believe that this White woman would do it. He began to prepare himself for ruin.

It wasn't just the harsh hits sparking off Mrs. Phelps lips. It was the whole look of the place. It had the tidy order of a place built on the lash. The entire plantation was placed in a gash between hills, a deep cut that might have been slashed by the White man-god himself.

Closest to where Jim walked was the big house and close to the big house were the quarters, the slave quarters, siting slip in the hip of the east corner, the corner where the sunrise stretches to wake a slave to his daily day-long, night-on and on strife. This was a severe bit of business when it comes to slave society life. The more genteel of the plantations hid the quarters elsewhere, to at least pretense that the slavers didn't smile with their teeth bared. But it was clear this here plantation was run by folk who didn't care about that. They wanted the slave shack as close as could be so they could whistle out the window and have labor ready to work or get ready for the lash. Any family that was proud of slaving in this type of way, was a family that would whip a man, woman, or child in the day and sleep at ease. Just from the lay out of this plantation, Jim knew he was in trouble deep.

Jim was led to a shack and welcomed with a shove. He stumbled forward and caught himself against its door. One of the man-hunters snorted and spit on the dirt as if it weren't the earth's floor. Old Gran had told Jim about that. Spitting on the earth was disrespectful, she told him. If you must spit, you were supposed to spit in the grass so the grass could drink it to grow. Spitting in the dirt was for show and made more mud to muck up the shoes of the next man who came along. Besides…

Gran (*Jim remembering*):
Spit ain't water,
'less you God.
Spit from a man's mouth is filth
as filthy as gut rot.
Keep you spit out the dirt
or the dirt will spit back

and cover you up under its skirt,
know that.

The state of the shack he was brought to didn't precipitate any improvement in his prediction about his predicament. It had a dirt floor and every indication of having been kept in a state of dereliction. It had a window with a plank hammered over it so that it let in a sliver of light, just enough to show Jim where he was and what had become his plight. He was a prisoner to farm justice and this shack was a stop along his path where he was to be held as a slave-catch stashed in a wood box burse. And yet he had certainly slept in worse.

After months on the high wire of the river, sleeping in swamp and rain, and after finding himself in every rattling snake of muck and mire, he didn't require much and had developed a superior tolerance for pain. And four walls and a window, and a bed, despite the chain attaching his ankle to its leg, wasn't so bad after all that. The first night he was there he couldn't help but to fall back into a hefty, dreamless slumber.

The first morning he awoke with the sun and the still softness of a non-raft morning was hard to overcome. His mind was clouded from not being rocked by the river. His body ached from being sunk into a mat. His feet were blistered from the long walk and his heels were cracked into tats.

So he laid for a while looking up at the roof, and he thought of what he couldn't and wouldn't do. He couldn't break through the walls of this shack, though they looked as if they were stuck together with horse glue. He could but he wouldn't lift the bed leg, certainly as easy as lifting a ladle to taste a stew, and walk off with his chain. He couldn't get to running on the river without Huck as cover, and with every man-hunting, catcher dog on his scent, that would be as daft as pissing into stiff wind.

286

What could he do? One thing to another meant trouble, and he was full of that already. At least here he had a roof and walls, and a place to raise the balls of his feet. There was food and water, and sleep. There was sometimes even company, adult company with people who understood the life enslaved, and understanding is something Jim hadn't felt since the Middle Pass days. As far as Jim could tell, Huck and the liars hadn't an ounce of empathy, couldn't muster a tick of compassion, treated Jim with the heart of a flea, and wouldn't share a germ of lasting friendship. They were small as small could be. But in the company of the enslaved, there would always be room for feeling. The enslaved were bigger than their enslavers, and greater still, than any who kept their human instincts in some cave under a mountain of will. *Their souls seem locked away, like a cold bell in a tower*, thought Jim, *while we keep soul close and walk with ours.*

Jim thought more and more, and came upon the Joker's speech about the nature of the White man's need for others to believe his superiority.

> Jim (*contemplating*):
> *It must be hard*
> *to need others so much,*
> *and to also hate that fact.*
> *It must be hard*
> *to convince yourself you are tall*
> *while standing on another's back.*
> *It's got to be hard*
> *to think a slave lazy*
> *for not wanting to work for free.*
> *It has to be damn near impossible*
> *to live with yourself*
> *when you treat people so dastardly.*
> *But then again*
> *they make it look so easy.*

When do they become like this, Jim wondered. *Are they born this way?* He wondered if their enslaver nature was a seed that took hold and grew bold over many days. He wondered if maybe they never grew and were grown folk walking around with the spirit of toddlers—greedy little robbers—prone to take whatever they bumped into. He thought they could be two-spirited, like the Indian people talked about; that there was one gentle spirit they kept for those within their tribe and one vicious spirit they kept for those without. But then how would they know who is in their tribe, by what folk say and do, or by shape of their face or their skin's hue, or by name or by rank or by language or past proof?

Jim considered what a complicated thing is the White man's way; it is a riddle pieced together by puzzle found at the end of a maze. And Jim was tired. Jim was tired of the matrix of shifting values and twisting laws. Jim was tired of the swelling and shrinking boundaries that, wherever they happened to be on a particular day, were always bayonet sharp and Minie ball hard. Jim needed time off their rivers and time off their rafts which had no rack nor pinion, nor rod or staff. Jim was glad to sit, even with a chain around his leg, and lay on a steady bed to ride the rapids, however tormenting, inside his own head.

And soon, he found that many simple people, even some friendly figures, haunted the plantation. There was enslaved Nat, chuckleheaded and not at all brave to any hint of a witch, who brought Jim food and told him all about the shack, about the big Miss and that yellow wench. The shack was a makeshift jail in this town without a bench or a sheriff or a constable or any sense of law. They would pay Mrs. Sally Phelps a tithe for the trouble of keeping any non-violent fugitive until they figured out what to do with this communal flaw. Jim was the first runaway they'd kept and Mrs. Sally was excited, Nat told him, to Christianize him into his senses with recited holy verses as old as sin.

Ch. 21
Jim Gets Religion

In Genesis,
God spoke between the lines.
In all the generations of men mentioned
throughout them beginning times,
hope begat hope.
Hope begat hope.

****

Mrs. Sally Phelps would come and pray with Jim about the Christian way, and the mosaic of laws the Bible laid to keep the enslaved in their place. Jim listened closely, as he was curious about how the Bible could both promote, according to Mrs. Sally, and prohibit, according to Middle Pass, the facts of slavery. Mrs. Sally read Leviticus 25: 44-46, where God supposedly said you can buy slaves, but just can't treat them ruthless.

Yet, Middle Pass had told Jim about this passage and about how a couple verses earlier God clarified that you may not enslave your countrymen and that this was why White folk had so much interest in making sure we Black folk would never be full citizens. Besides, he said, the only way to keep a slave loyal as Ruth was to make them happy with less, and that in itself was a violence against the hope God put into in every human breath.

Mrs. Sally read Luke 7:1-10 about a slave that Jesus healed, but certainly didn't treason to set free, and she explained this as the reason why God had sent her to heal Jim of his heathenry. But, Middle Pass had already clarified her confusion when he once told Jim that the bible made a difference between a servant and a slave, and that this particular passage was about a powerful man begging Jesus that his servant be saved, and by that humble faith, the servant was healed. Middle Pass preached that the powerful man was using something God-given, called "free will". According to Middle Pass, this "free will" was the power behind faith, since you had to *choose* to be faithful to make the way. Middle Pass said Jesus came to earth to heal us and show us our power if we acted like children of God, sisters and brothers.

But, according to Mrs. Sally, the true proof was a letter from Saul turned Paul sending a runaway slave back to slavery once he had been converted to Christ. She told Jim that being returned a Christian slave was his God-given right. Mrs. Sally said it wasn't Jim's fault, the nature of his birth. Being descended from Ham, it was the nature of God's curse. Middle Pass had simply said the god that made up that story was the devil. And since Jim had already questioned the foolishness of that story, Middle Pass' point seemed right level.

Mrs. Sally was well-versed in these justifications, and Jim had heard some of them before, but never with such conviction or with such a predilection towards *hands* as expressions of feminine force. She kept her hands on Jim's shoulders, rubbing and squeezing, as though testing the ripeness of fruit. Then her breathing would get to throbbing, speeding and heaving, as her hands would fall to his back to pat, claw, and root. Jim—on his knees between Mrs. Sally and the wall of the shack with his nose so close to her clothes, as her hands fell down his back— Jim felt like a tree where a bear might scratch its own back in the wood, if Mrs. Sally was a bear. It felt strange and damn near felt grown good. And he was glad when she was gone so he could chop some wood.

And Nat had some stories of the Phelps family plantation and the yellow wench in particular. She had an unknown White father who never confessed, and a mother Mrs. Sally Phelps nearly beat to death before she sent her down and far. But all the slaves knew and had saw that Mr. Silas Phelps was her paw. So Mrs. Sally hated the sight of her, but through Christian charity kept her around. Though, now that the wench was filling out all about, many thought she would soon be sent down. In New Orleans, a body like hers could fetch a pretty purse, and that fact was first on Mrs. Sally's mind as she watched the wench from behind with her lips pursed.

Jim, for his part, took the opportunity of Mrs. Sally Phelps's preaching, to convince her of his goodness by confessing sins. Not his own sins, but those of the Joker and the Jack, and the Phelps' were thankful to learn the schemings of the two thieving hacks. If Christianity was big enough to keep Jim enslaved, he felt it must have space for vengeance and hate, and so he let the Joker and the Jack have both that day. And that night, he slept like a log again, and in the morning woke with a natural grin, thinking prison might just be better than slaving. He had a preacher's wife humping his shoulders, consistent food to eat, and sleep, the sweet sleep he had been craving for days upon days over.

But his mood swiftly shifted as thoughts of his family returned every other second, and the burning yearning for his wife sprouted about him and beckoned. And the guilt over his children ate at his craw. And soon the hopelessness that awaited him down south is all he saw. He thought to run again, but knew if caught there would be no mercies. To them, a slave determined to escape was a catching disease.

So Jim sat and listened to Mrs. Silas preach, thinking of Moses on the mountain. He thought of the voice of God pouring from a fire fountain. Sitting, clawing his toes in the dirt floor, Jim thought of the burn of the lash and what his neck might feel like broken. He'd heard of hell. He'd heard the rip of rope around a throat yell. He'd dreamed of burnt skin after seeing smoke. He lipped a swear without being aware and wondered whether he would be spared the bared teeth of flames or the skin-curdling churn of rope or the back-splitting crack of a whip croaking in the grip of a pale horseman with hands pink and hungry as a hog. Jim tapped the outside bone bump of his wrists against the inside bone bump of his ankles and thought of hungry dogs.

The bone reminded him of coin and coin of money and of the $800 dollars he was worth. That was too much for poor Ms. Watson to burn or tear to pieces or bleed to death in spurts. She wasn't rich enough to make a public picnic of folding a slave into creases and ripping his body to the raws.

Thank God she was too cheap to donate him to the supreme cause and collect his value in the small print of an insurance clause.

But all this thought was robbing Jim of peace and he soon felt a misery much more deep. For Mr. Silas Phelps put a stop to Mrs. Sally Phelps lust to preach and seized his turn to earn his Christian keep. And Mr. Silas Phelps loved to preach about damnation and hell, and he was as deep at describing how fire felt as there is water in a mountain well. He said fire bit, pinched, singed, cut, ground, pound, punched, kicked, stabbed, ripped, tore, jabbed, bat, scratched, shot, blasted, peeled, cooked, and boiled a body. As Jim's spirit floated in the dark of his outhouse cell, his heart bloated with sorrow's swell, Jim began to ask the question that heats the fires of hell: Why?

Why be born if only to suffer? A real god certainly wouldn't need man's labor. Nature thrives in life with no help from man. The bounty of earth comes from her own flesh and sweat under the warmth of the sun, not from what men can shear from her soil to fill themselves with her crumbs.

Or maybe their god lives off man's prayer and plants him in trouble to treble his yield. Or maybe their god sees men as flowers and sends bees to the field because our tears are pollen for his powers. Maybe their god's money is the honey of our blood and his milk the silk of our sweat. Then it makes sense that their god would crown us in thorns to tap syrup from our flesh. Yet, why would such a god exist?

Is there a bigger thing that feeds on him? Is there a greater judge that judges his sin? There must be an end of all ends, an empty big enough to hold him and leave room for the wind to blow the longing that sent him spinning to his mission? If their god is all there is, then what prompted him to want to make us at all? Without space around a god, space into which his mind could stretch, where did his idea for the world come from and from where did he draw the breath he put into our flesh?

Jim held all these questions in the darkness within and while they were with him, he felt the company of his own existence. Even in his most leisurely day as a slave, Jim rarely felt that way—that he could ask why. He only had time for who, as in who was he dealing with, and how, as in how must he deal, or when and at what time must he fulfill his slave detail, or where and the distance between places and which routes might hasten the way's paces; but Jim never had time for why. Why is for dreams, and what things mean, and what seems at the seams between happenings. Why is not a question for the enslaved, no matter how much he must crave to know who gave him the lot of his days.

What does why matter with your family scattered to the winds of markets, with your hope shattered against a master's hardness, with your body shackled to the whims of heartless men who measure your essence in the darkness of your skin. What would why matter to Jim before now, when the milk and honey of hope of freedom had curdled and soured and left him pinned in like a sow.

Facing Mr. Silas' prayer for power, his hands on Jim's cheeks, Jim could see that their god was a man: a man with needs, a man that needed obedience in every deed. A man like this cannot exist without a slave, without someone to believe in every word he might say. *God must be that White-man god*, Jim thought that day.

And 'why' soon left Jim for the what of what comes next. And the 'what' that was in front of him began to crest and press upon his back that fact of the life he thought had left: the life of a slave. A nd that life was a road with all turns set, the wagon grooves where tattooed truths in which bloody ink had set and set him here, back in chains, the range of all possibilities set and arranged.

Jim racked his brains with 'what next,' and kept coming up with Huck, and the luck he'd had to ride with him, and the ways in which the boy had shown him something different: that in the White man, somewhere in the child of him, under the thin veneer of his skin and its coat of formless phlegm coughed up from his imagination, deep in his core, back of his mind, there might be a brother that might act in a spirit of family, or at least in the spirit of sport and being fair to someone other than his own kind, and with the liberty and justice he designed for his comrades and cohorts.

Somewhere in each of them there must be a Huck that might possibly understand that all beings are his brother and a man ain't nothing but a man. He decided he'd allow them the thought that he wouldn't slip the chain around his leg off the flimsy wood of the bed. All in all he would play the "good one" in the hope that there might be a Huck among them, a malleable heart that was open to the possibility of mercy against oppression.

Jim admitted to himself that this foolishness had no basis. There was no good reason that White men would be anything other than the bitter he had tasted. But the luck that was Huck had changed him somehow by showing him the White man at his best: a decent (at times) friend, sharp and smart, and willing (at times) to do what's right. There had to be another like him among the millions of Whites living under sunlight.

But regardless of whether Huck was the only one, Huck was enough. And as Jim thought back to the plays they had made to make it through the roughs along the river's thrust, he thought: *if there's one I can trust, it is Huck.* He thought that, if he ever found the boy again, they could hook and crook their way out of Daniel's den. For there weren't men made who Huck and Jim couldn't convince through debate, or trick with trades, or evade if fate would have it that way. Jim felt encouraged as he thought of Huck and the pluck of his ways and how, together, they could make freedom from ashes or dust, dumb luck or dim days.

And this little, this bit, this smidgeon of hope was all Jim needed to feed his energy. And as his energy became activity—became kinetic—his movement generated more energy in that way that hope can be self-fulfilling and prophetic. Equal and opposite, an empty space formed. And that space, like any hole, was prone to be swarmed by what was around it. And that rushing in to fill was like a magnetism, it was a gravity, and it attracted to Jim new options and new opportunities. And Jim, who was nothing if he wasn't ambitious, made his ambition a mission to find every slip and sliver of the efficacious—the hustle was on.

Ch. 22
Jim's Hustle is the Muscle that Turns his Tide

...lying right at the river's edge when the sunshots are low and drained. Often they are mistook for insects—but they are seeds in which the whole generation sleeps confident of a future. And for a moment it is easy to believe each one has one—will become all of what is contained in the spore: will live out its days as planned. This moment of certainty lasts no longer than that; longer, perhaps, than the spore itself.

Toni Morrison, *Beloved*

****

When it came to other slaves, Jim knew their ways and the best way to loop them into his wish. And, shamed as he was to do it, he at times had taken advantage of the more foolish. Nat was one such fool living on this farm. This could be seen in sacks of naps tied into stacks that Jim immediately recognized from a hustle he had run way back. This slave believed in witches, as most people do[3], and like many fools he was prone to seeing clues to what to do in anything new; a new sound, a new color, a new smell or taste.

Fools run a spectrum whether Black, White or in between. But for all fools, what they believe is what they've seen. White fools can see heaven in a werewolf, long as it's white and see evil in an angel if it has color, however slight. They only believe in math if it adds up to pay and only believe in God if he acts the way they say. A Black fool will see trouble in snakeskin and luck in a hairy chest. A Black fool can see a witch in a ditch and by opinion be depressed. And a voice? A strange voice will make them *both* whelp and this is how Jim knew the way to rope Nat into his personal help.

One night, when Nat was passing his shack, Jim pushed his face against the door and launched his attack.

> Jim (*in a slithery, whispery voice*
> *with a Caribbean accent*):
> *Hey, boy.*
> *Dat runaway dem devils got boxed away?*
> *Him a witch*
> *and him a work him a spell today.*
> *Him not a slave atall.*
> *Him a come to warn.*
> *Calamity soon fall.*
> *But keep him secret, ya hear me?*
> *And bring him a full plate, daily.*

And that's all it took. From that point forward, Nat brought him secret portions from the Phelps' own take, according to whatever whim Jim's witch voice ordered him to take, in addition to the watermelon and scraps the masters Phelps had thought to appropriate. And Jim ate good, or at least better and, for a fugitive without friend or peer, better is a blessing without measure or frontier. He took pleasure in it, just knowing that he'd gotten something better than what was, even if better was just crushed up mush. But then one night, just as the day had come to dusk, Jim heard a sound flush with the lush rush of hope only a bird can sing to fling up. It was a voice that chimed a familiar ring. It was, he was damn near sure, Huck!

Jim heard two boys talking, and the one that sounded of Huck was coming up with a plan to break the board that blocked his window and sneak Jim to freedom! But the other boy, whose voice was also a tad familiar, thought it would be better to dig Jim out despite the fact that it would take many a week's measure longer. Jim stayed quiet and feigned sleep, partly unsure if this was a dream, for why else would a fool make an escape longer than it had to be? He let himself fall back to sleep as the voices trailed off into the dark's deep.

The next morning, Jim remembered his dream and was sitting up and, to pass time, was listing up all the good favor they'd be whisking up if he actually had lucked up and got in touch with Huck and back to the raft. All of a sudden, he heard Huck's voice again and this time Jim knew he wasn't dreaming. But could his mind be creaking under the pressure of the trouble he was currently keeping? Could he be losing his grip on time such that he had fallen back blind into some memory of some moment of sunshine on the raft? Could he have gone daft, from all the thinking and winking up a witch's voice, such that he had cracked his own mind right at the center beam joist? Jim was worried.

But then the door opened and light flooded in. Jim's eyes huddled under his hands. As they adjusted their aperture, Jim was enraptured by the vision they would command. Despite what all known shucks Jim could ever conjure up, holy whiskey from water and gold from bread crust, it *was*, for goddamn, dumb-luck sure, Huck!

Huck! Is that old Tom?, Jim shouted without thinking he would need to hide his knowledge of the boys. Then, judging from the quick look Huck gave him and with the psychic connection two build when river rafting, he read that they were pretending ignorance as part of a ploy. Nat was right behind and asked how Jim knew the two of them, but Tom quickly jumped in to ask why Nat would think such a thing. Nat said he heard Jim call out names. Tom said no one called out. Then Tom told Nat that something must be wrong with him and the poor man's face drooped with doubt.

Nat:
It's the witches.
They won't leave me 'lone.
But please don't tell Master Silas
or he'll hide me to the bone.
He say there ain't no room for witches
in a Christian home
and I know he knows right,
but I wish he'd tell me
who that is whispering to me at night.

300

Tom told him they'd come check on him at night if he wanted, and Nat was sure grateful. And on the way out Tom whispered to Jim that if he heard digging, it would be he and Huck busting him free as the faithful. Jim grabbed their hands and squeezed them almost by instinct, as he couldn't contain the feeling of hope coursing through him, as foreign as it was distinct. And as the two boys left, Jim stared at the closed door and wondered what luck could bring him Huck at a time when his hope was so unmoored. He thought, *I bet it was all that mentioning him, all them thoughts that caught the good and only good wind of God's attention.*

Jim *(thinking):*
Maybe God's going to prove
He ain't White after all,
maybe God ain't got no color
like outside ain't got no walls.
Maybe God don't play no favorites,
maybe He just hedging His bets
and rolls with the front-runner
because they can do more for Him,
more or less.
And maybe I tapped into something
God thought was a gamble worthwhile—
the hope of all hopes
the future of a child.

Ch. 23
Huck, finally, protests Tom's foolery

There comes a point when one must
speak up,
when good intentions
and the absence of bad action
are not enough,
when they must speak
and act on their words
to ensure
that justice
as a deed
is done

****

Soon all God-loving thoughts left Jim, when he began to understand the nature of Tom's intention for him. Tom began to plan a most elaborate escape, one worthy of picaresque, an episode of largesse, a bildungsroman of compressed plot twists as part of the getting going process.[4] It's as is if he set as his mark a twain of mess, inane gests to make light of Jim and Huck's most deadly serious quest. At Tom's behest, they were to complicate the simple, elongate the brief, plant problems where none had sprouted, and trouble the waters of relief. Both Huck and Jim put up with him for different reasons, as Tom set traps on their path as if they were prey praying to get eaten.

Huck was quick to divine the solution with the most minimal confusion and Jim smiled at his steady evolution into a young man of sense and mission. He and Tom would sneak out at night and bust out the plank on the window. Then he and Jim would get in the wind to go back to the raft. Simple. But Tom wasn't having anything easy. He wanted hell. Especially when it came to this game he saw as a story to tell.

First, they were to dig Jim out, but pick axes were not allowed. Tom ordered that they use case knives to stretch the job out. But after the first few bouts of stabbing the ground, Huck expressed his doubts on whether the idea was sound. They compromised to using axes and pretending they weren't, like slavers calling themselves farmers when they were driving slaves, like owners dreaming slaves wouldn't run away for wanting to stay, then using lashing and lynching to keep them in place. It was typical and peculiar to southern charm to pretense one thing as another to prevent resentment and keep peace, even if peace was a stinking, dead body.

Huck protested then, and again when Tom wanted to write a note to give the Phelpses a hint that someone was going to attempt a theft, thinking they would consider the theft might be of their prisoner. Huck and Jim were flabbergasted at this ass of an idea to consider. But Tom was certain the Phelpses were too dumb to catch on to the break out without a note, which would drain the whole thing of its fun. And Huck and Jim thought less fun meant more doing, and was certainly better than sparking suspicion.

Why on earth, Huck and Jim reasoned, would they treason away the plan and give the Phelpses the upper hand in catching Jim and Huck once they got off land? But Tom was resolute and Jim had no power, so Huck was the deciding vote. Huck went along with Tom, begrudgingly, and so they wrote a note that claimed frontiersman were on the take, coming in a mob to heist Jim away.

Before planting the note there were a number of other plots that Tom seeded to ensure that the escape was tangled in knots. It was a power of work, days and hours and hours, every night while the farm was asleep, the scheme would flower. They had to steal candles, tin plates and a spoon, a sheet and a shirt, a warming pan, a giant grindstone, and a skirt. They made saws and pens to pen inscriptions with pictures of coffins and things and, of course, the anonymous warning letter. They dug the hole and made a rope-ladder and cooked it in pie, but that wasn't the worst of the ridiculousness they scattered like scat out of a bulls' single, back-eye.

They loaded the cabin with rats and snakes and spiders that Jim was supposed to sleep with, and let bite him so he had blood with which to write a journal he was supposed to be keeping. At this point, Jim broke from the plan, and gave the rats to the dogs to make friends of them and gave the snakes back to the land. The spiders Jim crushed and mixed with the blood of the rats, and pretended that he let them bite him to keep Tom off his back. Throughout this whole dumb affair, Jim did calculus to determine that he had to go along with the plan no matter how bad it was.

The clearest connection that a man of fields and work—men like the enslaved—can make, is between people and beasts since plants are too quietly complex to contemplate. A seed will follow rules as certain as the seasons. But which plant will succumb to which pestilence is as mysterious as God's own reasons.

But animals, God bless them, are as simple as can be. They sleep and eat and dump and hump in an order that matches their need.

Yet, animals have another dimension. They have distinct personalities. And therein lies the wisdom they hold for humanity.

Jim (*calculating*):
If Tom were a donkey,
he'd be the kind
that makes a show,
makes show of his stubbornness
to keep his pride aglow
as an act of self-righteousness.

If Tom were an elephant,
he'd stampede
to trample all the little things
that he does and doesn't see.

Either way, the boy is cocksure—
as sure as a cock in the morning—
that he's right pure
no matter who he leaves mourning.
Best to let a fool with power dream
he's bigger, stronger, and smarter than he is,
rather than fight his stubborn will
or the way he'll wield war and fits.

If Huck were a donkey,
he'd be the sheepish kind

that goes along quietly kept,
and will march his dumb ass off a cliff
if that is where he is led.

If Huck were an elephant,
he'd be the kind
that wanders back and forth
looking for a path long gone,
lost for his life's course.

Either way, the boy ain't sure—
as unsure as hind-wind—
best to let him find his way
or find somebody to follow to the end.

And such is politics when done with correctness. When two sides get to fighting they go looking for a tie-break to resolve it. And Jim was the tipper without a vote. He had input and a weight, but that weight was passed between the two sides, and often dropped to earth with a great thud, like a cast iron black shot put.

And some might say Jim kind of gave in when he may have had options, but with choices as bad as run to death or wait for death, Jim felt locked in. So Jim went along for the time being, but that didn't end up as the best plan neither, because next came the type of madness that would make a skeptic into a believer.

The final and worst bit of foolery that Tom thought up, was to outright warn the Phelpses of the whole plan. You heard that right, to give away the whole plan. In Tom's thrill-polluted mind, they needed one more variable of trouble to make the escape worth his time.

Tom sent two letters to Silas claiming Jim would be kidnapped, and his bounty stole. The letters claimed an exact time the crime would occur, just to make sure the trouble would hold. When Huck wrapped his head around this, he looked like he could have kicked Tom blind, and an argument commenced when Huck asked him what could possibly be in his mind.

Tom argued that propriety and tradition to all the trappings of civilization required that they make a proper presentation of their escaping Jim from prison. *How could they be White men and outlaws*, Tom reasoned, unless they did justice to the law breaking with a "flourish" that would leave even the most righteous lawmen in a guffaw about the plan's intelligence. He figured that White men—*being sharp and good and smart and able and hard when they needed to be*—should do everything, even bad things, excellently.

Huck disagreed about what constituted excellence, and he did so vociferously.

Huck (*irritated*):
*Excellence is
what excellence does
and, in this case,
what we doing
is getting Jim free.
Any other flab
we tack on our track,
ain't excellent,
it's reckless.*

Tom (*superior*):
*Well Huck,
I know you are ignorant
as ignorant as can be,
but I always thought you too quick
to miss the point completely.
I guess you really can't*

learn a Finn a thing.
Now look we got to take a vote
and make motions.

Huck (*humbled, but resolute*):
Yes, I'm ignorant.
Yes, I wish I had your brain.
But common sense done kept me dry
along a river's worth of rain.
I ain't read your books, Tom,
but I done read your game.
You looking for fun
in all the wrong places.
But Jim and me
got aims.
We aiming to get free,
Jim and me.

Tom (*perplexed*):
Jim and you?
What voodoo is this?
Has this slave got you brainwashed
into thinking you and him kin?
Are you serious?

Huck (*serious*):
He ain't my kin,
but he is my friend
and we both want to be free,
and we members of the same gang now——
a gang for freedom by any means,
by every means,
and by the means
that make the most sense.
Now cut the malarkey
right damned now
or you we can do without,

and you can have all your
votes and motions alone.
We 'bout to be out.

And for the second time in their young friendship, Tom looked at Huck with a cocked head. The first time was when he refused to lay a trick on Jim's sleeping head way earlier in the story. Tom thought a bit and came to a conclusion. Huck is what he is. He actually cares about Jim and wants to help him. Well help the two of them he would, with a helping of extra drama to make sure the boring story of this White boy and a Black slave had something good.

You got it, Huck. Let's leave tonight. Everything's set anyway. We might as well light out and hide till light, Tom gave in. Huck was unsure of why he had, but sure was glad to hear something sensical coming from the young cad.

Good. Right. Let's go get Jim and go, Huck was ready to get in the wind and flow, and Jim was thankful and surprised.

Ch. 24

Jim Escapes Again

And if they told me "yes"
to everything I asked,
I'd still ask
why,
because the thing itself
will never be
enough.

****

By now you know Jim was no fool. Other than from Huck and the two bastards who held him captive, he didn't suffer foolishness as a rule. But in his current circumstances, what could he do?

Jim figured they'd get caught, and that once they got caught in all the madness, they'd either think him crazy or that the children had designed the whole absurd tommyrot business. The boldness of it would also absolve Nat, since the Phelpses would know that fearful fool couldn't have had anything to do with that. At best the plan might work and Jim would go free, and if worse came to worse he might just end up returned to his family once they didn't hear back from the owner he was supposed to have way down yonder in New Orleans. He figured the longer the plan took, the longer the Phelpses would have to figure out that he hadn't escaped from further down south. And so he went along and only protested a bit, from time to time, to make sure Huck could see that he hadn't lost his mind.

In between dealing with Huck and Tom, he fed the dogs, pet the dogs and made sure they knew him on the chance they might be sent to sniff his scent and lead the Phelpses to him. He also used the time to observe the friendship of Huck and Tom, and tried to understand the strange nature of their bond. Jim saw Tom was no good for Huck, that one was the other's pet and fancy. Jim thought Tom made a bet against fate that he could make a buck out of Huck, a horse, a good mate for his captainship and whimsy. Their bond wasn't flimsy, be as it was built on being brother witnesses to murder and cousin co-beneficiaries of the treachery Injun Joe committed before he starved dead under the beam of a cave's girder[5]. Jim had heard of that whole calamity, but Tom was still what he was: a boy with rich family. And Huck was orphaned—a captive to charity.

Huck's more like me than him, Jim thought. He had no patience for the fun Tom sought, for the rush Tom found in making things harder than they ought to be, in going farther than what was required to be free. For Tom, life was craps, where survival is not in question. For Huck and Jim, life was risk, where another breath is a blessing.

Jim continued to consider his options. Now if they were caught and Huck was found and he was bound down to New Orleans, at least Huck would not be thought murdered and Jim wouldn't be blamed for that sin. Now he might even be able to convince Huck to claim Jim ran under his suggestion or request, to help Huck survive his own runaway quest. It was also possible that Jim could be seen as doing a slave's duty, protecting a White boy at all costs, even to his own ruin. Now that Tom was a part of the way, he could also blame Tom's well-known foolishness for the thought to escape.

Now that all this had been laid bare to Jim, there was only one place to stand—right where he was to let the stupidity pass. This ridiculousness would all be evidence that this whole adventure was just the kick of two true asses: one a poor, dumb boy and the other, a mischievous knave. Hapless slave was a role that Jim knew how to play to appease the limited imaginations of the White folks of his day. So there it was. He would ride this thing out, might even come out looking like a "good slave[6]," let it all die down and save his escape for another day.

The night had risen. By the function of the sun, the earth was flung into darkness. The time had come for the deed to be done, for the three to be strapped to the harness of their common intention. Either Jim would be free or the whole mission would crumble under the weight of fate's forgone conclusion. One could anticipate what happened next, but the story is certainly worth its weight in tonnage of text, for things thickened as the chickens of consequence commenced to rummage and peck.

Jim peeked incessantly through the seams between the wall and the door looking for signs of his team, Tom and Huck, to start the finish of the mess the two had made and get to the escape they had planned for. He saw a commotion of men motioning and coming toward him. Here was the first bit of bad, which came quick and in clumps of all sorts of trouble.

Just outside Jim's shack arrived a huddle of White men with shotguns ready to rumble. It seemed Tom's letter worked and had gotten the whole town stirred and whirred into frenzy on the lookout for imprisoned-escaped slave thieves. They were outside the shack cocking guns as Jim huddled in a corner sure the end of the thing had come.

Is this how it would end for him, riddled to bits by bullets because a boy made Jim's life a game of null bets, with nothing at stake in this boy's mind, but to make a toy of spent time? Did Jim's life even matter to Tom beyond the way it could flatter his sense of power to hold a life in his hands until its final hour?

Just as Jim was contemplating his end, Huck and Tom bust in through the hole they had dug. Tom told Jim to head out first. But Jim was sure he was doing this so that he would catch the worst.

Jim hesitated and waved Tom forward. Tom peeked out and said the prisoner must emerge or the whole plan would go to dirt. Jim thought that maybe the plan was to get him killed all along, that maybe Tom's true mission was to see himself a killing, something to build a story on. But what choice did Jim have? Even though the boy was just a boy, he could, at any time, yell out to the men and claim Jim had kidnapped him.

Now what should Jim do? What would you do? Would you trust a son of enslavers to tell you when you, an enslaved soul seeking escape, should move? Does he want to see a soul shot? Does he want to see a slave bled? Does he keep a secret desire to witness death in the depths of his heart and in the back of his head? Does he wonder what it would look like to see a bullet crack a skull? Does he wonder what it would smell like when a body sinks from live to null? Does he envision his witness as a story to tell? Does he hope the tweets of birds will carry the message of his witness of life's living hell—a murder?

Jim decided he couldn't choose based upon what Tom wanted. He would choose for himself, and whatever consequence came he would accept it and let it haunt him.

Jim:
Lil' boy,
I don't know what moves you,
but I have children I live for
and 'fore you sacrifice me,
I'd sacrifice you.
So, if you scared of getting shot
and want me to go first,
then nare one of us going out this way
to face a shotgun burst.

Tom:
No Jim.
No sir.
That ain't it at all.
I just want that if anybody gets away scot,
it's you,

And Saul turned Paul was a deep cut, a biblical expression of invitation to faith. We all know the story of how a sinner became a prophet under Jesus' weight. Jim looked at the boy, Tom, and thought to himself, *okay*. You done sealed your fate if you willing to play with the bible on such a consequential day.

Jim went and held his breath in wait for buckshot to cut roughshod through his chest. Huck followed. But there was nothing there but a clear path to the fence. Jim was breathing shallow. He and Huck dashed up and over the fence, and flew like a robin and a sparrow, but Tom's leg got latched on to a splinter and when he ripped it off the splinter broke with a loud crack. That's when the men yelled a warning that they should identify themselves or catch a blast. None of the three said a word and that was all the men needed. They believed the thieves had arrived to reap the theft they had seeded.

Jim and Huck looked back and saw barrels flash. They looked forward and heard blasts. They heard the men running in the thundering of their boots. They knew the dogs were coming ahead to lead the men through.

As the dogs approached, Jim welcomed them, due to the fact that he had coddled them time and again by feeding them odds and ends. The hounds sniffed the three of them, licked their hands as greetings and charged down the path looking for something else on which to unleash their wrath. Jim, Huck, and Tom hid while the men passed, waited until their voices died down and made their way to the canoe to shoot the river to the island where Huck had hid the raft. Good great gracious, Jim's plan had worked as sharp as a tack!

They were gliding now, riding the river easy. A few strokes of the oar and they were in the groove moving freely. That hour slid by as easy as bacon is greasy.

They spotted a good island to camp and as they turned the last oar to set foot on land, Huck turned to Jim, barely able to contain his excitement, he spoke in a roar to him, *Jim you're a free man again! I bet you won't be a slave no more!*

Tom was silent with a smile bent, he winced a bit as if there were something biting him. And just as they thought the waters had parted enough to make room for a laugh, trouble came back like a lightening crack. Tom had a bullet in his calf.

The farmer's shots that they thought had whizzed to a miss had struck Tom's flesh and left it torn and ripped. Tom told them to leave him and go; he'd find his way back. Jim and Huck immediately went to doing the math on that.

Huck:
*It's now
or it ain't Jim.*

Jim:
*We can't leave him.
What if the boy bleeds to death
on this island
on account of us getting in the wind?*

Huck:
*Well then you go
and I'll stay.
I'll go back with Tom
and we can figure out another meeting spot for you to wait.
I'll find a way
to slip away some other day.
And we'll be off
to skiff and skate.*

Jim:
*No. I ain't leaving two children
in such a state.
What kind of man would I be?
I got to make sure the boy get some help
or I won't ever be free.
Not only would I feel like an eel,
but they'll add that to my story.*

They'll say I ran away,
shot the boy,
and left him with a bush for a grave.

Damn life for the ways it plays. It'll leave you locked and loaded in a gun of *this, and ain't no other way* while in the midst of what looks like choice. For the enslaved in a circumstance of trouble, every word is like the thunder clap of God's voice.

Jim:
I got about as much choice
right now
as a blackbird has
in being a thrush.

Huck:
I'll get a doctor, Jim.
I'll rush.

Jim:
We rid the river for an hour.
Huck, what if he dies
while you getting a doctor?
What if he dies alone?
Either his body won't be found
or we will have to bring
it home to the Phelpses.
What do you think they'll say, Huck?

Huck struggled under a few breaths, stunted words really. He kept starting to reply, but couldn't form a thought that didn't sound silly. Jim was right. They'd blame him, and they'd be blame certain to tack that on to his bill—a fugitive slave crazed enough to kill and leave a child for dead. It would double the bounty on his head, and were he caught he wouldn't be sent to Orleans, he'd be hung instead.

Then it dawned on the boy: the only good that would come of Jim going on would be if he left and didn't wait for Huck. Huck almost said he should take his chances on his own, until his voice choked on a thorn. *Then Jim would be gone*, Huck thought. Then Huck remembered the moment he got back to the raft and found that the Joker had sold Jim for a few draughts of draft. Huck remembered how, in the realization that Jim was gone, something inside him cracked.

At the moment he realized Jim had been sold, Huck, a boy who'd seen enough rough and scuffle to crumble the roughest grey-shelled river mussel; Huck, one of the toughest little knuckle heads this side of Duckhead; Huck, when he found out Jim had been sold back into slavery; Huck buckled over in tears. He wailed and ran through the woods screaming Jim's name like the sum of all fears. He crumpled in a pile at the thought of his partner gone for good. After all the rapid wild he had seen on the river, Jim was the one solid piece of driftwood he'd clung too. With him gone, Huck had faced the uncertainty he'd been flung too, and it left him the scared little boy he was.

That whole moment came back to Huck in a rush and he held his tongue as his mind looked for rational reasons Jim should stay to help Tom rather than get on the run. The boy had long since decided that conscience wasn't a reason, because things you did in conscience for one, for another would constitute treason. Like helping Jim get free, which was certainly a good thing as sure as a thing could be good, was a sin to Ms. Watson and everything for which she stood. Like faking his death, the only way to escape the fate of Pap beating his back to a filet, caused a great deal of trouble for everyone in the town who now thought a child murderer might be lurking around. Conscience was a weak motivation for a thinking boy, who could think of all the sides of a situation, who could see every angle to a ploy.

So he looked for logic and Jim's logic was the only solid play. He had to stay. If he left, his chances of success would be frail. Even then he'd need a whole pond's worth of toad croaks of luck to find his way back north with every dirty duck hungry for a buck hot on his trail. *Jim was right again*, Huck reasoned. He should stay. And this was mighty fine with Huck since it meant that he and Jim could be together another day.

Jim interrupted Huck's thought with a reminder of the urgency. He spoke with a hardened certainty, like a father to his son. His tone left no flexibility, the color of his voice didn't run.

Jim (*with command*):
Go get the doctor,
and I'll hide in the bush.
I'll wait till the doctor gets back,
Then I'll push.

Huck (*disappointed, but compliant*):
Oh.
Yes. I'll do that.
But will you stay on the island
'till day?
That way I can slip away from the farm
and we can get back on our way.

Jim didn't answer, just nodded and looked away. He could tell the boy meant 'our' when he said it, and he didn't want to sour the boy's hopes for a companion, but wasn't no way Jim, in the hour of moment, wouldn't leave Huck abandoned if he had to. As much as he had come to appreciate the boy's help, and his heart, and his basic goodness and his smarts, and his humor and his quiet, he would walk away from Huck if that's what it took to get to the other side. It just so happened that Huck was his best play so far, and that staying with Tom shot was the next best play, so stay with Tom and Huck he would, for the night, but he couldn't promise a thing about the next day.

Go now, Jim spoke with the coke of the force he'd already thrown, and Huck hopped to it and got gone.

Ch. 25

Jim Comes to a Crucible

More weight.

-Arthur Miller
The Crucible

****

While Huck was gone, Jim had that time again, that time to think. And he began to waver on the brink. Tom had been an evil little heathen as long as Jim had known him. And who knew, with a bullet in his body, what the boy would say. In the pain and embarrassment of having done something so dumb, he might figure that he should save face. Jim had known White people to blame a slave for their own guilt, and claim they'd been persecuted when one tells them the truth of what they done did. In a puddle of milk that they spilt, they'd be quick to wilt. They had a masterful skill at claiming victim when it came time to sleep in the bed they done built.

But then, Jim thought, Huck wasn't like that at all. Huck stood tall above all the low down hypocrite, scapegoating bigots, claiming righteous ground while acting wicked, heartless child-selling, wife-raping, degenerate White men, whose spines—in rough times—shook with rickets. Huck was different.

And as much as Jim tried to harden his heart to Tom, who showed all the signs of Whiteness at its worst, Huck had gotten this boy on board with getting him free. So somewhere in the little bastard there was something worth a rusty penny. Huck had made something out and clear. The little fool continued to risk his life for him, to commit what was, for White men, an unforgivable sin. It is because he knew him, Jim reasoned, because Huck knew his heart. Huck knew that he was smart and that his sense was sharp. He knew Jim had thoughts and considerations, Huck knew of his wife and child. He knew that Jim was no domesticated beast, but a man, like he hoped to be, born to be free to wild.

Then Jim, dwelled on his father, the wildest man he'd ever heard about, who'd strut like a stallion without a doubt, who didn't live long enough to raise his own son, but lived full enough to leave a story for generations to come. Jim thought of his father and thought, *he had one thing right even as he had a lot of things wrong:* a man must be a man, must live out his choices and their consequences, like a bird must sing its song. Even though the cat hears the trill and whistle, and uses it to track the bird as prey, the bird sings, as if there were no danger, all day. The bird flies till it dies, and that's what Jim's father did, and that's what he had right.

So Jim was clear. He would be a man to every end, even the tragic. For what good is freedom if you have to trade the joy of living right in order to have it. Despite all that enslavers had inflicted to try to break Jim—to rape his courage, to drain his hope, to poison his thoughts with self-hatred, to rob him of his labor's profit and then claim him lazy, then name him 'slave' to frame his life as debased, inherently, along with all his progeny to the last generation—despite all that White slavery done to try to curse him with perpetual degradation, despite all that, Jim had kept himself a man. And it is upon his own judgment that a man stands. And Jim judged that a man would never leave a boy to bleed to death no matter the circumstance.

It was set, and Huck was getting the doctor. Jim would stay with Tom and wait until it was certain Tom would be cared for. And that was that.

But then Tom, in his delirium, was babbling on about being a legend for having '*saved a slave free*' and being so good that Jim, the slave, stayed '*so faithfully.*' He mumbled that Jim '*was a good boy*' who knew how to '*behave gratefully.*' Tom pondered that Jim would probably '*stay with me for life*' even when he was free. Then Jim would '*raise his children to be faithful too,*' Tom dreamed, and all Tom's children would have Jim's as slaves '*for all their days to rise atop like cream or morning dew.*'

Hearing all this, Jim rubbed his fist as doubt came rushing back. He knew this boy Tom could never appreciate Jim's choice to sacrifice for the skin on his back. White men like him could never see a Black man for his worth, since to them Jim's skin was a God-given curse. They believed Jim's kind and kin were given to them as burden and purse. To them, dark skin meant a person was dim. And to them a dimwit was bound to bow down to those greater than him.

So that's it, thought Jim. *That's why he did it.* As sport and pleasure to test his mettle, Tom meddled in Jim's journey to freedom as if it would earn him a metal, as if his role in Jim's transition were a trophy he could mount and revel in, as if his reward would be to get the submission of Jim and all his kin. If that was all Jim was reduced to, even to a White boy offering help, what could possibly come of Jim sacrificing himself? So his own children could suffer fatherless, so his own wife would be left behind, so the potential of their freedom could curdle and lay curled and sour, dry as lemon rind?

Jim was back in the world of why as in why should he risk his life? Why should he stay here and watch over Tom as if that would somehow be right? Why shouldn't he leave this boy to die and relieve the world of one more slave master? Why should he give this boy his life as a gift when he will grow up to wield a whip and leave half-Black bastards? Why not save some Black man from lashes, save a Black woman from rape, save a Black child from being shrunken by hate? Why save this White boy? Don't nits breed lice? If you lay with snakes, don't snakes bite? Don't one and one always equal two? Why give slavery another White man to spoil and rot from the evil he is bound to do?

Jim began to back away from Tom with the intent to leave, just as he heard the sound of someone coming through the leaves. It was the doctor, and he was without Huck. Jim jumped into the bush. His heart sank into his belly, he had missed his chance to push.

The doctor was an old man with a kindly face, but Jim couldn't mistake his Whiteness for what it was, more leverage to levy against him in any discussion about the trouble and its cause. Chances were that every ounce of it would be laid on his back and would be counted out in strikes of the lash. This was as good as fact, so Jim stayed back.

He watched the doctor work Tom from a distance as the injury got worse something relentless. Tom was even more out of his mind, and Jim was sure enough that Tom would mention a runaway slave was sitting out in the rough. He decided to stay close and wait to know for certain whether Tom had given him up. But Tom didn't, and Jim wondered if the boy was just that committed to the escape that he would suffer so and still keep everything in place. Or maybe he'd forgotten Jim altogether, so lost in the pain's full measure.

The doctor for his part worked hard. Tying Tom's limb and digging under his skin to try to fish out the scattered shattered bullet parts. Tom's cries were clawing, gnawing at Jim's bile. Jim had heard pain before, but coming from a child it was always hard. There's something pure and raw about the bleat of a hurt kid that stirs something deep in anyone who hears it. Jim was moved by each yelp, by each grunt and moan, by every whine from hell. Jim was moved to stay still even after it was clear that Tom had long forgotten him and wouldn't tell. Even with the doctor too occupied with Tom's fate to hear a hint of Jim slipping away, Jim couldn't push his will to get on with the escape.

Time passed so slow as Tom's pain refused retreat. The doctor's worry increased until he began to entreat to the sky, to the earth, to the animals, to anything that could hear him, for some help, any help to save this boy from the terminal pain that seared him. Jim heard the sorrow in his call and felt the greatest stirring of his will since the beginning of the whole ordeal. He wanted badly to step out and help, but better sense kept him from following what he felt.

But then Jim started calculating a rationalization. Maybe if he helped, the doctor would speak up for him. Maybe when the time came for things to get rough for him, Jim's act of help would be enough for them to reconsider his death sentence. Maybe the relentlessness of slavery and the White man's code, would be bent in deference to the doctor's story once told. Maybe his help would actually save Tom's life, and all those people that love Tom would thank Jim for his life.

It would be better no doubt to help than it would be to run and as he had discovered, better is the best thing a man could ever hope to be, and despite being on the edge of freedom, Jim knew then that he would never be free. Tom would haunt him if he ran. Huck would haunt him too. That's two more children beyond his own, and those are two seeds he would rather leave unsewn.

Slowly he stepped from the shadows. His feet moved before he was ready, but once he was in full view of the doctor, he knew he had to speak.

I will help you, said Jim unsure of what else he could say. The doctor thought about the way he just appeared and must have known he was the runaway the whole countryside had been talking bout since the other day, but he also couldn't find words to say. So he told Jim what to do and Jim dove in, giving as much help as he could possibly offer him.

The work went long, but Jim was faithful about it, and before long, Tom got better no doubt about it. The doctor thanked him, but never let on whether he'd concluded him a runaway.

Jim figured that at the right opportunity he'd fly. He was dead tired, but the doctor worried him in his quiet. The doctor didn't ask questions. The doctor didn't make comment. The doctor would just work on Tom, then wait, work on Tom, then wait. He wouldn't even glance at Jim to indicate that he was glad for Jim's aid. Yes, Jim could see he would need to get gone shortly.

But at some point, Jim, awake for the better part of two days, needed rest for his eyes and bowed his head on his knees. Against every effort to keep himself in the waking world, he fell himself to sleep, with his head on his knees, and dreamed. He dreamed of himself on some sort of beach, like the sort he had heard of at the end of the West where the sun plunged into the ocean for its nightly death.

Jim was on a long trek, a walk through those same massive trees so tall that they wore the clouds like a shroud around their leaves. Those same trees from an earlier dream that at their base were reddish, the color of cinnamon, and they were so wide that a carriage could fit through a hole in one of them. The earth was soft, covered in moss, things were quiet as a flea's cough. Jim was sitting by that same stream from his earlier dream watching water-spiders skeet across. The water itself was air clear, so shear at the surface that it sheared the light into colors and made rainbows ripple in circles.

Jim turned to a fern, that same fern from his dream before, and looked closely at its structure and immediately the green of its leaves began to rupture. Jim's sight was sucked down into its veins. He could see its cells, little rectangular bricks busy with business. He zoomed in further and couldn't believe his witness. Each cell was a city unto itself. Each city was full of beings living and working in its miniscule dwelling. Each being was as full a creature as Jim himself.

A feeling of great and enormous power in Jim began to swell. He felt as big as all life itself. It was a warm bigness, as if the sun was included in it. It was a limitlessness, as though freedom couldn't even contain it. Jim, in his dream, was raining tears at this feeling of perfect, whole, complete peace. He thought, *this must be the life God leads.*

Jim looked again at the water and it was bright as light itself, and smelted smooth as a diamond at its surface, and as soft as if the diamond had melted. Jim leaned and fell face forward in with no intention, nor any need to swim. He began to take water in, which constricted a bit in his neck, and, as the discomfort settled in, he stirred awake to find his fate had once again been reset.

Jim opened his eyes and there stood a White man with his hands on a rope and that rope strung around Jim's neck.

There was no need to struggle at this point. Nothing could be gained from resisting arrest. Jim was caught and whatever were to come next, he was returning to slavery, life or death.

Ch. 26

How Jim Became Free

The whole world—a show,
we all—earth props,
and when ends means end
we reap dust
and loved ones' tear drops.
In that dust—the seed's cradle,
the earth turns just
as the seed pops
and life thrusts.

****

There was nothing new on the walk back to the Phelpses. It was the same walk that brought him there from the first. It was full of the dread that hangs in an enslaved head, the dust that rusts in his thirst. Except that, while Jim's wrists were bound, his feet were free. This gave him just enough of an ability to move any direction he might need.

The patter-rollers and catchers had rested their guns against the Phelps's porch. Clearly they intended to do violence hand to hand. As he approached the big house, the White men began to put on their show, to show the slaves of the Phelps plantation what they surely already did know. Runaways get the savage-full fury of the White man.

But, Jim was no longer a runaway. Inside he felt free, despite the ropes that had him restrained. Something in him had changed. He had helped to save Tom's life. He had sacrificed his chance to get free. A feeling bubbled up from Jim's gut. If these White men couldn't respect that Jim had acted in peace to save one of their sons, maybe they would respect getting their asses beat one by one.

If one tries to take an inch of me, I'll give him a foot, Jim thought and the thought visibly furrowed in his brow. It was clear in his direct eye-contact searching the hearts of the whole crowd. A couple of the White men winced at the sight of it. A couple became enraged with fear. One patter-roller approached Jim from the rear. Jim heard his feet sliding with apprehension. He wasn't charging in, which gave Jim time to make his decision.

The catcher swung and Jim kind of felt it come and so slipped him quickly. He pivoted his foot to turn and blasted him with a shoulder followed by the full weight of his body. The catcher tumbled far and hard. He cracked his back against a fence with the crash of a runaway horse cart.

Jim heard Mrs. Phelps gasp. That was the shoulder she had rubbed and pawed. Several men backed up with slack jaws.

Another catcher stepped forward and Jim didn't wait for him to throw, Jim charged him and hooked his bound wrists around the back of the catcher's neck and slung him in what made a wild show. The catcher's limbs went to flailing like he was a rag doll. The man was crumpled as he rolled several yards like a human ball.

No one else stepped up in attempt to subdue Jim at the risk of a very public failing. These catchers had reputations to protect and none dared expose a truth they all surely knew: without guns and a deputy's back up, they'd be dusted from hat to boots. Yet, as you might expect they'd moved to retrieve their guns to shoot. They flung cusses and howls. That's when a blood curdling yell tore through, wild and loud.

> Tom (*screaming franticly*):
> *NO!*
> *Stop!*
> *Jim's free!*
> *I busted him loose because he's free!*
> *I got the letter here with me!*

Jim heard Tom, but didn't pay him much mind. He figured the boy had gone mad with pain. The catchers probably figured the same since, on Jim, they kept their guns trained. The Doctor who he'd helped to save Tom then yelled, his voice at first strained, before calming himself to be heard clear as rain.

> Doctor (*making a plea*):
> *PLEASE!*
> *Don't be no harder on him*
> *than you have to be.*
> *He was a most true ally*
> *a man'll ever see.*
> *He helped me save this boy's life.*
> *And despite the fact he ran away,*
> *he stayed through the night*

and held the boy
and helped the boy
and done what was right.
Now I know he done roughed a couple of you up.
But that just shows that he could have done it to me.
Instead he stayed and helped.
Lord, have mercy.

Mrs. Phelps then ran toward Jim in a rush. She wrapped her arms around his shoulder in a gentle touch.

Mrs. Phelps (*pleading*):
Praise God, we saved him!
We brought him to Christ!
I prayed over him and
shown him the light!

Mr. Phelps eyed the way his wife was pawing Jim with a bit of consternation, but he had also pet Jim with prayer and commenced to make a statement.

Mr. Phelps (*somewhat quietly*):
What she means is that I prayed over him
and Christ must have possessed him to stay,
and because he stayed
my nephew Tom was saved.

Then Huck spoke up and left the whole lot of them broke up. He choked up as he started, then he came to steady, and the words he spoke left everyone who heard them believing. All this time Jim was unsure of Huck for good reason. But now the boy's wisdom had come into season.

Huck (*haltingly, till his momentum come*):
I ain't who you think I am.
From my Pap, I done run.
He beat me vicious every day,

332

and I could have kept taking it,
but I made a decision.

I pretended to be kilt,
and they blamed it on Jim.
And that's just as backward as a night sun,
because if there's a reason I'm alive.
Jim ain't the one.

See I made a choice to run.
I figured I'd be better off on my own
than to keep getting beat to my red meat,
and bruised to my white bone.
But some of the things I seen on the run
left me scareder than a pup.
I seen a friend my own age, Buck,
snuffed… all shot up.
I seen crooks thieving whole towns,
stealing girls' girlhood and such.
I seen a man blast dead a harmless drunk.
I probably seen too much.
Probably seen too much.

But through all the danger,
one thing kept me safe and hopeful,
at least safe in my mind
and hopeful in my heart you see,
even when the raft was smashed,
even when Tom got shot,
the one thing what kept me
was Jim.

But Jim ain't a thing—
some thing to own.
I know that now.
I seen Jim tossing you men in the wind,
after he was as gentle with me as any man been.

I see it clear now.
Jim is a man.
He has children.
Them children have a maw,
Jim's wife.
And he has the most goodness
I ever seen a man have in my life.
His children need their father.
His woman need her man.
He's got to live.

Huck walked over and stood in front of Jim and took a breath to speak. *If you shoot him, you have to shoot through me.*

Jim's heart broke open and he sucked up a tear, quietly.

The White men's sentiment changed and softened. They lowered their aims. Yet Jim was still a prisoner again. So they let him walk of his own will back to the shack, but this time no White man would get close enough to try to put him in chains. Bread and water is all they gave him, but they did call him by his name instead of cussing him something untame.

Jim sat in the dark that night and prayed to dream again, to taste that stream again, to see those magnificent trees, to be that free even in his imagination. But the dream never came. Instead he was weighed down with his situation something so blue. For all the effort he'd made to escape, his life was to remain the same. From all he came from and all he came through, this—back to slavery—is where it all came to.

Jim (*to himself with a grunting moan*):
Ashes ain't ashes,
unless there's something to burn.
Dust must have something to cling to.
A womb ain't a womb till it bears a life,
and a tomb is just a room without a view.

A man ain't nothing but a man.
Blues ain't nothing but a song.

334

From cradle to grave we crawl to fall,
wailing the whole way long.

Trouble tends to double every day,
then treble under the moon.
Worship or work, sleep or wake,
one day all breath will swoon.

A man ain't nothing but a man.
Blues ain't nothing but a song.
From cradle to grave we crawl to fall,
wailing the whole way long.

I'll die enslaved if I must.
I'll die a man either way.
I'll die and that's all I know for sure,
but I'll die a man that day.

A man ain't nothing but a man.
Blues ain't nothing but a song.
From cradle to grave we crawl to fall,
wailing the whole way long.

Jim awoke from his dreamless sleep with no interest in the
day. There wasn't any reason to look forward, nor back. There
wasn't a thing to say. There was only the dirt floor under his
feet, the boarded window at his back. There was only thought
weighing him down. There was only this, and that was that.

But the door soon opened to let in light and something
in him jumped up as if it were Huck, but it wasn't. It was just
one of the slave-trading men. Jim swallowed his hope and
didn't give the trader an inch of his attention or a moment of
his trust. The trader came over and Jim was ready, ready to
return any blow. He was turning over in his mind whether he
was ready to go. He could end it all now and get it over with
by beating the man's face to a pulp of crimson gore. Then, no

matter how slow they tortured him, once he was dead suffering would be no more.

But, to his surprise, the man stood to the side and said for him to get up. Jim looked up at his captor in no particular rush. Whatever evil the man was lusting for could wait till ashes turned dust. Then the man said something that didn't make sense to Jim, so he asked him to say it again, and he did. Jim was clearer on what was said, but still not sure what to say, so he kind of stood up and took a step and got ready to see his last day.

Jim thought that this must be one of those things he's heard about. They wanted a reason to shoot him so as not to pay his owner, and so would let Jim run out. Yet, Jim wasn't running from a damned thing. If the cowards wanted to shoot him in the back, they could. He was going to walk away like a man, goddamn them all where they stood.

Jim laughed a bit of a huff, and walked out ready to die, and, right at that moment, the sight of Huck startled his eyes. Jim looked for a while and squinted a bit. Then he cracked a half of a smile, the half of his mouth bunched behind a bit lip. Huck was wearing a smile so wide that it seemed as if he was crazed. After all they had been through together, Jim wondered, what could bring him to smile on this day?

Then Silas and Sally Phelps walked up and placed money in Jim's hand. Jim kept his eyes on Huck. Jim thought, *is all this necessary to make it look like I ran? Is Huck a part of all this truck?* But then Jim thought of Tom and his convoluted plan.

> Jim (*thinking*):
> *This must be what White men do*
> *to make themselves feel better*
> *when they do things*
> *for which they know they'll be damned.*
> *Pretense.*
> *They must pretense some reason*
> *that justifies their daily, lifetime treason*
> *against their fellow man.*

336

Jim took the money, money he wished he would have time to spend, and he enjoyed the feel of it in his palm. The momentary feeling of luck was just enough of a balm. But then they led Jim to a table and offered him some food. And once again Jim was as confounded as he was confused.

They told him he had no work to do, no more chains to wear. He said he wanted to take a walk through the woods, they said he could walk anywhere. He tried to give back the money, they said that it was his. And for a brief moment Jim thought he might still be asleep, because there was no explanation for this.

But then it came, the news that explained what was happening. Though Jim found it hard to believe at first, it became clear—the reason for his unshackling. Jim was free. You heard me? Jim was FREE!

Jim was free and had been all along. Ms. Watson had willed it so. She had died ashamed of herself for selling Jim so far away from home.

Jim was free and had been all along.

How was HE supposed to register this? How would this come to sense? All the harrowing turns of his journey should never have been? All the risks, all the trouble, all the rough for Huck and him, it all was just unnecessary adventure, a bunch of shuck and jiving.

Now, how would you take such news—that you had been free the whole time you were risking death to get free? Would you feel gratitude or relief? Would you feel rage for all the dealing with trouble you had to waste in order to be what you were born to be.

Jim was free and been all along? Jim was free to work for himself? He was free to save up his money to buy his family from his own wealth? He was free to go West, where there wasn't slavery? He was free to live by the want of his will or by the whim of his fancy? What now, Jim was not sure. But the thought jumped up that he had something to discuss with Huck to keep his mind and heart pure.

Jim talked to Huck of luck and laughed out a bold '*told ya so*' as an entry point to a tough story that had to be told. Huck was thinking there wasn't a thing for him to go back for, thinking that Pap had taken all Huck's $6000 and would be drinking it until both of them were again dirt poor. But Jim told Huck what he knew, *your Pap's dead Huck. It was him in that body we found in that half-sunk house way back. You as free as old Jim to do what you want to do.* Jim felt warmed by the thought that Huck was forever through with Pap's abuse.

Jim told Huck he kept it from him to save him a horror no boy should see, having to see his father reduced to decrepit half-fleshed dead body. No matter how bad his Pap had been, he was still his blood. And Jim said he thought it better that Huck live without an image so rough.

Of course that was only part of the story, though it was a part true. But Jim had also kept Pap's death from Huck to keep Huck's help in getting through. But Huck didn't need that part of the story, not at fourteen years old. He didn't want to confuse the boy with thinking that he'd been used. If he ever met Huck as a man, maybe he could handle the full story true, since by then he'd understand that a man's got to do what a man's got to do.

And Huck, to Jim's surprise, still had no intention of going back, even with $6000 dollars sitting in his lap. He asked Jim if they could stay a team and head out west to run from "civilization" and slavery. Jim laughed at that, hard as he might ever have. And told the boy don't be a fool, that he must go back.

There were private moments between the two friends, but this bit of it can be shared. For it was such a tender touch Jim took so that Huck's heart could be spared.

> Jim (*with the weight of last words*):
> *We don't need to know what luck comes next.*
> *The best is always yet to be.*
> *The worst too.*

Jim drew an X in the dirt with the toe of his shoe and continued.

> Jim (*with preacher's soul*):
> *Life spills river to sea*
> *and always offers something new.*
> *It cuts left and cuts right*
> *and rolls ever down.*
> *It rips deep*
> *and slips free*
> *and floods whole towns.*
> *Rich, poor, and all life,*
> *will rise and fall*
> *and from a first crawl till a funeral pall*
> *life will never pause nor stall.*
> *For some she comes young*
> *to snatch the sapling before it bears one plum.*
> *For others she wait for their backs to bend,*
> *'till the winds crack their skin*
> *and drains their color grey.*
> *But life,*
> *she come for what's hers either way.*
> *They say death is an angel and a mystery.*
> *I say death is life in disguise*
> *making space for more life to be.*
> *And that's you and me, Huck.*
> *We history.*

Jim kept his eyes wide to dry as they got a bit misty.

> Jim (*with fatherly feeling*)
> *Time'll move on past anything,*
> *anything we could dream,*
> *past anything we could believe,*
> *past anything we ever seen.*

At this Jim looked above Huck's head and thought about what he'd just said.

> Jim (*with brotherly love*)
> *Time will move on*
> *to where we could be brothers,*
> *and when that time comes*
> *we'll be bound one to the other.*
> *We'll be the warm*
> *in the breath of the storyteller's word*
> *and in the light*
> *that makes a shadow*
> *of the listeners who heard.*
> *We'll be the truth,*
> *whether told or hid.*
> *And life will carry on*
> *with all that we did.*

At that, Jim stopped and the moment was washed with silence.

Jim? Huck called, with a bit of a hesitance.

Yes, Huck?

And there was silence again. The same silence they had carried since they'd cried together over Jim's children. The silence welled up in them till Huck leaked a bit of his longing into the moment.

> Huck (*hopeful, with a bit of pleading*):
> *Jim, we could just head West as a team.*
> *We could go to where there ain't no slaves,*
> *ain't no civilization,*
> *no Jokers, Jacks, or Toms.*
> *You know what I mean?*

Huck hoped he did so he could stop talking, and him and Jim could just get to walking to the raft. Jim felt his anxiousness and laughed.

Jim (*with a teacher's touch*):
No, Huck.
Civilization is everywhere,
and slavery is too.
Civilization is built on slaves,
and slaves have been
since men lived in caves.
You'll grow up
and know what I mean one day.

Jim was a little haughty with this last word and Huck
was unconvinced. He spoke again with more than a little
insistence. *No, Jim. We could be a team. Us and snuff the world, Jim.*
You and me.

And there it was. Huck's half of the silence broken.
The quiet thing Huck had been all along hoping: that Jim—the
closest thing to real love he'd ever known, and the best
example of love that a man could offer—that Jim might stay
with him and take the place of Huck's father.

Jim, knowing Huck would make a good son, knowing
that he had basically become one, that they were a team
through all the rush of the river and the risk of the shore;
knowing what Huck was asking and sure that there would be
some joy if their adventures endured; Jim knew he had to shut
the door on any of these child-like hopes that gave poor Huck
some false comfort. No. They couldn't be father and son or
brothers, or teacher and student or travelling friends. No.
Huck and Jim's time had come to an end, and Jim brought a
sense of seriousness to counter Huck's hope and imagination.

Jim (*with a coach's firm tone*):
Huck, I am not a boy.
I'm done with games.
I got a life to build.
I don't even have a name.
Nothing to pass to my children.

341

Nothing to carve into to stone.
When life come to death me gone
to make room for some other one.
Huck, I don't even have a name.

    Your name is Jim, Huck said and saying it sounded as ridiculous as it is. Jim knew he had a name. Yet, even though Huck was perplexed by how he was sensing it, the sense that Jim was saying something different came, something clear and important and different that made sense and explained the whole impossibility of them being family.
    Your name is Jim! Huck shouted as his eyes welled up. Jim, a bit angry at the boy for not understanding, swelled up.

Jim (*with a wronged father's fury*)
Jim what, Huck?!
You are Huckleberry Finn.
If you had children
that name lives on with them.
And six thousand goes
where that name goes.
If I ever get enough luck to save a buck,
how will any bank ever know me
from any old Jim Crow?
I need a name so I can pass my work
down my family tree.
Without that, what am I but a passing breeze?

Huck (*sounding more like a child*
than he ever had):
You more than a breeze to me, Jim.
You more than a brother or a friend.
I don't know what to call it,
but I think of you like kin, Jim.

    Huck was about ready to cry now as Jim steadied himself with a smile.

Jim (*with a clown's comforting*):
Huckleberry Finn,
if we kin,
then day and night is the same.
Ha! Us kin?
Then I'd have Finn as a name.
And that name ain't even yours.
That belongs to your Pap
whether you want it or not.
Ha! We kin?
Jim and Huckleberry Finn?

Jim smiled wider in pause for the sound of that together. Huck noticed the change in his smile.

Huck (*confused*):
What is it Jim?

Jim (*enthused*):
Jim and Huckleberry.

Huck (*still confused*):
Yep, me and you Jim. What is it?

Jim (*more enthused*):
Jim Huckleberry.
Got a nice ring, I think.
Jim Huckleberry.
Jim, the man for the job.
Jim, the man you looking for.

Maybe, I'll just make it Jim Huck.[66]

Jim was really smiling now.

What you keep saying my name for, Jim? Huck was as lost as a half-wit cow.

My name. It's my name now, Jim brandished a brilliant smile.

How? Jim what you talking 'bout?

> Jim (*with the joy of child*):
> *Huck you can find me now.*
> *Go West.*
> *Go grow.*
> *Go see what you can be.*
> *And if you ever want to know*
> *what came of me,*
> *say your name*
> *and there I'll be*
> *with some luck.*
> *Jim, as always,*
> *but now, Jim Huck.*

Jim Huck? Huck was starting to get it.
Jim Huck. Jim said with a lifted spirit.

> Huck (*with pride*):
> *Yes, that name has a ring Jim.*
> *It has a ring indeed.*

---

[66] A huckleberry is an edible fruit which is tart when lighter colored (red) and sweeter when darker colored (blue or purple). According to the online Urban Dictionary, the Historical Dictionary of American Slang asserts that, in the 1800s, the phrase "I'm your Huckleberry" meant "I'm the man for the job." Since language is arbitrary and ultimately malleable to the needs of communication, since the purpose of language is to transmit meaning, Jim is going to make "Huckleberry" do what it will do—it will be a new root.

And that will be the name
of your children, too?
They'll be named after me? Shoot!

I reckon so, Huck, Jim replied with a little bit of hesitancy.
Jim wouldn't want his kids named for another man. But since
Huck was actually the name of a boy, and since Jim was
choosing it, it felt a bit better than a brand.

Huck:
Well damn if that ain't luck for me.
I'll never have to have any heathens of my own
to have my name carry.
That's the best thing you could have done for me.
Now you done set me free.
Now I can go on and go
and I'll always know
that what I've been
will continue to be
with the children of
Jim Huckleberry.

And it sounds too mature for Huck to have said, but
trust that it is what he meant.
The free children of Jim Huck, Jim corrected him.
May the children of Jim Huck forever be free, Huck said with
his head lifted in determined sincerity.
May the children of Jim Huck forever be free, Jim agreed.
Forever free. Huck said it as if it were a blood swear.
Forever free. Jim repeated it as if it were a life's purpose.
One thing though, Huck, Jim started.
Anything Jim, Huck replied, wide open-hearted.
How do you write it? Jim laughed and Huck laughed back.
Jim pulled from his pocket the quill he'd bought way
back and said, *write it for me, Huck.*
Huck found a scrap from his own pocket and wrote it
down. He handed it to Jim.

Look like chicken scratch to me, Jim frowned and stuck it in his pocket.

One day it'll be chicken scratch you can read, Huck smiled from eye socket to eye socket.

And write, Jim said with a chuckle.

Huck looked proud happy, pushed his shoulders back, handed Jim his quill back, and adjusted his belt buckle.

And with that and a laugh they shook hands and hugged a little, and turned backs to solve their two parts of the same riddle in their two faces of the same wind. But Jim turned back, slightly pained from having let Huck loose and with a slight pride in having the freedom to choose. He handed the quill back to the boy.

> Jim (*with the hope of the formerly enslaved*):
> *Take this, Huck.*
> *Write about us.*
> *Tell the truth of two friends.*
> *And I will take my remembering*
> *and tell it 'till my end*
> *for it to pass down through my kin.*

Jim handed him the old quill he had bought off an enslaved man among the provisions he'd made for returning to the river. It was a tool for writing, which was something Jim always wished he could do. Huck took it and looked down at it. He laughed at how ancient it was, this silly gift. His laugh settled into a smile. His smile faded a bit. Huck didn't want to look up, knowing Jim was already on his way, gone on to a new day. And when Huck did look up, that fact is exactly what hung round his face.

Jim, for his part, still thought he was dreaming. As he looked forward into the distance—Huck behind him—over the tops of the trees, towards far away clouds, over the sinking sun, his mind leaned him forward toward what was to come: Freedom.

His first thought as a free man was this: *I need a gun.*

346

THE END

A word

All through school, my last name—Huckleberry—felt like a stain. I mean Huck does rhyme with **** and berry rhymes with fairy. It is what it is. You can't really blame kids for being kids. Back then, I felt my father was to blame.

My father could have changed the name to something rugged, like King or Douglass. He could have coached me on how to roll with it or maybe taught me how to throw a fist. He could have encouraged me to ignore the bastards or return the ribbing with quick wits. But he couldn't do any of that from prison. By the time I turned sixteen, I felt like "forget that man's dumb name and forget him."

But my Big Mama, rest in peace, told me the story of this strange name, Huckleberry, when I asked for consent to erase my father. I didn't want his name anymore. Instead, I wanted hers. *She* raised me and *he* gave me nothing. Her lips pursed.

"He gave you your life, dodo bird. And that name."

Needless to say, permission to change my last name was not granted. But Big Mama, being who she was—a tree planted by the water, the flesh and bone of love, and a master-teacher-storyteller preacher's daughter—she didn't just tell me no on the spot. She told me a long story of why not.

What follows is that story.

But before I tell it, a bit of context may serve notice as explanatory[67].

Mark Twain once wrote, "there is no age at which the good name of a member of a family ceases to be... an asset, and worth more than all its bonds and moneys."[68] In America, a land built on the theology of meritocracy over genealogy, a name and the story attached to it is a legacy, a kingdom, a crown. And in America, the same holds for the burden of a name of bad renown.

My father's great, great-grandfathers and their grandfathers were enslaved, and the story of their names is the story of the plantations where they were degraded and chained. Thus, their legacies seem to be kingdoms of scorn under crowns of thorns. For the millions like me who descend from the American enslaved, all we seem to have gotten from our ancestors is a skin everyone seems to hate and the mystery of why our people seemed to accept being enslaved as a centuries-long fate. Thank God things are not always what they seem.

Big Mama told a different story about slavery. In her story, the enslaved were heroes who endured so that we might be. And their resilience in the face of violent oppression is what makes us, their progeny, so mighty. And her story has weight today. It could be a root in a world untethered and

---

[67] *Adventures of Huckleberry Finn* begins with an ironic "notice" that 'anyone looking for motive, moral, or plot, would be prosecuted, banished, or shot.' Those were the consequences of challenging white supremacy in Mark Twain's day. Twain also offered an "explanatory" that the dialects that his characters speak, most notably "the Missouri negro dialect", have been crafted "painstakingly, and with the trustworthy guidance and support of personal familiarity." Clearly, tongue in cheek (Twain is the same person who wrote "I am not one of those who in expressing opinions confine themselves to facts"), Twain seems to admit his own biases ironically. Today, I offer that my "context may serve notice as explanatory" as a nod to Twain and my context and biases. I write this book as a descendant of the enslaved and that is the point— now that you've purchased this book (thank you very much!), if you want to skip the trouble of reading it, the moral is such: The journey is the means and the end.

[68] Twain, Mark. "Why Not Abolish It?" *Mark Twain Collected Non-Fiction,* Volume I. Knopf, Everyman's Library, p. 801, 2016.

loose. A new history such as this might let us off the noose that the long rope of nostalgic amnesia has tangled itself into.

To tell the truth, this story might have been half made-up. Still, it was a root of hope in my family. It was a trunk from which we could branch. It was a perch on which we could stand free. I will share it with you as it was shared with me.

Big Mama told the whole story in rhyme. It has a flow that reflects the human impulse to align, that celebrates life's infinite between—the energy that moves in, through, and around everything. Big Mama not only knew this cosmic wisdom, she applied it religiously. And I believe this is why she told the story in rhyme and beat—to bind form and function, to set meaning free *between* any illusion of binaries like pride vs. shame, good vs. evil, slave vs. free. And she told the story in rhyme, most importantly, to sear it to my memory.

And so I'll share her story, our story, with you now, partly out of hope and partly out of fear—hope for a future cleared of the shackles of the past and fear of the way we seemed to have forgotten what got us here, forgotten how this raft we call America has weathered currents of change, and the balance it took to make some sense of a history so strange. After all, only one ultimate truth remains no matter the trouble or the rubble left behind; if we are to move forward, we must move forward in some form, for some function, and forever together.

To create our destiny, we must face our origin story. The future demands that we understand the past. And it is in this mold that *Jim Huckleberry* is cast.

Ase',

Marcus James Huckleberry, III

350

Afterword

By Samuel Sawyer Finn

I promise I'm different from other White people. Most have their privileges and immunities, but I have the crumpled humilities of a self-aware writer of trash. And that is why I was the perfect White person to receive a letter from Mr. Marcus James Huckleberry, III.

For most White people, feeling superior to Black people is like gravity. We don't think about how it holds us every moment of our lives. We might even design machinations to overcome it while walking upright because of it. We use it to erect everything from ivory towers to prisons. White supremacy is our inertia.

For most White people, the ultimate proof of our superiority is 400 years of slavery. How could we possibly enslave people for that long unless we are smarter, stronger, and more determined? Our dirty little secret is that every Black complaint of racism only feeds our certainty of superiority; if you had any choice in the matter, then you wouldn't let us keep doing this to you. Most White people think like this.

But thank goodness I'm not like most White people or I would have probably missed the brilliance of *Jim Huckleberry*.

When I received a letter from a man named Marcus, my first thought was that this must be some low production scam.

We've all seen the emails from that African prince in Nigeria asking for a bank account number so he can transfer his treasure somewhere safe. But, this was a genuine US Post mailed letter bearing a strange and familiar name: Huckleberry.

I hadn't thought much about my great-great-great grandfather Huckleberry Finn since I'd seen the novel he wrote about his childhood in the South before heading out West. I say I'd *seen* Finn's book because I never actually read it. Once, I cracked it and numbly thumbed through a chapter about some thieves scheming to hustle an entire town. From what I could tell, the book had no moral and no plot, and I had no motivation to keep reading it. I probably had the last remaining copy on earth sitting dusty on my shelf for a decade, and had long left it behind as a worthless and weird family heirloom. Huckleberry Finn was just a story to chase a glass of scotch with, an ancestral premonition of my own flailing career as a writer.

Then I got Marcus' letter.

Marcus had written down his family's oral history of his 4X great grandfather, a story passed down over generations. It was the story of an enslaved man named Jim (fyi, I learned from the endnotes of *Jim Huckleberry* to use "enslaved man" rather than "slave"), and it was the story of how my 3X great grandfather, the boy Huck Finn, had helped Jim escape slavery. Immediately, Huck Finn went from a story to a personal fascination. Like most White people (fyi, I learned to capitalize "White" from the footnotes of *Jim Huckleberry* as well), I had imagined that my ancestors' hands were bloody with slavery at some point. I had never considered that one of them might have actually helped someone escape. And here was a Black man telling me just that.

I dug up Huckleberry Finn's book to verify. I read it voraciously.

It was a shocking, funny, horrifying, heart-warming, disgusting, amazing, troubling, hard-edged, deeply conflicted portrait of the life of a wild child in a wild time. Huck Finn ran from a horribly abusive father to a bloody and chaotic sojourn down the Mississippi river, deeper into the savage heart of the Dixie South. Death lived on every bank. His one help along the way was a beautifully sincere and painfully ironic relationship with an escaped enslaved man, Jim. The irony stinking at the core of this relationship may have been lost on a reader of Huck Finn's time, but in the 21st century, it reeks of the White supremacy we postmodern White people love to hate (and hope to hide).

Huck Finn dehumanizes Jim by labeling him with the "n-word" over 200 times (I lost count after 200), and meantime he admits to loving Jim as his mentor, spiritual guide, teacher, and truest friend. Jim had escaped slavery in order to work and buy the freedom of his own children, yet in order to get to freedom he had to act as a surrogate father figure to a runaway potential enslaver in Huck Finn. Jim is alternately described as a human pet, a human toy, and a human moral dilemma on Huck's way to a rejection of his society and the slavery it is built on.

Any present-day reader would likely feel more empathy for Jim than for Huck Finn. As the book progressed, I wished for Jim's empowerment and rooted for him to dump Huck and get on to his freedom. To me, Jim was the true hero and actual protagonist of my ancestor Huck's book about his own life. The irony of that might be lost on a reader of today. This irony is at the heart of the confusion of the 21st century American White man who is waking up to the nightmare that he is not the hero of America's story as he has told it. That irony is not lost on me.

With this awareness as a light shining on each page, I ravaged Huckleberry Finn's book and read three-fourths of it in one long night before getting to a particular page and, like a miracle of deus ex machina, a yellow-greyed slip of paper fell out. I picked it up and was dumbfounded. I held in my hands an envelope with a typed return address for James "Jim" Huckleberry. My hands shook as I read it:

Dear is Huck,

I learn to read so I read your book. Good job. I learn how to writer so I could writer you this. You a damn lie.

You know that you never put no dead snake on me in my sleep. You know I might wrung your little red neck if you did. Most them jokes you say you pull on me made up.

And why you write me like I dont know how to talk? You make me sound like a damn mush mouth fool.

Look boy good luck with your book. And I'm thanking that you made me out as good and smart as I kept to you. And you a good boy to me. This why I keep your name for mine. But one day Ima tell the real story and you best not say nothing to disagree or Ima tell the truth about all them nights you cry like a baby in my arms when we kidnap by them two crooks. Or Ima tell all that piss in your pants and scream in your sleep about your Pap. All that is your business. And a sad business it is. Just dont dare fight with my book when I writer it you hear?

Anyway Im glad you done tell your story. Its a wild one. Ima just let you know Ima tell mine.

Again with the good luck.

Jim

I had to cover my mouth not to scream! Part of me had wondered if Huck Finn had made Jim up to make himself look like a hero, too blind to see how he was making himself look like a racist. But, Jim's letter verified for me that I had a decent (though inescapably racist) ancestor. Here I had that truth in Jim's own words.

I got my bearings and wrote back to Marcus. He sent me his self-published novel, *Jim Huckleberry*. I read it and was stunned by how it confronts slavery with brutal clarity, handles

Huck Finn with the skepticism he deserves, and shows Jim to be deeply empathetic and empowered despite being enslaved. It contains footnotes that describe unique perspectives on the Black American experience (and yes, I capitalize "Black" because of those footnotes). The footnotes provide resources that inspire further research on enslavement. In an America that seems to perpetually play around with a return to White nationalist sentiments, we need this book.

I finished *Jim Huckleberry* and immediately got on the phone with every agent and publisher I knew. I pushed this book down Park and up Broadway. When one agent said it had no market, I called her a corporate shill. When a publisher said the author had no platform, I called him a lazy coward. It became my personal mission to free this novel from obscurity.

Now I am proud that *Jim Huckleberry* lives here in the book flesh as a clarion call for White Americans to face their history, as a shout out to Black Americans for keeping theirs, and as a bridge between the two. Maybe Mr. Huckleberry and his 4X grandfather Jim will turn out to be Black princes with treasure to share after all.

Post Script

******

Big Mama (*speaking church*):
Change your name?
Just because your daddy is a damn shame?
Your daddy couldn't sully Huckleberry if he tried.
And you will keep that name
till the day that you die.

For five generations
a family done carried this name,
through wars and depressions,
wars and migrations.
And worn as it's done been
under the pressure of our skin,
it's had a direction from Jim,
from him that wrestled it from the imperfect union
of he and a young brethren of another skin.
Together, they went against a slave society.
The reach of this name,
from him to you,
is the long arc
of a covenant unbroken
and a flame growing
to light a path to justice
despite us not knowing where we're going,

baby trust this.

Your father,
he went wayward,
slipped into a crack.
He fell into the abyss
off the edge of lack.
He left you to me
and thank life that he so did,
because I raised you hard-headed,
like my own goat kid.
Now you call me mama,
and that is a pride I will take.
But the name Huckleberry you can't change,
like you can't change night to day.
Your father didn't make that name
and though he did not carry it well,
you must keep your name
and draw from its history well.
Huckleberry ain't a brand
a slave was burned with.
It ain't some monument to enslavement.
It was chosen
by your great, great, great, great, grandfather—
a brave of escape—
who carried the lay of the lash
from his ass to his nape
and still rose.
His life wasn't no crystal stair.
It swung low—his dream deferred,
his time as a caged bird singing.
It wasn't sweet Cane
being caned, being Strange Fruit[7]—black and blue—
an Invisible Man possessed by the ghosts of his Beloved
still enslaved at the roots.
The Songs of Solomon humming in his red heart,
in Another Country[8] than his own,

were sewn to raise a Native Guard scarred,
but lifted to march on.
Jim was born into slavery,
and still he rose.
Like a rose from concrete,
like water from a stone,
like a feast from a single loaf,
like gold from everywhere the sun shone,
like diamond—hard as heaven is to get to
and clear as no shame—
like any poor man,
Jim had nothing to give his children
but the name he claimed.
And that ain't nothing your daddy's shame can stain.
You will keep this name till the day you die.
Now let me tell you why.[69]

---

[69] This monologue is constructed of references to some of the texts that inspired this story, including poems, novels, and songs. There are many other non-fiction works that lay a trail for anyone hoping to understand the African-American experience from late-period slavery forward. There are multiverses of histories left untold and I hope that you will join in the mission to unearth them so that we can humanize the millions of enslaved African Americans who helped to build this country by memorializing their resilience, intelligence, creativity, brilliance, entrepreneurial excellence, and indomitable hope:

- From "Mother to Son" a poem by Langston Hughes
- "Swing Low, Sweet Chariot" was composed by Wallis Willis, a Choctaw freedman sometime after 1865.
- "Harlem" a poem by Langston Hughes
- "Caged Bird" a poem by Maya Angelou
- *Cane*, a novel of narrative prose, poetry, and play by Jean Toomer
- "Strange Fruit" a poem by Abel Meeropol, transformed into song by Billie Holiday
- "Black and Blue", a song by Louis Armstrong
- *Invisible Man*, a novel by Ralph Ellison
- *Beloved*, a novel by Toni Morrison
- *Song of Solomon*, a novel by Toni Morrison

- A reference to Sethe, the protagonist of Morrison's novel *Beloved*, who took ultimate action of freeing her child from slavery by sacrificing the child's body to keep the child's soul free from the horror of slavery.
- *Another Country*, a novel by James Baldwin
- *Native Guard*, a book of poetry by national poet laureate, Natasha Trethewey
- A reference to "Lift Every Voice and Sing" a poem turned song, and ultimately the Black American Anthem, written by James Weldon Johnson
- "Still I Rise", a poem by Maya Angelou
- "The Rose that Grew from Concrete" a poem by Tupac Amaru Shakur
- Matthew 14: 13-21, The New Testament of the Bible

A Resource

****

Below is excerpt from a three-session unit, titled *Ironically, all lives matter,* is designed by the author to help teachers use this text to engage students or DEI practitioners engage adults. Teachers in English, History, Humanities, Art History, Creative Writing, Biology, and Chemistry may find value in it.

This unit contains sessions designed to accomplish the following:

1. create brave-space for conversations about race, class, and gender
2. engage a challenging text of the American literary canon that is often the center of school controversy (*Adventures of Huckleberry Finn*), and
3. inspire creative responses to contemporary controversies by introducing an afro-futurist historical fictional response to that text (*Jim Huck*)
4. Create connections across academic disciplines in the humanities and sciences to provide broad context for understanding race, class, and gender

Each session requires participants to read, listen, research, converse, and create. They are designed to produce mutual understanding that supports challenging, healthy conversations about subjects in controversy. This unit offers multiple options of specific activities that can be used in part or whole, in or out of sequence, asynchronously or synchronously, with late teens or adults. Practitioners are encouraged to bring their own diverse knowledge and perspectives to the units that they craft for their participants.

Appropriate for ages: ≥ 16

Learning Objectives:

L.O.1.   Understand irony and how it can be useful for comprehension and conveyance of complex meaning in a text and in the real world
L.O.2.   Communicate understanding of a complex text and complex societal constructions such as race, class, and gender.
L.O.3.   Compose original works of self-expression that engage complex ideas

Formative Assessments (if applicable): Mining texts for meaning through guided analysis
Summative Assessments: Exhibiting understanding through creative writing/expression.

<u>**Session One:** *Isn't it Ironic?*</u> **(70 – 90 minutes)**

Asynchronous Pre-work - Video to Frame Lesson (15 min.):
Lil Baby, The Bigger Picture" (4:16)
Link - https://www.youtube.com/watch?v=_VDGysJGNoI
Lyrics - https://genius.com/Lil-baby-the-bigger-picture-lyrics

Chorus: "It's bigger than Black and white/there's a problem with the whole way of life/ It can't change overnight/ but we gotta start somewhere…"

1.   Advise that there is strong language and that they should listen using headphones if possible.
2.   Share the chorus lyrics as a teaser.
3.   Have students watch the above video and read the lyrics on their own prior to the synchronous session.
4.   Tell students that after watching the video, they should find the following comment by "JT" posted on 7/9/20
5.   Have students read the comment and read through the replies – Here is a portion of JT's comment: "For everyone saying or trying to correct and saying "all lives matter" you are not explicitly racist…You're just ignorant. BLM is not intended to say that black lives matter more than all others. It's implying that there is an imbalance and once that is corrected then all lives will show to matter…."

Contemporary Connection (synchronous):
Read and discuss the following framing essay (45 - 60 minutes)

I don't believe you when you say '_____ Lives Matter'
By Michael Otieno Molina, teacher and author of *Jim Huckleberry*

———

361

Irony abounds in contemporary conflicts around race. Take the Black lives matter – *all* lives matter debate. "Black lives matter" is a clear and direct assertion that Black people's lives should matter as much as any life. That some attempt to contradict the statement that "Black lives matter" by saying "all lives matter" is textbook irony. "All lives matter" cannot be a true statement unless "Black lives matter" is a true statement. So why would people say "all lives matter" to challenge the fact that all lives matter? Ironic, don't you think?

- *Check for Understanding:* How do people use the word "ironic" in everyday conversation? Think of an example of people using the word "ironic" in colloquial speech and then *Google Race* to find a good definition of how "verbal irony" is used in literature. Distinguish between the two. (5 min.)
  - Here is a relatively clear definition of irony – when the intended meaning of words contradict the surface meaning expressed by those words. Think sarcasm.
  - Here is a description of how verbal irony is used in literature from Encyclopedia Brittanica, "Irony has often been used to emphasize the multilayered contradictory nature of modern experience. For instance, in **Toni Morrison**'s novel *Sula* (1973), the [Black] community lives in a neighbourhood called the Bottom, located in the hills above a largely white town."

- *Building Mutual Understanding Pro-tips:* Make room for the heart-space in order to allow for awareness of emotional responses. Be generous when people use imprecise language. Be quiet. Listen. Breathe. Listen more, and ask clarifying questions. Be more curious than certain. Value subjective experience.

This author's completely subjective opinion: I am confused by people who say "all lives matter" as a response to "Black lives matter." It seems that people say "all lives matter" to shut down discussion about whether Black people's lives matter as much as other people's lives in America or in the world. It also seems that the discussion of the value of Black people's lives is an important step towards making sure that all lives in deed do matter.

I am also confused by people who say "Black lives matter". My personal response to the statement has been a series of questions starting with this: *to whom?* Who is this statement attempting to persuade? If Black lives matter is just a statement or an appeal for the world to see the value of Black people's lives, that appeal or that statement assumes that it is possible for Black lives not to matter. Every Black person's life matters to themselves or to someone who loves them. If a Black person's or Black people's lives don't matter, we are in a discussion that is bigger than one confined by racial constructs. That bigger discussion is about the worth (or lack thereof) of human life. This the ironic nature of the Black lives matter vs. all lives matter conflict is as clear as a nutshell – individually, each statement undermines the common truth they share. Ultimately, that gets us nowhere.

- *Mindful Think Time:* What are you feeling or thinking in response to this perspective? Do you agree, disagree, "agree to disagree"? Are you as confused as the author is? What might be a contrasting perspective? How might you make space for the author's perspective and a contrasting perspective? (3 min.)

More subjective opinion of the author: Mark Twain fans will not be surprised that his particular brand of *anti-racism* can help with contemporary conflicts around race. Twain critics will not be surprised that his racist characterization of Jim in *Adventures of Huckleberry Finn* reaffirmed the dehumanization of Black life during post-reconstruction America, a historical period when America may have needed Twain at his most directly anti-racist. How might we build a bridge between these two versions of Twain? How might we build a bridge—a base, a rise, and a landing—between people who say "Black Lives Matter" and those who say "All Lives Matter"?

(Asynchronous or Synchronous) *Thought Questions – Take some time to consider (5 - 15 min.):*
- What circumstances do you think people are responding to when they use the slogans "Black Lives Matter" or "All Lives Matter"?
- What do you think people mean when they make these statements?
- What unspoken assumptions might help us understand what people mean when they make these statements?
- How might both of these statements be examples of verbal irony?

Learning about verbal irony helps us understand how to apply literature study in daily life. If we ever hope to decode the Rubik's Cube of race relations, understanding verbal irony is a good start. Mark Twain can be helpful here. Verbal irony was Twain's most potent tool in critiquing aspects of American society that still need critique today.

In the second of the three session anti-racist unit *Ironically, All Lives Matter*, we engage an excerpt from *Huck Finn* and one from Jim Huck a new work of American fiction that contrasts and connects with Twain's most famous work. Verbal irony is at the core of Twain's work. For generations, teachers from Illinois to Ireland have taught Twain and, likely, missed some of the point. For at least one generation, cool English teachers have either challenged the following song for its frustrating misuse of the notion of irony or praised it for exhibiting irony to perfection. Take a listen and judge for yourself if it's ironic or not, and get ready for the complex and contradictory world of Twain.

Closing Connection: Isn't it Ironic, by Alanis Morrisette (5 min.)
https://www.youtube.com/watch?v=Jne9t8sHpUc
Lyrics - https://genius.com/Alanis-morissette-ironic-lyrics

Session Two: ***Do all lives matter to King Solomon?*** (90 – 120 minutes)

Trigger Warning: The Twain excerpt included contains the "n-word". As prep for this lesson read Toni Morrison Taught Me The Challenge Was Worth It: Teaching Twain for Anti-Racism, from The Teaching Mirror teaching resource blog which gives a specific lesson plan for preparing students to engage with the word in a way that promotes a 'safe space to be brave.'

Opening Connection/Pair Share (Synchronous or Asynchronous):
Situational irony is when events occur that are the opposite of what is expected. In *This is America*, Donald Glover, aka Childish Gambino, creates situational irony through a string of contrasting images and occurrences that offer critique of present day America. Watch the video for *This is America* and discuss the following in pairs: *What are Glover's critiques of American life in the video for "This is America"? Give 2-3 specific examples of imagery that signals these critiques. (10-15 min.)*

This is America, by Childish Gambino (4:05).
https://www.youtube.com/watch?v=VYOjWnS4cMY
Lyrics - https://genius.com/Childish-gambino-this-is-america-lyrics

Pyramid Discussion (Synchronous): Combine pairs into groups of four to discuss their responses with other pairs for 5 minutes. Combine groups of four into groups of eight to discuss their responses with other pairs for 10 minutes. Bring the group back together for the next step. (15 min.)

To access the rest of this session, unit, and more resources for how to engage this text with adults and young adults visit www.molinaconsulting.org

Made in the USA
Middletown, DE
11 October 2022